Sins of Prometheus 2

Paradise Lost

BY
ZACHARY
HILL

Published by White Feather Press. (www.whitefeatherpress.com)

ISBN 978-1-61808-151-3

Printed in the United States of America

Edited by Nichole Ridner

Cover design created by Ron Bell of AdVision Design Group (www.advisiondesigngroup.com)

White Feather Press

Reaffirming Faith in God, Family, and Country!

Here's a list of other great
White Feather Press Titles !

Sins of Prometheus by Zachary Hill

The Lost Promise by Zachary Hill

Uprising USA by George Hill

Uprising UK by George Hill

Uprising Italia by Zachary Hill

Blood and Tequila by Colin Webster

Blood on the Mississippi by Colin Webster

Available on amazon
and anywhere books are sold.

In Loving Remembrance

Zachary Hill, the author of this book, passed away suddenly and unexpectedly the morning of January 15th, 2016. He leaves behind his sweet young bride of almost a year, Mackenzie Hadlow Hill. Zach is a gentle soul with big heart. He was an Artist, a Historian, a Teacher, a two-tour Combat Veteran, and a prolific Writer. He was a true Warrior Poet that always sought peace. He loved to play games and spend time with his family and friends.

Zach was also a Traveler. He adventured in other countries. He served his two-year mission for his Church in Mexico, taught English in Japan, and spent time in Italy. He served his country in the darkest places in Iraq. Now he's gone to the Undiscovered Country. Though he's away from us, for the time being, we know we will see him again.

We believe that he too is grieving for having to leave behind his friends, his family and his new bride. He would not have wanted to leave her now. But he was called back to his celestial home far too early. Our Father in Heaven has a plan for Zach, as he does for all of us. Things happen for a reason and it's our struggle to make sense of it in this mortal world... through our limited and narrow optics that are full of confusion, distraction, and pain. We take comfort that through the Gospel of Jesus Christ, we can be together forever.

Through his writing, Zach will always be remembered.

1

THEIR SMALL CONVOY PULLED INTO THE GROWING TOWN square of Promised Land and the truck came to a sputtering halt. The biofuel mixture needed a bit more refining.

Alex climbed out the passenger door and saw Alma waiting for him on the front steps of their house. Her arms were folded and her mouth was crooked to the side. A sure sign she was upset about something. It was a look she had more often, usually directed at him.

She had been different ever since the attack in the library. Almost dying would do that to a person.

It didn't matter because he was home. It was much better to suffer through Alma's wrath than get shot at by crazies or bandits.

"Had fun in Farmville?" Alma asked as he walked up to the house.

He paused before answering. This was a trap and no matter what he said it would be the wrong answer.

"The meeting went well, if that's what you're asking."

"While you were off driving through the country side, I had to stay here and deal with escaped cows, three escaped buffalo and four camels. Do you have any idea how hard it is to get a camel to do something it doesn't want to do?"

"As hard as it is with you?"

Alma didn't smile.

He patted her on the shoulder and did his best "disarming smile" he could. Alma's expression didn't change.

"You handled things wonderfully. I'm proud of you. The houses are still standing. Everyone's alive. What more could you ask for?"

"A better place to put these animals than a wooden fence."

"What about Walmart? It's empty. Just take out the shelves and use it for our barn."

"Hard to defend if we get attacked."

"We'll set up an outpost there. We are getting crowded here as it is."

"Temporary solution at best, Alex."

It seemed like that was all he had, band aids for big problems.

"Well, when temporary runs out, we'll have a permanent solution by then."

He looked around at Promised Land and saw that there were now two houses built from scratch that fit the new paradigm of life. They were simple, insulated and with wood burning stoves for heat and cooking. They had electricity from solar panels and old army generators that could run on anything but needed to be built for times when electricity wasn't available.

There were fifty three people now and everyone had a place. There was a lot of work to do. Animals had to be fed, wood had to be chopped and patrols had to be sent out to look for canned food, ammo, solar panels, batteries and anything else useful.

Then someone else emerged from the house.

The graceful form of Lisa walked down the stairs like a stalking tiger and she stopped with her hands behind her back. She was the most beautiful creature he had ever seen. She was smart, powerful and for some reason she loved him. Any hardship he had out on the roads was forgotten as he looked at her.

"We expected you yesterday," Lisa said.

"Farmville kept us late. They're pickier about the details than the big picture. They accepted the treaty in the first hour, but spent the next two days arguing about trivial little things."

"Can you blame them?" Lisa asked. "This is a new beginning. Those trivial things could become large down the road."

"I missed you too."

He put his arm around her and brought her in for a kiss which drew out a groan from Alma.

"Are you guys teenagers? We have more important things to think about," Alma said.

"Yes we do," Lisa said. "James made his first batch of hand made ice cream."

"I expected better of you, Lisa," Alma said.

He led them inside where he unslung his AR-15 and took off his gloves and sock hat. Inside the house was nice and warm from a burning fire. If there was one thing Virginia had plenty of, it was trees.

Alex sat down on the couch and let Lisa slide in to his shoulder.

Alma didn't sit. She crossed her arms.

"Okay, what about the treaty then?" Alma asked.

"We have a mutual defense treaty. If the Provisional Government comes after one of us, it comes after all of us."

"You think they'll help if it comes to it?" Alma asked.

"I do. We all realize how dangerous they are."

"Especially if they come with armored vehicles," Lisa said.

"Well, we have a few .50 cals, and mines," Alex said.

"It might not be enough," Lisa said.

"For once I agree with Lisa. We need to find more armories and military bases."

"Get a patrol together then," he said.

Alma smiled.

"Already have my team together."

He had fallen in to her trap like he always did.

"Just make sure to take Jason with you. I want at least one grown up going along."

Alma nodded but he suspected that Jason was already on her list. Those two were unofficial partners. They didn't hang out or even really talk to each other, but when there was a patrol those two were back to back.

Alma had never had a boyfriend before and he wondered if she even knew how to get one or what to do with one once she had it.

Then a short, furry shape charged inside and jumped up on his lap. The Basset Hound started licking his face despite his objections. The dog wasn't tall, but it definitely wasn't small and it always had an uncanny way to find just the wrong place to step when climbing on his lap.

"Okay, okay. Caesar, I missed you too."

Once Caesar said hello he settled down into a nap while half draped over him and Lisa. She smiled and scratched Caesar's belly while her mind was elsewhere. He recognized that look. She was thinking.

"So, where do we stand?" Alma asked.

"Well, we're closer to the PG so we're more likely to get hit first, but that's not guaranteed. The PG could bypass us and do a surprise attack on Farmville. The truth is, we're really too far away to help during an attack. We have to start building up our defenses. We also need to train everyone to fight."

"So, what you're saying is that we need to prepare for war," Alma said.

"Yes we do. It's coming and we're not avoiding it."

"Then let's get our plan together. Any idea how soon we can expect a visit from the PG?" Lisa asked.

He had thought about it the entire ride back home. He didn't have an answer.

"Let's get that .50 cal set up in the attic window with sandbags. That's our first priority. Second, Alma, get your patrol and look for anything we can fight with that isn't bolted down. APCs, missiles, cannons, anything. Go to every National Guard armory, gun store and military base you can get to."

"I'm on it,"

Alma got a wolfish grin and hurried out of the room.

"Rebekah will want to go as well," Lisa said.

"I wish she wouldn't," he said.

"Why? Because she's a girl?"

"No, because she's too young."

"None of us are young anymore. She did great on her last patrol."

"Was that the one where the hippy was shooting at them?"

"No, after that, it was the guy that thought they were all alien hybrids."

"Ah, yes."

He tried not to laugh but when he saw Lisa trying not to he lost it and they surrendered into laughing as a very confused Caesar raised his head to see what was going on.

After getting a jelly sandwich they walked outside where the garden was growing and beyond that was the cold river. Some of the kids were fishing and Jennifer and two others were working in the garden getting it ready for planting in the spring.

Against all odds, the Promised Land was doing well. It was the middle of their first winter and everything was okay. He couldn't ask for more than that.

That night they had a dinner from their supply of canned food while he told them about Farmville. They had about thirty people and were also preparing for war. The settlement of Luray was only about ten people and had agreed to come if anything happened.

Then there was a furious knock on the door. Alex was the first out of his seat and ran to the window to look out on the porch. Two of their men with thick coats and slung rifles stood there.

He opened the door and waved them in.

"What's going on, gentlemen?" Alex asked.

They didn't take a seat and their faces were still white and red from the cold and smelled like dirt and horses.

"We were doing a patrol south of here, near Natural Bridge," Jeremy said. He was the taller of the two men and had been a car salesmen before.

"Yeah, and we saw trucks. Military trucks," the shorter man said. He was new and Alex couldn't recall his name.

"But they also had a big army tank with them," Jeremy said.

"Tank? What kind?"

"I don't know."

"Describe it."

"It had eight wheels and a machine gun up top."

Alex went to the bookshelf and grabbed a military vehicle recognition guide and flipped to the "Stryker" armored vehicle.

"Is this what you saw?"

"That's it," Jeremy said with a nod.

"Which way were they heading?"

"East."

He looked over at Lisa and Alma. They knew what it meant.

"Alma, get on the CB and warn Farmville that they might have company."

"Should we send some or our people over?"

"Not until we know more. It could be a scouting patrol or a raid somewhere else. Or they could be planning on hitting us too."

Alma nodded and ran up the stairs to where the radio was.

"Thank you, gentlemen. Get something to eat and rest."

After they left he sat back at the kitchen table across from Lisa.

"Trucks. Maybe they found a stockpile somewhere."

"Let's hope that's all it is. But if they got that many trucks, it means they have fuel to spare. A Stryker doesn't exactly get great gas mileage."

"But what if it's not?"

"Then let's get our trucks gassed up and our people ready to go."

He went over to the houses and told the 'sergeants' to get their patrols ready.

Strategies raced through his mind as he thought of an attack on Farmville. He calculated how many people he'd need to keep here and how many would need to go.

The simple fact was that they weren't ready for a war. Promised Land only had basic defenses, nothing that could stop a Stryker or heaven forbid, an actual tank.

It's too soon.

He went to their armory where the stockpile of weapons and ammo was kept. It was a brick building they had made just for that purpose and had several gun safes for the more dangerous weapons they were saving for an emergency.

In the back of the small armory building was a single .50 cal machine and two chains of ammunition. He hefted the enormous weapon into his arms and carried it up to the top window of his house. Next he brought up the tri-pod and then the ammo.

Lisa poked her head up into the attic.

"There you are. I've been looking for you," she said.

"Just getting things ready."

"Everyone's on alert. I think Alma's angry that her patrol is postponed."

"She'll survive."

He checked the headspacing for the fifty's barrel and then loaded a belt of ammo and slammed the lid down.

"What's wrong?" Lisa asked.

Her dark eyes looked up at him without judgment or expectations.

"We're not ready for this," he said.

"We'll do what we have to."

"That's the problem. We're always on the defensive, always reacting to the aggressors."

"What do you want? You want us to go attack the PG?"

"No. I don't know what I'm saying."

She stepped up into the attic and sat down next to him. Lisa peered out the circular window and then at him.

"We'll be alright, Alex. A fifty will take out a Stryker. We have explosives for bombs and our people know what to do."

"Not all of them."

She put her arm around him.

"You worry too much. Thinking is good. Worrying is not."

"If we fail, it's on my head." He paused and waved his hand at the Town Square below. "Look at those people, Lisa."

Down in the "Town Square" were a dozen people loading ammo and food into the trucks. All of them had survived so much and to be threatened now was unacceptable.

"We'll be okay," Lisa said and kissed him on the cheek.

They sat there for a few moments but the list of things to do only grew in his head.

"You've seen Cass around?" He asked.

"I saw her a few minutes ago talking to Adam."

"Maybe we should get her to train up more sharpshooters."

"Your mind's getting ahead of you. Think about the immediate problems."

"You're right."

He picked himself up and helped Lisa to her feet. Then they went down to the radio where Alma was sitting.

"They getting ready?" Alex asked.

"Yes but their scouts haven't seen any sign of them."

"If they've found some other place to loot, I think we should know about it," Alma said.

"We don't exactly have a spy satellite."

"That's no excuse to be blind."

All night they waited by the radio for the signal to move out. Everyone kept watch with weapons at the ready. He kept his 1911 on his hip and his M-14 within arm's reach. Lisa kept her AK-SU slung across her chest, ready in a second to take a life that threatened their people.

When dawn came they organized a rotation of rest. The PG would have attacked by now if they had went directly to Farmville. Still, they could double back or even come after the Promised Land with whatever they had gone after.

The idea of the PG getting an Apache helicopter made him want to invest in Air-to-Air missiles. There were too many threats that could come from too many directions.

He went over to his house and sat down on the porch steps. He was tired. He tried to ignore it but his body wouldn't let him. It was like he ached all over. He hadn't slept much at all during the past week. Long nights of negotiation with the Council of Farmville left him with little energy to do much at all.

He had seen what a fully armed military was capable of. If the PG rolled in with everything they had, there would be nothing they could do to stop them.

Lisa sat down next to him and handed him a cup of coffee.

"We need a plan, Lisa."

"You'll think of something, but not before you drink that."

He took a sip and looked around the dirt field that had become the center of his world. People stood around talking to each other like any small town, but they all carried guns. For now the concept of "civilian" was meaningless.

Whatever it took, he'd keep his people safe.

2

THIS WAS THE SECOND TIME MIRIAM'S WORLD HAD BEEN destroyed. The first time was when she was ten and the extremists overran the city of Basra. Even though she was young she knew why they were running. She had seen the pictures on the news and heard the people talking. A live beheading on TV wasn't something a young girl could never forget.

She remembered hearing the distant '*thuds*' of explosions and the hammer strike sounds of machine gun fire. Her father had woken her in the middle of the night, threw a few things in a suitcase and the next thing she knew they were running through crowded streets while her father carried her. She remembered Basra was filled with screaming people holding on to their families. The only light came from the explosions in the sky.

The second time her world ended was more subtle. She went to work on Monday at eight in the morning. Two people had called in sick. By noon, three others had gone home with fever. There were hardly any people out on the streets and her manager called it an early day.

Miriam broke a stick in half and tossed it into the fire. As it cracked and sizzled she looked out the window of the old house and wondered when the rain would stop. It had been raining for two days and it was a cold rain. She couldn't afford to get sick now. There were no doctors, no medicine and no one to help her. Unlike the last time the world ended, she was now alone with no father to carry her.

This was an old house along a narrow country road. There were less chances of being seen on a country road and more chance of finding a house with a fireplace or stove. It turned out that the fancy modern houses weren't much good without electricity.

The last time she saw living people was three weeks ago. She had hid in some old house while she watched the five people on horses ride by. They had saddlebags and backpacks filled to bursting.

She couldn't tell if they were good people or bad. She couldn't risk falling into the hands of bad people. She remembered the images on the evening news.

The light outside was dull and gray and the rain didn't seem close to ending.

Miriam stretched out and lay down in her sleeping bag she had taken from an empty sports store. It had felt so strange to take things out of the store and she had expected a cop to come arrest her at any minute. But no cop came. No alarm sounded.

She pulled a book out of its plastic sandwich bag and continued where she had left off. It was the last in the series and if it ended in a cliffhanger she'd throw the book as far as she could.

There would be no more adventures of this hard boiled detective. There would be no more super hero movies, no more number one hits and no more latest fall fashions. Every one she knew was gone.

All that she had of her father were a few old photos and the two guns he had owned. He had been a historian and bought two Russian surplus guns that mother made him promise to keep locked up and unloaded. Now she carried them with her wherever she went. On his deathbed, Father had shown her how to use them but neither of them knew how to shoot. Before the power went out she had looked the guns up and wrote down everything she needed to know. She had never fired the guns in anger or even to hunt with and she prayed to God that she'd never have to.

The old Mosin Nagant was a long heavy thing with a canvas sling and the Nagant pistol was a revolver with strange looking bullets that looked like lipstick when it was retracted into its case. She wore the pistol on her hip in a holster with a big flap on it like she saw in older movies. After two years it still felt foreign and uncomfortable.

Two years.

Two years was a long time to be alone.

When the gray light outside faded away she put down her book and settled in to sleep. She had a lantern and flash lights but didn't want to waste them.

She paused for a moment. All her life she had prayed before going to sleep like her father had taught her.

Miriam pulled the sleeping bag over her shoulders and went to sleep.

In the morning she woke to a bright, blue sky. It was cold out there and the ground would be muddy, not great for traveling but she had been through worse. The boots she had pillaged from that old sporting goods store kept her feet dry and as comfortable as she could hope for.

She packed her gear, had a can of peaches and walked out into the cold

January morning. It was sometime around the fifteenth, though she couldn't be sure. It also didn't matter.

Her breath clouded around her as she took a moment to look at the map. She had left Philadelphia and was going south. It didn't matter where, as long as it was warmer. Someplace by a lake sounded nice.

Growing up in Iraq she was used to hot temperatures. It had been a shock when she spent her first winter in New York. She couldn't believe people could live in such cold.

She slung the rifle over her shoulder and started walking south. An hour later she came to a small sign almost covered by bushes that said, "*Welcome to Virginia.*" It had a faded picture of a cardinal.

Virginia had a bunch of American history, though she couldn't remember exactly what, Virginia hams and a beach. That was about the extent of her Virginia knowledge. No one was left to remember the rest. The human race was dead now and she was just buying time until the end.

"Stop right there," a voice said from behind her.

Miriam froze as her heart pounded in her chest.

She hadn't been paying attention and now she was caught. The rifle on her back was too clunky and awkward and the pistol she barely knew how to use. She'd fumble with it while whoever this person was shot holes through her.

She thought a quick plea to Allah though He was no longer listening.

Please don't let me be captured by bad men.

"I've been watching you for a while," the voice said.

It was a woman's voice. That was much better, but women could still be thieves and murderers.

"Who are you?" Miriam managed to say.

She felt a hand open her holster and pull out her pistol.

"I don't want you shooting me. Now turn around," the woman said.

She turned to see a woman in a military uniform, though none too clean. Her face was filthy and her unkempt hair hung in front of her face and down to her waist. Her skin was brown and she had the large eyes and round nose like someone from India. Her name tag said "Bhattathiri."

The woman also carried a big gun covered in gadgets. It was pointed right at her. She hadn't had a gun pointed at her since Iraq and the barrel looked like a massive cave staring at her.

"Where you going?" The woman asked with a musical accent.

"Please don't hurt me."

"Where?"

"South."

"Where?"

"Don't know, just south."

The woman narrowed her eyes like she didn't approve of the answer.

"It's dangerous to travel alone," the woman said.

"It's dangerous to meet people."

"Just the wrong people."

"Are you the wrong people?"

A hint of a smile played at the woman's lips.

"I'm not."

A wave of relief swept over her even though the woman could be lying. Just hearing the words made her relax.

"Then give me my gun back."

"Not until I know you're not going to shoot me out of fear or by accident."

"I'm not useless."

"We'll see. What's your name?"

"Miriam Al-Basri."

"You're Arab?"

"Iraqi."

"Muslim?"

"Is that a problem?"

"Is me being Hindu a problem?"

"If you're not going to hurt me, I don't care what you are."

"I don't care what you are, I just want to know if you're being honest with me," the woman said.

The woman lowered her weapon and her stance grew a little more relaxed.

"What's your name?" Miriam asked.

The woman raised her eyebrow.

"Can't you read?"

"Your first name."

"Shakti Bhattathiri, Specialist, United States Army. Saw the smoke from your chimney. Watched you for a while to make sure you were really alone."

How long had she been watching? This woman was scary. She was a soldier with a big gun, probably a veteran of the war against the Chinese and EU. Shakti could probably kill me without trying and if Shakti decided to walk off with all my stuff, there is nothing I could do to stop her.

"And now what?" Miriam asked.

"Haven't decided. I can travel with you. You don't know what you're doing, your guns are garbage and I doubt you know how to use them. You could use the help."

"And what do you get out of it?"

"Two is better than one."

"Won't I just slow you down?"

"Probably, but speed isn't everything."

"Then why?"

Shakti let out a long breath and her shoulders slumped a little.

"Maybe sometimes I can't open a jar on my own."

Sure, this Shakti chick was a little scary, but she was also a human being that was as alone and frightened as she was. Maybe she wanted company. With the bands of armed men she had seen from a distance, she knew why Shakti was wary of strangers.

"You're safe with me," Miriam said.

Shakti extended her hand with the pistol, handle first.

"Please don't shoot me by accident," Shakti said.

"I won't."

Once the gun was holstered Shakti asked where she had gotten such 'antiques.' She told the story as they continued walking south. She talked about fleeing Iraq, moving to New York, then Philadelphia for college.

"What did you study in college?" Shakti asked.

"Business."

"I was going to be a chemical engineer."

That wouldn't have been her first guess.

"Don't look so surprised. I wasn't always a soldier."

"You signed up when we were invaded?"

"Like many others from my University."

"Where are you from?"

"Peoria, Illinois."

She nodded like she knew where that was. Shakti already thought she was useless, no need to throw ignorant in there too.

The road grew more overgrown and windy as they went. The sky they saw through the trees was crystal with a few high up clouds that were nothing more than wisps. It was the clear days that were always the coldest. Pretty, but cold. They passed by a gas station with broken windows. The place looked like a tornado had passed through. Almost everything was gone. Even the large sign had fallen to the ground, crushing a Prius.

Shakti didn't talk much for the rest of the day. That was alright because

Miriam found her mouth going and going without pause. She talked about waking up to a silent Philadelphia and trying to call anyone. Even Facebook had been empty. It was like everyone disappeared overnight. The news she did watch hadn't been comforting.

"Where were you when it happened?" Miriam asked.

"New York."

"What happened?"

"I got up for roll call and half the platoon was gone to sick call. The Platoon Sergeant didn't look good either. By afternoon we knew something was going on."

Shakti fell silent and didn't say anything for the next hour.

They found themselves in a narrow valley surrounded by thick forest. Night was coming and she hadn't seen a house in a long time. A half hour later they spotted a trailer half buried in vines.

"No place for a fire, but it beats sleeping outside," Miriam said.

"I found you because of the fire. Maybe we don't want anyone else to find us."

They went into the trailer that was free of skeletons. That's all the people were now, skeletons. Sometimes they had leathered skin and hair, but they were no longer corpses. That was the worst thing. She had left Philly after the smell got unbearable.

Even the cars were decomposing. The tires were going flat, weeds were growing up around them and soon the roads would be impassable for anything that wasn't made for off-road.

There were two beds and after dinner Shakti disappeared into her room leaving Miriam sitting in the living room alone and staring at the widescreen TV that would never work again.

Shakti didn't talk about herself. She wasn't dangerous and probably needed company, that much was clear, but everything else about the woman was a complete blank.

She took out a photo of her parents and her two brothers at the Statue of Liberty. They were gone now. Maybe they were watching her from heaven. They probably wouldn't be happy with her spirituality right now. The Quran in Arabic was still sitting at the bottom of her backpack in its plastic bag.

Sleep didn't come easy. In the other room Shakti would moan and call out in unintelligible ramblings. Shakti was having nightmares. Couldn't blame her. That first year all she saw in her sleep were the emaciated corpses she found in houses and stores and her lying down to join them.

It could have been much worse. If Shakti had been a man, she would have ran, even with the chance of getting shot. In Iraq she had seen what men did when there were no laws.

In the morning she awoke to find Shakti in the small living room opening two cans of beans. Dim light came in through the closed blinds illuminating one side of Shakti in rays of dust mites. She was wearing her uniform pants and boots and a black skin tight body suit top that looked like something professional runners wore.

Shakti looked up with her large, almond eyes and mumbled something about a good morning. She made a faint smile.

"What's for breakfast?" Miriam asked.

"I found these in the pantry."

"Excellent. I love a free breakfast."

"So, Miriam, what did you do before all of this? Do you know anything useful that can help us?"

"Unless you have budgets to balance, then no."

Shakti shrugged and handed her an open can with a plastic spoon.

She took a bite and sat down on the dusty sofa while she tried to think of a way to get this woman to open up.

"You think they'll ever make plastic spoons again?" Miriam asked.

"I don't know."

"And what about airplanes? I wonder if we'll lose the ability to fly."

"I doubt it. Too many books around. Hurry and eat. We need to get moving."

"Why the rush?"

"I don't like wasting time."

After she ate she put on her boots again, strapped on her backpack and shouldered her rifle. Shakti was waiting for her outside. The air was cold and stung her cheeks and nose. Shakti's gun hung from a carabineer near her shoulder and she wore wrap around sunglasses.

"Ready?" Shakti asked.

"I guess so."

They started walking down the road.

"We need to get you a better gun," Shakti said.

She didn't know how to use anything fancy like Shakti had so she had never tried to find a better gun.

"Nothing wrong with my guns."

Shakti just shook her head.

Their pace was slowed because they were going uphill again. She was tired of these mountains and was ready for some flat land. Her legs were used to it though. She had been walking for a month now. She had left the resort cabin she had found and decided to head south. It was too cold up north and she was sick of it. It wasn't too cold to travel though, so she hit the road.

At the end of the day they came to a small town called "Warm Springs." It looked like something out of a history book or a tour agency calendar. The houses were red brick with white porches done up like Greek temples. Farm houses were scattered everywhere the place looked like it had been a quiet getaway with lots of expensive folk art shops.

They walked down the main street that was empty of life. It probably had been a peaceful place before everything, but now it felt more like a cemetery. Darkness and cobwebs filled the shop windows and grass and weeds were peeking through cracks in the roads.

Then Shakti's hand came up to Miriam's chest and stopped her in place.

"What?" Miriam whispered.

Shakti pointed to a telephone poll. She didn't see anything unusual and was about to ask. Then she saw it. There was a flier on the post that looked brand new. It also looked like it was printed out from a computer.

Shakti's gun came up to her shoulder and she looked around before approaching the flier. Miriam mimicked her and unslung her long Mosin. She peered through the rifle's sights, not sure what she was looking for.

The flier was a map. At the top were big bold letters that said, "Safety and Refuge." Below the map were normal black font letters that said, "We have built a small community and welcome anyone looking for peace and comfort. We have farms, water, heat and electricity. We are peaceful but very well armed. If you're looking for an easy place to steal from, keep looking. If you don't mean trouble then follow the map to the Promised Land."

She looked to Shakti who had her brow raised.

"What do you make of that?" Miriam asked.

"It's too good to be true, but too good to ignore."

3

MIRIAM'S FEET HURT. SHAKTI WALKED FASTER THAN SHE WAS used to and didn't take nearly as many breaks.

Shakti hadn't said much all day. She just walked on in silence.

"It's time for a break," Miriam said.

Shakti didn't respond and kept walking so Miriam sat down on the edge of the road and put her camel-back's tube into her mouth.

"What are you doing?" Shakti asked.

"I'm taking a break."

"Take it at noon."

"I'm taking it now."

Shakti walked back to where she sat and looked down on her.

"We have to keep going. The sooner we…"

Shakti went silent and looked down the road they had come.

When Miriam made to talk Shakti held up a finger.

"Get off the road," Shakti said.

Shakti grabbed her by the shoulder straps and pulled her into the trees just as a truck came around the bend.

They plunged into the bushes and branches scrapped her face as they ran further in before she tripped on a root and fell face first. Shakti landed on top of her almost knocking the wind out of her.

The truck's brake's squealed and three men jumped out. They wore Army uniforms and carried black guns.

There was no more government which meant no one to control these armed men. Perhaps they wouldn't do beheadings but there were plenty of other terrible things to do. Men had powerful imaginations when it came to causing pain.

The soldiers raised their guns and faced the woods.

Shakti rolled to her back and raised her gun.

The soldiers might be there to help them. It was possible. But all she could think about were the lawless soldiers in Iraq and the horrible things they did.

She scrambled to get her heavy Mosin up and ready. She looked through the sights at the dark shape that was walking towards the woods.

"Come on out," one of them said. "We're here to help. We're from the Provisional Government and we got food and medicine."

She looked to Shakti who shook her head. Her eyes were wide and her breathing was heavy.

"You know these people?" Miriam mouthed in silence.

Shakti didn't answer.

Miriam's hands shook causing her sights to bob all over the place. She tried to steady the Mosin and put her finger on the trigger.

The three soldiers walked into the woods while the one kept calling out that they had food and anything else they wanted.

"Take the one on the right," Shakti whispered.

"What? I can't shoot anyone."

"You have to. Shoot the one on the right when I open fire."

"I can't."

"Do it."

Shakti stayed on the ground and took aim and Miriam lined up her sights on the soldier's chest. She took a breath and tried to calm her pounding heart. She lay belly down in the wet leaves of the forest.

Then Shakti fired. The gun shots were like blows to her head. She had no idea a gun was so loud but now she knew with painful clarity.

The man at the end of her gun ducked down and looked around for whoever was shooting.

She either had to fire or let the man shoot Shakti.

Without further thought she pulled the trigger. The gun kicked in her hands and slammed her shoulder hard. There was thunder that hurt her ears and the man fell backwards.

She crawled up onto her knees to get a better look. All she could hear was ringing and her heartbeat.

Did I just kill him?

A wave of nausea spread over her and threatened to overflow.

Next to her Shakti had her gun up and the two other soldiers were lying on the ground. Smoke rose from the barrel of her gun.

"You got yours?" Shakti asked.

"I think so."

A moan came from the bushes where her soldier was. Shakti jumped up and ran over to the soldier with her gun up at her shoulder.

Miriam yanked back the silver handle and the empty shell flew out. She slammed it forward to load a new round and hurried over to see what was happening.

The man she had shot was covered in blood, most of it around his shoulder.

"Who are these guys? Are they actually from the army?"

"They're from an army and they're not here to help."

She looked over to the truck and saw that it looked like the army trucks she had seen on the news.

"Did we just kill soldiers from the army?" Miriam asked.

"They're nothing more than bandits. Trust me," she said and aimed her gun at the soldier's head.

Shakti fired and Miriam stood there with her mouth open until she managed to form words again.

"Why did you do that?"

"He was dying, now grab his gun."

"What did we just do?"

Shakti lowered her gun and stood right in front of her.

"Look at me." Shakti waited until she looked at her. "Those men are from the Provisional Government. I used to be with them. They're nothing more than bandits with uniforms. If we went with them they'd put us in a labor camp where we'd be little more than slaves. You want that? I don't."

She looked down at the dead man. He looked like any other young man. Either Shakti was right or she was a murderer.

"Grab his gear and let's get moving," Shakti said.

She kneeled down and removed the man's body armor that was covered in pouches. She barely managed to lift it.

Shakti opened the door to the truck and looked around.

"Do we have the keys?" Miriam asked as she carried the heavy body armor over to the truck.

"It doesn't use keys, just a button."

"Really? That's easy."

Miriam put the armor and ammo in the cab of the truck and then went back for the gun. It looked just like Shakti's with the same gadgets and everything. Perhaps she really was from this Provisional Government.

They removed all the ammo, gear and weapons and threw them in the truck. Then they climbed in with Shakti behind the wheel. She started the big gray truck and the engine rumbled to life. Then they were driving down the road and the trees to either side seemed to fly past them at impossible speeds.

"We'll be there in just over an hour," Shakti said.

"What if this Promised Land is a trap? What if they're just like these Provisional Government guys?"

"We either give them a try or remain by ourselves for the rest of our lives. This is the best bet I've seen."

"What else have you seen?"

"Nothing good."

"Tell me."

"Just a few small groups, like ten at most. They're moving away from the Provisional Government, trying to find someplace where they can be left alone."

"You think that's what this Promised Land is?"

"Maybe."

She settled down in her seat and got comfortable. She wished she had some music to listen to. Music always made long drives feel shorter.

Miriam turned around in her seat and tried to see what was in the back of the truck but it was too dark.

"What's back there?" She asked.

Shakti raised one of her black eyebrows and stopped the truck. She pulled out her pistol and climbed out. They walked to the back of the truck that was covered by a light gray tarp. She unstrapped the tarp while Miriam covered her.

Did she think a bear would jump out?

Once the tarp was open they lowered the gate. Inside were large wooden crates, the kind that needed a crowbar to open.

After a lot of work with Shakti's camping hatchet, they managed to get one of the crates open. Inside were plain white boxes with a bunch of random letters and numbers that military people seemed to like. Shakti picked up a box about the size of microwave.

"Spare parts for Chinook helicopters."

She tossed the box back in and went to the next crate. This one was filled with spare bolts and barrels for M4s. Shakti explained it but she only understood half of it.

Then another crate was filled with boots and the last crate contained what Shakti called "sapi plates" for body armor.

"I was hoping for food and ammo," Shakti said.

"Well, if we come across a Chinook helicopter that needs fixing, we'll be set."

They got back in the cab and continued on their way.

As she settled in for the drive her mind kept going back to the man she had shot. Before she would never have pulled the trigger. She had shot a man and it was all she could see in her mind. She could feel the kick of the heavy gun and see the dark silhouette fall down.

Why had she done it?

Then images of armed men in Iraq and their daily beheadings floated in her mind. Whatever it took, she would not end up like those poor people.

The flashing of the sun through the trees kept her awake and the truck's nominal heating felt better than a fire.

Shakti slowed the truck and came to a halt.

"What's wrong?" Miriam asked.

"Before we get to this place, I want to give you a shooting lesson."

Shakti climbed out of the truck and Miriam followed.

"A shooting lesson? Now?"

"In case things don't turn out well."

Shakti reached up into the cab and grabbed the Mosin.

"We'll practice with this first so you can learn the basics. Aim the rifle like you're about to shoot."

Miriam obeyed.

"Good. Now aim at that tree down the road, the gray dead one."

The tree stood out like a skeleton among all the others.

"Fire."

She pulled the trigger and again there was the painful gunshot and the kick to her shoulder. She lowered the gun and looked.

"Did I hit it?"

"No. You jerked the trigger and flinched before shooting."

Shakti had her fire a few more times, making corrections after each shot. Then Shakti pulled one of the army guns from the cab. She took her Mosin and shoved the black gun into her open hands.

"Now we'll try a real gun. This is an M4 with an Aimpoint sight. Look down the sight, see that red dot? That's where the bullet's going to go."

Shakti ran her through how to load, unload and clear a jam. It took a few times and Shakti's normal, even paced tone grew sharper with each mistake, but she got it down to a level Shakti must have found acceptable because she moved on.

"Now, using the stance and grip I taught you, take aim at that tree and try to hit it."

Miriam raised the M4 and steadied herself. She put the red dot on the tree and squeezed the trigger like Shakti had taught her.

The gun kicked but it was nothing compared to the old Mosin.

"Miss. Try again. Don't anticipate the shot. Let the gun surprise you."

She aimed and fired.

"Hit."

She emptied the magazine one well placed shot at a time. She hit the tree about two thirds of the time. Once the magazine was empty she lowered the gun and smiled.

"Not bad, huh?"

Shakti narrowed her eyes.

"If we had ammo to spare I'd have you doing this all day. Remember, if it comes down to it, don't hesitate. And above all, find cover."

They climbed back into the cab and continued on their way.

As they drove the small towns and houses grew nicer and more common. Instead of scattered pre-fab homes and trailers, they were passing the kind of houses doctors lived in when they retired. They passed a small town called Goshen that was almost swallowed by vines and weeds. The few houses they saw were old but well kept and some of them were quite big. It looked like a nice town to settle down in.

"We're almost there," Shakti said. "Keep a cool head and eyes open. Follow my lead. If I start shooting, you shoot. If I run, you run. Understood?"

"Are we going to talk to them first?"

"After we scout them out."

She looked at the map with a pink highlighter circle around Lexington. There were directions on how to get to where they lived. Apparently it was near a Walmart.

An address and GPS would have been so much easier.

They came to a sign that said "Welcome to Historic Lexington."

Shakti pulled the truck to the side of the road and got out. Miriam had to put on the armored vest which must have weighed half as much as she did. But Shakti insisted. Also, it was where all her ammo was.

"I hope I don't have to use any of this."

"Me too, but if we do you'll be glad you have it."

After tightening down the vest she felt like a Ninja Turtle.

"What about those small vests people ware on those cop shows?" Miriam asked.

"Only good against handguns. This'll stop a rifle round."

Good to know.

"We go in by foot. Stay out of sight. I want to see them before they see us."

She had gotten used to riding in the truck and took a last look at it before following Shakti down the road into the town.

The houses here were very nice with wrap around porches, towers and what were once well cared for gardens.

They went down a hill into the town that undulated from more hills. Church steeples and buildings that looked like they were falling apart before the end of the world dotted the town.

"This is the main street," Shakti said while looking at her map. "We go down there and take a left towards VMI. We go past that, over a river and this Promised Land should be around there."

"Lead the way."

Shakti stayed out of the street and walked through people's lawns and once they got to the business district she lead them through the back alleys and side streets. The parking lots had dead cars that all needed washing and weeds growing through the new cracks.

The store front windows were covered in dust and she put her hand up to her brow to look inside. The old store was filled with books. Some of the shelves were empty. She tested the door and found it unlocked.

"We don't have time," Shakti whispered in that sing-song accent of hers.

"Very well."

They made their way through the old part of town and onto a college campus. The wide green lawns needed mowing but other than that the campus looked almost normal, like it was a holiday for the students. The sign said, "Washington and Lee." She had never heard of it.

They continued on to the VMI campus right next door. They stopped before a giant parade ground with flag poles and a statue at the far end. Castle looking buildings surrounded the open weed filled field with an impressive castle looking building on the far side.

"Why didn't they take this place over?" Miriam asked.

"Don't know."

Shakti led the way and went from building to building. The drive way led down to the street where a bridge was.

"That's the bridge. Up the hill should be Walmart," Shakti said.

"If they look bad, I'm not going in," Miriam said.

"Define bad."

"If they look like they'd cut people's heads off."

Shakti nodded and continued on. They rushed across the bridge and hid in some bushes while they waited to make sure they weren't spotted. Shakti waved them forward and they continued up the hill past a gas station that looked abandoned before the end came and past a French restaurant.

In the distance she saw rolling hills and beautiful farm houses. The place was gorgeous and she hoped this Promised Land was everything it said it was. After two years she needed a place to rest.

But "Promised Land" was a religious term and this was the country. Religious country people didn't have the best reputation for liking Muslims. She didn't want to go in there and be turned away or worse. She hoped the old hatreds were dead along with the old world.

At the top of the hill the land leveled out and in the distance she could make out the sign to Walmart. There wasn't a whole lot of cover around.

"Stay low," Shakti said.

A part of the road was an overpass with another highway below. A broken down semi-truck was there but other than that the roads were empty.

Past that were a few scattered restaurants then the Walmart.

When they came to the shopping center that held the Walmart they found a Chinese place with a fallen down sign and on the other side of the Walmart was one of those huge home improvement places that she never went to.

"Okay, now what?" Miriam asked.

"Hold on."

Shakti took out a pair of binoculars and looked around. It was a long time before she spoke again. Her hand shot out and grabbed Miriam's arm.

"I see someone," Shakti said.

4

SHAKTI SAW MOVEMENT INSIDE THE WALMART. IT WAS A LONE figure in the shadows. She lay down and pulled the clueless Miriam down with her.

"What is it?" Miriam asked.

At least she had the sense to whisper it.

Miriam wasn't a fighter. She was civilian through and through. It seemed cruel that she had survived to see this new age. This was an age for harder people that did hard things.

She was pretty with large eyes and perfect skin. How did she get perfect skin in this age? Genetics didn't give out its gifts freely. Jerk. She had a round waste that western fashion magazines didn't like because they didn't conform to what they saw as beautiful, pale, skeletal and bitchy. Miriam was none of those things yet was quite beautiful.

"There's someone inside the Walmart," Shakti said.

As she watched she saw the person emerge out of the shadows and walked out into the parking lot. It was a woman with long black hair and a rifle slung on her back.

The woman waved to someone in the store and then another woman emerged. This one had graying hair tied up into a bun. Instead of a rifle she carried a large broom. They were laughing and talking.

She passed the binos to Miriam.

"What do you think?" Shakti asked.

Despite her lack of knowledge about survival, Miriam was a smart woman. No one left alive could be completely stupid.

"They look friendly."

"Let's go introduce ourselves."

"Are you sure? Should we wait and see?"

"There are two of them. Only one is armed. If they turn out to be the wrong kind of people then we outgun them."

If this turned into a Charlie Foxtrot, her plan was to run. Despite how she acted, she was no fighter. She was a lab nerd. Even during the war she hadn't fired a shot in anger. It was only recently that the PG had made her fight. "Lack of manpower" was their excuse.

This was their safest chance to make contact. It was now or they'd never do it.

"Let's go," Shakti said.

She stood up and Miriam scrambled to her feet. She flipped the safety off her M9 Beretta but kept it in its holster. She raised her hands and nodded to Miriam to do the same.

Together they walked out into the parking lot that was little more than a wide area with weeds and broken cars.

A moment later the dark haired woman spotted them and raised her rifle faster than she would have guessed.

"Stop right there," the woman shouted out.

They stopped and the two women came forward. The other woman pulled a pistol out of the black-haired one's holster and aimed it at them.

When they got closer she saw that the black haired one was young, probably not over twenty. She looked Latina and had a wide mouth and long nose. She was pretty but in a unique sort of way. The other woman looked older, maybe in her forties. She had a peace symbol on her necklace and a sock hat that said "save the whales."

"Who are you and what are you doing?" The Latina asked.

Her face scowled at them and her gun was steady like it was held by a clamp. Whoever this girl was, she knew what she was doing.

"I'm Shakti and this is Miriam. We saw your flier in Warm Springs."

It was lame but it was all she could think of to say.

The Latina's eyes went to her uniform and stayed there.

"You in the army?" The woman asked.

"Was," Shakti said.

"Was?"

"I left."

"Which army?" The older woman asked.

The way she asked sounded like there was something more to the question. Maybe they'd had run-ins with the Provisional Government.

"United States. I was up in New York. I went to college at VCU in Richmond. Thought I'd go back there."

The two women looked at each other and some unspoken conversation passed between them.

"We'll take you to our town and get this sorted out," the young woman said.

"What's your names?" Miriam asked.

"I'm Alma, this is Jennifer. I'm going to take your weapons but you'll get them back when we find out if you're safe."

"Understood," Shakti said.

She let the women take her weapons and fought the urge to pull her pistol and shoot them. The idea of being unarmed was not a comfortable one.

"This way," Alma said and pointed with her gun.

They walked behind Walmart and down a hill where a path had been worn down. Below and across the river was a collection of houses and small buildings. People were walking around and there were pens for cows and other animals. It was also much larger than any other group of survivors she had seen.

"So many people," Miriam said.

"We got a nice community here," Jennifer said. "Where are you two from?"

"I'm from Philly," Miriam said.

"How is it up there?"

"There's nothing."

"What did you do before?" Jennifer asked as they climbed down the steep dirt path to the small wooden bridge across the river.

"I was a bank teller. Not very impressive, I know."

"It takes all kinds," Jennifer said.

"How long have you two been together?" Alma asked.

"Two days," Miriam said.

Shakti let Miriam do the talking. Miriam seemed the type that liked talking to people just to talk. Useless chatter was just a waste of time at best and annoying at worst.

They got to the bridge that looked hand made. It was made from solid logs with rough planks to walk on. It was good for foot traffic and not much else.

When they reached the small settlement she saw that it was more involved than she could have seen from above. There was a machine shop, solar panels, buffalo and even children. She hadn't seen happy children in years.

"This is amazing," Miriam said.

"Isn't it?" Jennifer said.

They were led to the largest house, a farm house with a large porch with a Bassett Hound laying on it and looking around with its sad eyes.

"Look at the cute puppy," Miriam said.

She saw Alma roll her eyes.

A man came off the porch and walked towards them. His hand stayed near the pistol at his hip. He was a good looking young guy with a black sock hat and an X-Men shirt under his thick coat.

"Who did you find, Alma?" The man asked.

"Found them near the Walmart. They came out with their hands up."

The man took a moment to look them over then he held out his hand.

"Alex Attaway. Glad to meet you."

Miriam took his hand first and then she did. She hoped she wouldn't come to regret it. She had been fooled before and was in no mood to be fooled again. His smile felt genuine though and a part of her wanted to relax.

It would be nice to finally find a place to settle down. Running from the Provisional Government hadn't been a dream vacation.

Please, Ganesh, don't let this place be like the last.

They led them to the porch and sat them down in old fashioned rocking chairs. She had never actually sat in a rocking chair before. She didn't move to America until she was fifteen and in the small city apartment she hadn't had any rocking chairs.

"Okay, tell me your stories," Alex said.

Alma stood behind him with her rifle in hand.

Miriam started with being born in Iraq and escaping when she was a girl and all the way to being a bank teller in Philadelphia. Then she went on to say how she found a small cabin by some lake but it was too cold so she decided to walk on down south to someplace warmer.

Alex asked a lot of questions about family and what she was looking for. Then his attention turned to her.

"I was a Chemical Engineer student at VCU. I was heading to Richmond to see if anyone was left."

"You were in the army?"

This was her moment of choice. They might have met the PG and feared them. If she told them the truth the might fear her and not let her in. She had just found someone and she couldn't go back out there again all alone.

But if she lied they might find out somehow and then they'd never trust her again.

"I was up in New York when the virus hit. In two days almost everyone I knew was dead. The senator took me and his bodyguard and a few others to Kentucky. From there me and a nuclear engineer took a helicopter to all the nuclear reactors and shut them down before they caught fire and spilled radiation all over the country."

"Wait, you helped shut down all nuclear reactors?" Alma asked.

"I did."

"The senator and his body guard all survived?" Alex asked.

This Alex was smarter than he looked. She thought he was just a dim strong man.

"It wasn't coincidence."

"Then what?"

"They had injections."

"Those rat…" Alma started to say but Alex held up a hand to quiet her.

"They knew it was coming and protected themselves," Alex said.

"They didn't think it was going to run wild like this. It was released in other countries first but somehow got released here as well."

"And then?"

"And then we met up with a few generals and politicians at Ft. Knox. I assume you've heard of the Provisional Government of the United States."

"We've heard of them."

"They started rounding people up to man their farms and oil wells. That's when I left. I didn't want to work for anyone that stripped families of their food and forced them into labor. It was all for the good of the country, they said."

"You left them?"

"I did. I have one of their trucks. It's parked on the other side of town. There are two more M4s with ammo and crates of machine parts and uniforms."

"Or it could be a trap," Alma said. "For all we know you're a PG agent."

"Then why would I come dressed as one? I could have just come as any refugee," Shakti said.

"I saw her kill three of them," Miriam said.

"You did? Tell us what happened," Alex said.

She let Miriam tell the story. It would sound better coming from someone else and right now she needed all the credibility she could get.

"Very well," Alex said. "Then tell us what they have. Manpower, guns, vehicles, assets, resources and what they are planning. Everything."

"Of course. Do you have a pen and paper?"

Alma disappeared inside and came out with a notebook and pen. Shakti drew a quick map of Ft. Knox and showed where the new HQ was, the motor pool, fuel storage and armory were. She then listed what she could remember of their vehicles. They had five Strykers, three Bradleys, four MRAPs and a

Paladin self propelled artillery that no one knew how to fire indirectly.

Alma said something in Spanish that was probably cursing and Alex cracked his knuckles.

"Well, that complicates things," Alex said.

"What are we supposed to do against that, *hermano*?" Alma asked.

From watching 'Arrested Development' she knew that "hermano" meant 'brother.' Since they looked nothing alike she assumed it was a metaphorical meaning.

"Listen, they want to expand," Shakti said. "They're swallowing up every settlement they come across and centralizing resources at Ft. Knox. Whatever they told you, don't believe it. If they know you're here they will come after you eventually."

Alex sat back and thought in silence for a while.

"We spotted them heading east. What are they doing?" Alex asked.

"Is there a military base out that way?"

"Yes."

"Then they're going there to secure what assets they can."

"In the truck we found a box of helicopter parts. Maybe they want a helicopter," Miriam said.

"Wonderful," Alma said.

Then a woman walked out onto the porch. She looked Chinese and the way she walked and examined them with a long glance said that this woman knew what she was doing. She would have bet money that this Chinese woman had military training. It was just something in the attitude that she had seen for the past four years. Whenever she saw a contractor or special forces, she saw that same look.

Alex handed the woman the paper.

"What our PG friends have."

"They're hitting all the major bases first and then going after National Guard bases after," Shakti said.

"Alright, Alma, get your team together and go to Ft. Pickett. Get what you can there. We'll find the fuel."

"Right."

Alma took off down the steps and ran across the little town square.

"Okay, you've been honest with us, now let me share. This is Promised Land. It's our home and we're not going to let anyone take it from us. We have survivors of all kinds. Everyone is welcome.

"We have fifty three people, only a handful are capable of fighting. We're working on getting everyone trained though."

"They have almost a hundred, but only about thirty of them are professional soldiers and they won't let the others be armed."

"Thirty professional soldiers, but they have APCs and who knows what else," Alex said.

"Launch a pre-emptive strike. Destroy what we can before they come after us," the Chinese woman said.

"And start a war?" Alex said.

"The war's started. They will come after you, it's only a matter of time," Shakti said.

"We got some thinking to do. In the meantime I'll have you shown to where you can stay if you choose."

He waved over a dark haired, pale skinned girl. She had on a tight black jacket the kind joggers used to wear and a gun at her hip. She didn't look older than sixteen.

"Rebekah, take our two guests to an open room and help them get settled in," Alex said.

"I'm going with Alma no matter what."

"Yes, yes. Of course. I'm not trying to stop you. You were just the first person I saw."

The girl looked up at them and smiled.

"Welcome to Promised Land! I'm Rebekah. Follow me please."

Shakti looked over to Miriam who had an even bigger smile. Miriam had to know that this place was better than anything she had any right to expect. If she didn't stay here she'd be crazy.

But then the Provisional Government was on its way. If they took this place over she'd end up as a farmer. The PG weren't a bunch of moustache twirling villains. They did want to restore civilization and keep as much of the old world as they could. They had a very valid point. But the way they treat people is not the kind of world she wanted to create.

After getting their guns back, Rebekah led them across the sandy area of their town square to one of the rectangular houses with small windows. They looked simple and had several metal chimneys sticking out the top. What set these two buildings apart from some utilitarian barracks were the solar panels on top. Almost every building had them.

Inside there were florescent lights, the kind that wouldn't go out for many years and a hallway with several doors on each side. At the end was a staircase that went up. Rebekah led them to the stairs and up to the second floor where there was another hallway. At the end was an empty room and Rebekah waved them in. It was a small room with a desk and bunk beds. It looked like an unpainted version of her barracks when she was going through Advanced Individual Training in the Army.

"Here you go. Hope you like it. Maybe next year we'll get houses in Lexington but until we get self sufficient we're all staying together. The communal bathroom is at the end of the hall and the kitchen is down stairs."

"This is great," Miriam said.

"I live downstairs in room three. If you need anything, let me know. Oh, wait, I'll be gone for the next day or so, but just ask anyone. They'll be excited to meet you. We don't see a whole lot of new faces around here."

Then Rebekah waved and hurried off.

"What do you think?" Miriam asked with a huge grin.

"It's not bad and probably better than anything else out there."

"That means you like it."

"I like it."

Miriam then ran to the end of the hall and looked in a door.

"No shower," Miriam said.

"I doubt we're going to see any hot showers any time soon."

"Let's go and meet everyone."

She followed Miriam outside and looked around. There were people all over the place. She took a deep breath and smelled the smoke in the air from wood burning stoves. She heard laughter and conversations that weren't in the terse military cadence she had gotten so used to.

It felt normal here. Normal was good.

5

REBEKAH JUMPED INTO THE OLD TRUCK AND PUT THE RIFLE between her knees, barrel down. She had on her body armor and mag pouches and her hair tied back in a bun to stay out of the way. She had on a pair of Oakleys that she'd never have been able to afford. She also had her first aid pouch, camel back and knife. Her pack with her sleeping bag was in the back of the truck. Everything had been checked and double checked. She was ready to go.

The rifle was the one Tavor they had in the armory. She chose it because it was Israeli and as a faithful Jew she felt it her duty to choose an Israeli weapon. On her hip was a Glock, the same pistol Alex had trained her on back at Virginia Beach.

She liked living there. She'd go out and watch the dolphins play in the waves and watch Adam fish. Promised Land was technically better. It had a small river and lots of open space, but it just wasn't the same.

Adam climbed into the driver's seat.

"You ready, Bekah?"

"I'm ready."

No jokes or funny stuff. This was serious.

In the truck ahead of them she saw Alma and that big guy, Jason get into the cab. Cassidy and her husband, Chris, got into the bed of the truck. Cass had her big "Broadsword" rifle and Chris had a shotgun.

Cass found a hubby of her own religion. Maybe there was hope for her too. With all that was happening it was even more important that she preserved her religion. She couldn't be the last Jew.

Before the end of the world she hadn't really paid much attention to it. She went to school and cared more about the latest song and what her friends were doing.

Things were different now. Everything was different.

The two truck convoy rolled out three hours before sunset. They'd get there when it was dark. Alex wanted them to wait until next morning but Alma refused because "The PG could be there any minute."

"Think we're going to find anything useful there?" Rebekah said as their trucks turned onto the empty highway.

"Sure. There's got to be lots of stuff there. If its worth using the fuel to get is a different question."

"Even a National Guard base has got to have good stuff."

"If not, we'll go to the nearby armories. I know by the Richmond airport there's some artillery."

This could end up being a long patrol.

Driving no longer felt natural. It was like they were doing something unique and special. Almost every patrol was on horses now.

"Did you see the two new people?" Adam asked.

"Yea, I showed them around."

"How they look?"

"One's Indian, former army. She looks kinda serious. The other...I think she's Arab. She seems nice enough."

At first she had wanted to ignore the woman. She didn't want some holocaust denying anti-Semite near her. But she knew she had to let go off all that crap from the old world. Things were different now. Maybe the new girl was the nicest person in the world.

"Word is the Army woman was with the PG," she said.

"I'll keep an eye on her."

They drove over miles of empty road. Sometimes there would be a long dead car on the side of the road or a crashed truck. In the hills by the highway were abandoned farm houses and truck stops. Everywhere she looked was a whole lot of nothing.

As the sun went down she saw that there were no distant lights. There was no one out there.

They pulled up to the gates of Ft. Picket at 9:15. The metal gate was closed. That was a good sign.

Jason got out of the lead truck and opened the gate one handed. The other hand held his giant AK-shotgun he named, "Lucy" after a character in Dracula. He looked mean but Jason was nice. Very quiet though. He let her shoot Lucy once. It was pretty awesome.

They continued on into Ft. Picket and passed some boring small buildings that army bases seemed to be filled with. Virginia Beach had been covered in them. The road curved and came to an area with several large storage warehouses.

The lead truck stopped and they got out.

"We'll start here," Alma said. "Mark down everything you find and after we do a complete check of this base, we'll decide what to take with us. Keep your eyes open. If some wacko's here I don't want to get surprised."

Each team was assigned a warehouse and they got busy with their flashlights. Almost everything was in cardboard boxes. The first box she tore into held boxes of MREs.

"Got some food here," Rebekah said.

"Same."

They went through several boxes of MREs before getting to boxes of boots and uniforms. Then blankets, ponchos, poncho liners, back packs, mag pouches, and a billion different things that soldiers needed to carry. She wrote everything down in a little notebook.

When they finished they met back up with the others by the trucks.

"What did your team find?" Alma asked.

"MREs, uniforms and gear," Adam said.

"We found radios, GPS, batteries, and a bunch of other things we didn't recognize," Cass said.

"We found ammo, a metric crap ton," Alma said and burst into a huge, toothy grin.

"You were waiting to say that," Cass said.

"Yeah, I was."

"What kind?" Adam asked.

"Grenades, 5.56, 7.62 and 9mm. Crates of it. Also found a few M4s and two SAWs," Alma said.

"I think that's a good haul for one night," Adam said.

They made camp inside one of the warehouses and Rebekah laid her sleeping bag down on some of the foam pads they had found. Alma, Cass, Adam and Chris were talking while eating their MREs but Jason sat off to the side reading a book with a flashlight.

She crawled over to where Jason sat.

"What are you reading?" She asked.

"Book two of the 'Foundation trilogy' by Isaac Asimov."

Sounds boring.

"What's it about?"

"The slow collapse of an empire."

"Ours wasn't so slow." She waited for a response but when he continued reading she spoke up again. "You don't talk much."

"I talk when I have to."

"Any advice you can give me?"

"About what?"

She waved her hand.

"This. Everything. How do I do a good job on patrols?"

"Stay focused. Don't let your mind wander. When bullets start flying accept the idea that you're going to die and do what you have to do. Don't be a hero."

"Accept that I'm going to die? How does that help?"

"You won't be so worried about living so your mind's free to think of the important things that will actually keep you alive."

"Sounds depressing."

"War isn't pretty." He put down his book and looked at her. "Why are you doing this?"

"Going on patrol?"

"Yes."

"I don't know. I want to be useful."

"You can be useful taking care of cows or getting the fields ready for planting."

"That's work for kids and old people."

He nodded.

"You want to be an adult."

"Yeah, so? I'm not a kid."

"No, you're not. You're as adult as any of us now and that's the problem."

"What do you mean?"

"You'll figure it out eventually."

She went back to her sleeping bag not sure what had just happened.

Her turn at watch was just before sunrise. Cass shook her awake and with unfocused eyes she went outside into the freezing cold. Her Tavor hung across her chest as she paced back and forth trying to stay warm.

She had never been an outdoors person and had only been camping once. This waking up before dawn to stand around in the cold wasn't her favorite part about patrols.

I hate it, so why do I do it?

She thought back to her family dying in the hotel room. Her father had managed to get permission to get enough gas for vacation. With wartime rationing, vacations were a luxury few could afford. But dad was a lawyer and got what he wanted. All she could do was stand there and watch them die. She had been useless.

Now she could do something though. She didn't have to be a spineless witness. Now she could pick up a gun and fight back.

The others awoke after another hour and they packed their things into the trucks. Everything in the warehouses was marked and now to continue searching the base.

They drove on and came to the barracks area that was covered in two story wooden buildings that looked like something from a hundred years ago. The paint was peeling off, doors hung off their hinges and roofs were sagging.

Civilian cars sat in a gravel parking lot. There were about thirty of them. Army trucks sat in another parking lot and there was a tiny PX store.

They parked on one of the streets in the middle of the barracks area and got out.

"Same drill," Jason said with his low bass voice. "Search every building. Also look for signs of people. I see a lot of cars so maybe a unit was here training when it happened. We might have to go out on the ranges and search for them there. Keep an eye open for movement. Someone could still be hiding here."

Adam and she got to search the section of barracks that was closest to the PX.

"Feel like a snack?" She asked.

"I'm always in the mood for little chocolate donuts."

They shouldered their weapons and looked all over before crossing the street to the tiny PX. A red sports car sat in the parking lot on flat tires.

The glass door was unlocked and Adam went in first. He cut to the left and she cut to the right to get out of the doorway.

It was dark inside and she had to wait a few seconds while her eyes adjusted.

She saw magazine stands and the check out isle and beyond that were the shelves and fridges.

They moved in but something became clear very quick. All the food was gone.

"Alpha team, this is Charlie," Adam said over their walkie-talkie.

"Charlie, this is Alpha actual."

"Alpha, we're here at the PX and all the food is gone. Keep eyes open for survivors."

"Understood."

The electronics weren't touched but tools and food were gone.

"Right, let's get going," Adam said.

He lead the way outside and back across the street where the wooden barracks were. He moved with precision and focus that didn't match his growing weight. He spent more time in the kitchens now than patrolling. He had been drafted into the army when China and Russia invaded and knew what he was doing though.

She did her best to be like him as they moved into the first barracks. The floor boards creaked under their feet and the stairs looked like a danger to climb.

They checked the barracks one by one until they met back with the others.

"Barracks twelve is filled with stuff. Looks like a unit was here for training," Cass said.

"Right, then where are they?" Alma asked.

Jason pointed out towards the woods.

"If they're still here, they're out there on the ranges."

"Great. That'll use up a lot of gas," Alma said.

"At this rate we'll eat up all our fuel without finding anything useful," Cass said.

"We need something big to take out the PG APCs," Chris said.

"If you got any suggestions on a better place to look, I'm all ears," Alma said.

They had brought a lot of their gas in case they found a vehicle to bring back, but they didn't have a lot to waste. She was just glad that she didn't have to be in charge of all that.

"Let's continue searching the area before moving out to the ranges," Adam said.

They went as a group to a cluster of nearby buildings. The first was a machine shop filled with equipment. They wrote down everything there with size and weight and then went on to a nearby white painted house.

"Garrison Commander" was written on a still new looking plaque on the front of the house.

Adam and she went in through the front door. Cass and Chris waited outside to keep watch and Alma and Jason went through the garage.

After clearing the house and finding nothing useful except a scoped hunting rifle, they went outside and found the others in the garage. They had large smiles on their faces.

She looked inside the garage and saw an old fashioned jeep and a tiny artillery cannon.

"What is it?" She asked.

"It's an old WWII Willys Jeep with a 75mm pack howitzer," Jason said.

He squatted down next to it and ran his hand over it like it was some long lost pet.

"Does the jeep work?" She asked.

"It's too simple and rugged not to," Jason said. "The cannon looks alright, we just need ammo for it. Might have to make it ourselves."

"Alright, this is going back. It's the closest thing to a big gun we've found. Too bad it's actually not very big," Alma said.

It was big compared to a person, but small compared to a tank. It was nice but they needed something bigger. She didn't want this patrol to fail. She was a part of this and a failure here would be a black mark on her record. She had been sent out to find stuff to kill the PG and she would not return until she found it. The Promised Land was counting on her.

They continued moving past the barracks and came to some large garage buildings. This time they found something that looked like a fat tank without a gun.

"What's this supposed to be?" Rebekah asked.

"It's a recovery vehicle. It gets tanks out of ditches," Adam said.

"Useful?" She asked.

"Not really, but we could make it useful," Jason said.

They found nothing else so they went out in one truck to search the ranges. There was a sign with a map of the whole area. The place was like a bunch of loops with a long empty area for artillery to shoot at. There was a small fake town to practice urban combat so they went that way first.

As they rode over the rough dirt roads they saw a field with three cannons and three trucks sitting in a field.

"The cannons might have too much rust after two years of sitting there," Adam said.

"We should still check it out."

"We will."

They continued on and found the urban combat area. The buildings were mostly plywood but what all their eyes went too first was an armored vehicle sitting in the middle of the town surrounded by some humvees. It was sleek with eight wheels and a small turret with a big gun.

They spread out and went from cover to cover until they cleared the town. It was empty with no sign of the people that left the vehicles there. They met in the middle next to the armored vehicle.

"What is this thing?" She asked.

"It's a Stryker with a cannon," Adam said.

"It's an M1128 Mobile Gun System," Jason said.

"Is it good?" She asked.

"It's alright, but for our needs it's perfect," Jason said. "It's fast and hits hard."

Jason smiled for the first time. Then crawled up top and opened the hatch. He went inside followed by Adam. Not wanting to be left out she crawled up and looked inside. It was cramped in there and filled with a whole bunch of controls that she didn't understand.

It didn't matter. They'd figure it out and bring this baby home. She did a fist pump when no one was looking. Her mission was a success.

"Found the manual," Adam said.

She looked up and sat on the tank while the boys figured out how to drive it. As she sat there she saw something.

"Movement," she called out without pause.

Near the entrance to the urban combat area she saw someone. It had been a blur but it was someone crossing the road toward them.

She pointed for the others and everyone took cover and aimed their guns. She jumped down and crouched behind the Stryker.

A lone figure emerged with their hands up. It was a man with a beard and a camo jacket. She placed her red dot sight square on his chest.

"Please don't shoot, I'm unarmed," the man called out.

"Who are you?" Alma called out.

"My name's Brian. I live here."

"What do you want, Brian?" Alma asked.

"You're looking for something. I can help you."

Rebekah kept her sights locked on the man. If he so much as twitched wrong, she'd blow his head off.

"And why would you do that?"

"If you help me, I'll help you."

"What kind of help do you need?"

"I got a son. He's sick. If you have any medicine, I'll show you something I think you'll like."

"What?"

"You're looking for hardware, right?"

"Yes."

"I know where they keep all the artillery rounds. Hundreds of them."

Alma turned back to her people.

"Think we can trust him?" Alma asked.

6

ALMA LOOKED AT THE BEARDED MAN AND TRIED TO READ HIM. She knew little about people from being friendless most of her life. Her teenage years had been spent practicing her competition marksmanship and not going to parties.

"Well? What do you guys think?"

Cass came up next to her and peeked out from behind the Humvee.

"He looks alright. I don't see a gun," Cass said.

But Cass thought everyone looked alright.

"Jason," She called out.

He popped his head out of the Stryker.

"Turn around," Jason called out.

Brian turned around.

"Now walk backwards toward us," Jason said.

Brian obeyed.

When he came close Chris went out and searched him with a thorough pat down.

"No weapons," Chris said.

Alma came out with her gun still pointing at Brian. She didn't look at him. Her eyes were at the tree line from where he came.

"If anything happens, you die first," Alma said.

"I swear, I'm no threat. I have a boy who's sick. Do you have any medicine?"

"We don't, but we know where to get some. How many of you are there?" She asked.

"There's me, the boy and an old man."

"If you're lying I'm shooting you between the legs," Alma said.

Cass came out.

"What's wrong with the boy?" Cass asked.

"He has a fever that we can't get rid of. He's been sick for two weeks and its only getting worse."

"We have a settlement we can take you to," Cass said.

Brian looked around and then shook his head.

"I can't go nowhere. We like it here," he said.

"Sir, it's not safe here. Come with us and we can help your boy," Cass said.

"What do you mean it's not safe?" Brian asked.

"The Provisional Government's going to be here any day and if they see you they'll take you to their work camps," Alma said.

"Provisional Government? So there's still a government?"

"No," Jason said as he climbed down. "They are not the government. They're just a few politicians and officers that got a vaccine before anyone else did. They are not here to help you."

"But you are?" Brian asked.

"If you show us the arsenal, then yes," Alma said.

The man looked them over one more time.

"I'll take you to it, then you take us with you."

"Deal," Alma said.

As they climbed back into the truck she prayed that this would be worth it. They would need everything they could get their hands on to stand a chance against the PG. Alex gave off the impression that with some preparation they'd be able to hold off any attack. Not hardly. If the PG came to their doorstep they might be beaten back but they'd lose too many people and possibly see Promised Land destroyed in the process.

If they were going to win they had to go on the offensive and do a complete guerilla war against them. Stopping the PG before they arrived was the only way.

They drove to a cement bunker that was covered in grass like a small hill.

"It's all in there,"

Brian said from the passenger seat. Jason sat cramped in between them.

They got out and Brian opened the metal door that shrieked from rusty hinges.

Inside were pallets and pallets of artillery shells.

"Alright, gather around," Alma said and waited for everyone to get in a circle.

"Let's load up the ammo from the warehouse, then these cannon shells. Let's fuel up the jeep and the Stryker and get them ready to go. Brian, do you have transportation?"

"No."

"Alright, we'll have to come back for the rest of this stuff. Let's go get your boy and load up."

The boy was about ten and was pale with a high fever. They had been staying in one of the houses on base. The old man was a Vietnam vet with an old style M16. He looked older than dirt but could probably outrun her and give Jason a challenge. They had a fireplace and their kitchen was filled with cans of food.

They'd be coming back for those as well.

A jeep, ammo, artillery shells, a Stryker, food, armored recovery vehicle and gear. Not a bad haul.

The Jeep was easy to start with the old man's help but it took them a while to get the engine going on the Stryker and even longer to figure out how to use it. It was late afternoon by the time they got everything loaded and on the road. Brian, the boy and old man were in the back of the truck on top of artillery shells and covered in blankets to stay warm.

The Stryker with the cannon was a great find and Alex would be very happy. She had done good and couldn't wait to hear what Alex said. He'd get that big goofy smile of his and that would make all the effort worth it.

Behind her the Stryker with its big cannon kept up without a problem. Jason in the Willys jeep and the towed pack howitzer stayed in front. He was showing off.

She still hadn't thanked him properly for saving her life. In fact, she hadn't talked to him much at all. They were partners now but they never talked.

It didn't help that he was a huge beast of a man that probably had more bear ancestors than human and he never seemed to talk unless spoken to. She just didn't know what to say to him. It wasn't like she could ask him out to a movie.

How did Cassidy do it?

Cass used to be her partner but when Chris came around she was kicked to the curb and left on her own. Alex had Lisa now and things hadn't been the same. It used to be her and Alex and that was all they needed.

Now she had no one. It was like just after the plague hit, she was all alone.

They pulled into Promised Land well after dark.

She was the first to jump out and run toward the main house where Alex would be.

She jumped up the stairs two at a time and knocked on the door.

Alex answered the door as he put on his bomber jacket.

"Alma, you're back already. That's either really good or really bad."

"Look for yourself," she said and got out of the way.

She watched every movement of his expression.

Alex stepped out onto the porch and that smile grew on his face.

"I don't know what that is, but I like it," Alex said.

"It's a Stryker with a big gun. Come see what else we got."

"Who are they?"

He pointed to the three people being let down from the back of her loaded truck.

"We found them at Ft. Pickett. The boy's sick."

"Make sure they get anything they need."

"Look, we also got a jeep."

As Alex walked around looked at their haul she listed off everything they left behind.

"We'll get a patrol out tomorrow," Alex said. He then turned to her and put his hand on her shoulder. "Good work, sis."

She smiled and knew that she was blushing. She stuttered as she tried to think of something to say.

Lisa came up and read from an armored vehicle identification book about their new cannon-armed Stryker.

"Alma," Alex said.

"Yes?"

"I'd like you to lead tomorrow's team. Take Jason again."

"Alright," she said and the watched as he and Lisa walked off talking about their new acquisitions.

She was left standing in the square while everyone rushed around ignoring her.

Alma walked up to her room and took off her tac-vest with all its magazines and gear and placed her competition AR in the gun rack above her bed.

She lay on the bed and stared up at the ceiling.

I should probably get something to eat, maybe inform my team that we're heading out in the morning.

But she lay there for a long while, doing nothing.

Her eyes went to the map on her wall. It was of the United States and showed the route she had taken to get to Virginia to find her brother.

It seemed she was the only one that remembered that. Alex was too busy to care anymore.

When her stomach growled she got up and went to the kitchen. She made a boiled egg sandwich because there were always boiled eggs for whoever wanted them and went out to find her team.

As she walked toward the building where Jason and Rebekah lived she saw the two new people sitting on a bench and talking to each other. Then she remembered that one of them was prior military.

"Shakti, right?" Alma asked as she approached.

Shakti looked up with no warmth on her face. For someone who had just found a place to live after the end of the world, she figured the woman would be a little happier.

"That's me."

"Have they given you a job yet?"

"Not yet."

"Good. I got a patrol going out in the morning. We're heading to Ft. Pickett again. You're coming with."

Shakti nodded.

She didn't know if she could trust this former PG woman, but it was better to have her in sight than sneaking around unsupervised. Alex was welcoming to everyone. That wasn't her job. Her job was to protect the Promised Land no matter what.

"When do I report and where?" Shakti asked.

"By the trucks at seven."

"I'll be there."

Alma nodded and went inside.

She found Jason's room first. She knew right where it was but had never knocked on his door before.

Alma took a deep breath and knocked.

Jason answered the door in his cargo pants and "Babymetal" T-shirt. Behind him on his bed she saw his gun in pieces for cleaning. He filled the doorway and looked down at her.

"Hey there," she said and tried to act natural. "Alex wants us to go back out tomorrow, so get some rest."

"Alright."

"Umm…meet me by the trucks at seven."

"Okay. I'll tell Rebekah."

"Okay, thanks."

She didn't need Rebekah on this because she had chosen Shakti, but she didn't want to contradict Jason and look like a jerk.

"Alright, see you tomorrow then," she said and left as fast as she could.

She had survived without embarrassing herself.

The next morning she was bundled up in her tan jacket with the fur collar and her sock hat. She kept her gloves on as she looked over the maps on the hood of the old jeep.

Jason was the first one there. He came up and placed his huge Saiga shotgun on the hood. He didn't say a word, he just started putting his tac-vest on.

"It's going to take a lot of fuel to get that recovery vehicle back here," she said to sound conversational.

"Not sure it's worth it. Maybe if we stick extra armor on it and mount a few big guns."

"I think we're going to need everything we can get," Alma said.

"Probably true."

Then she saw Shakti coming up. Jason turned around to see her and his expression changed. It became that statue version of himself like when he was about to do something dangerous.

He picked up his AK-shotgun, shouldered it but didn't aim it.

"Shakti Bhattathiri, what are you doing here?"

Shakti looked up from putting her gloves on and stopped in mid stride.

"Jason Kaminski," Shakti stammered out.

"Alma, this woman works for the PG."

Shakti held her gloved hands up.

"Hold on, I don't any more. I left, I swear it."

"Why leave now? How do I know you're not a spy?" Jason asked.

He was a big guy with a big gun, but she knew Jason was fast. Competition fast.

She saw that Shakti didn't move. Her hands were up and her almond eyes were wide. Spy or not, the woman was terrified of Jason.

"You two know each other, I take it," Alma said.

"She was working with the brains at the PG."

"And he was a mercenary sent in when they needed something killed."

"I left," Jason said.

"So did I," Shakti said.

"I don't have time for this. Jason, we're taking her along. Keep an eye on her but Alex believes her."

"I'm not Alex."

Jason slung his shotgun but followed Shakti with his eyes.

"What are we doing at Ft. Pickett?" Shakti asked.

"Collecting a vehicle and some more supplies."

Shakti nodded.

She was pretty enough to be a Bollywood star and didn't look at all like a soldier. She acted the part though. The woman probably wasn't like that, but the end of the world had a way of changing people.

What would mom think of me now? Have I changed? Alex hadn't said anything, but he wouldn't notice even if I have.

"So, Shakti, can any of your chemical engineering help us here?" Alma asked, changing the subject away from questionable loyalties.

"Sure, give me the tools and books and I could come up with some way to make chemicals, but unless you got a real good chemist, all I can do is basic stuff."

"Make high explosives?" Alma asked.

"I can do that if I had the materials."

"But will she, is the better question," Jason said.

Adam, Rebekah and Cass showed up and then they mounted up, giving her a break from Jason and Shakti.

She was alone in the cab with Jason. Cass and Shakti were in the bed of the other truck.

She plugged in her iPod and went to her classic rock list.

"You like classic rock?" She asked.

Alma tried to smile and act normal.

"Yeah."

"What's your favorite?"

"Zeppelin."

"Robert Plant, right?"

"Yeah."

She couldn't think of a thing to say as her mind went blank so she let the music play for a while.

"What's your favorite band?" She asked.

"My own band."

"Huh?"

"I was the bassist for a metal band. We called ourselves the *Sarmatians*."

"You played the bass?"

"I used to."

She had always wanted to play the bass. Cass was supposed to have taught her but when Chris came along any thoughts of lessons fell to the side.

"Can you teach me?"

It came out before she could think about it.

He looked over to her and nodded.

"Find a bass and I'll teach you."

"Awesome. I always wanted to learn."

"It relaxes me."

For the rest of the drive she imagined being in Jason's small room alone with him while he wrapped his arms around her from behind and taught her how to play. His mouth would be close to hers and his instructions would turn into a gentle, slow kiss.

They arrived at Ft. Pickett at ten and went to the warehouses to load up. The new girl worked as hard as the others and kept her eyes looking around. That was a good habit to have.

Once the food and gear was loaded up, they went to the recovery vehicle. Jason and Adam got to work on it, draining the fuel tank of the bad fuel so they could put the good stuff in.

She sat on the hood of the truck while they worked. She knew nothing of mechanics and would only get in the way.

Shakti came up and sat beside her.

"Why are we bothering with this thing?" She asked.

"We're going to add armor and put guns on it I think."

"Doesn't sound like the most effective thing."

"Well, if you have a tank lying around, let us know and we'll use that instead."

"That's not what I'm saying. The PG have a lot of stuff to bring against you. But I don't think they'd bring everything at once. Too much fuel. They can only refine so much at a time. They'll come in with two or three armored vehicles at most and move in with infantry behind them."

"That's their MO?"

"That's their MO."

"Well, then this thing we'll use against their infantry."

"They're good. They made sure their best survived."

"Is that what you are?" Alma asked.

"I don't know why I was spared," Shakti said.

That didn't make any sense but the woman did appear to be telling the truth. She let it go and looked up to the recovery vehicle.

"How long?" She asked.

"Not long," Adam called back.

Adam was inside doing something and Jason was pouring fuel into the thing's tank.

She looked back at the way they came and opened an MRE. Beef stew, her favorite.

As she let it cook in its own water heater, she leaned back against the windshield and let her mind wander. She thought about her journey across the country and wondered how many people were really left out there. What was Mexico like? She imagined Mexico City as the world's largest graveyard.

Then she saw birds fly up into the sky. They were far away but there were a lot of birds.

"Shakti, is that by the gate?"

She pointed at the birds.

"Yeah, I'd say it's near the front gate."

She turned back to Jason.

"I think you guys need to hurry up."

She was about to tell him about the birds but off in the distance she heard a muted mechanical rumble of engines. Large engines.

"It's the PG," Shakti said.

Rebekah jumped up onto the bed of the truck and looked out.

"The PG are here already?" Rebekah asked.

"We need to go now," Alma said and hopped down.

"Just a second," Jason said and poured the last of the fuel.

He tossed the can and climbed up into the recovery vehicle.

"Mount up." Alma called out and jumped into the driver's seat. She started it up and waited for Shakti to get in. Rebekah and Cass grabbed the other truck.

The recovery vehicle roared to life and lurched forward.

"Front gate's a no-go. Is there another way out of this place?" Shakti asked.

"There's a back way through the ranges."

But it was a maze through there and it would be more luck if they actually found the way out.

She took lead spot and handed the map to Shakti. The other truck was behind her and the recovery vehicle was in the rear. It rumbled forward much slower than she liked.

They had to drive down a gravel field, past more repair bays to the road and take the road to the ranges.

Her eyes kept going back to her rear view mirror.

Two humvees came into view. She almost slammed down on the gas but then saw that they didn't have gunners up top.

"Shakti, see what you can do."

She grabbed her walkie-talkie and called up Cassidy.

"Cass, get your Broadsword and do something about our friends."

In the mirror she saw Cass lean out the window with her .308 AR and take

49

aim. She fired but she couldn't see anything else. In the seat next to her Shakti leaned out and let loose a few shots with her M4.

She heard the distant 'pops' of return fire.

They got to the road and she smashed the pedal down to get the recovery vehicle between her and the PG. The recovery vehicle could take it but her truck couldn't. Bullets went right through cars and trucks and would go right through her. She was wearing her vest but that meant with her luck the bullet would just hit her in the head.

A quick glance showed that the humvees were charging at them full speed. They were tearing down the road, speeding past the crumbling barracks. It was a matter of time before they caught up and she didn't doubt that each humvee had four people in there, all fully armed.

If they didn't do something they'd be killed. The problem was, they couldn't return fire while driving.

So, stop driving, genius.

"Shakti, I'm going to stop, get ready to unload on them."

"Understood."

This is either going to be brilliant or the stupidest thing I've done.

Alma rolled down her window and grabbed her AR. She then yanked the wheel to the left and came to a screeching stop. She threw her gun up and took aim out the narrow window.

Both her and Shakti opened fire. She didn't have her earplugs in and inside the Humvee the concussion of the gunfire was like jackhammer blows inside her skull. She ignored it and kept shooting. She fired as fast as she could while still being accurate. A steady drumbeat of death sent empty brass flying around the cabin of the humvee.

Now that she was still she could use the skills she had been training most of her life. She saw her shots hit the hood of the humvee and also saw Shakti's shots hit the front right tire and move up the side of the vehicle. Alma walked her shots up to the driver's side windshield and watched it turn opaque from spiderweb fractures. If they'd had uparmored humvees there wouldn't have been anything she could do.

Next time I'll bring a grenade launcher or something.

The humvee veered off to the right, almost crashing into the other humvee. The other humvee came to a stop and Alma gunned the gas again to get the recovery vehicle between them.

She didn't hear any more returned fire and they tore down the dirt road toward the rear exit that was somewhere in the maze of ranges that made up

Ft. Pickett's maneuver area.

Alma tried to remember the map of the range maze and lead the way with the slow recovery vehicle behind them. The massive hill of a vehicle kicked up a cloud of dirt. If the PG followed, they'd be easy to find.

"Good move with the truck," Shakti said.

"I do what I can."

Ever since that night at the Southern Virginia University library where she had come so close to death, Alma had had bad dreams almost every night. She had been shot at before but she'd never had to consider the possibility of dying.

Cass said she had mellowed out since then. Maybe. She didn't yell so often. So many things didn't seem as important. What was actually important was shown in a higher contrast. Living was important. Her family was important. Promised Land was important. Everything else had faded away.

Maybe something broke inside of me. I don't know. It's like I'm lost in my head and the real world is a dream.

7

SHAKTI CONTROLLED HER BREATHING AND TRIED TO CALM down. She had been surprised to find that she was good at being a soldier, but like math, she didn't enjoy it.

After driving around empty dirt roads they found the exit that lead out to a highway. They pulled out of Ft. Pickett's land and took a route that would go around the entrance to Pickett. If the PG were around, they'd be there. She knew their style. They always sent scouts ahead.

The tracked recovery vehicle only went about 29 mph. That meant it would take them twice as long to get home. *Wonderful.* That was twice the opportunity to be found by the PG.

"This dumb thing better be worth it," Alma said.

"It might be. If the PG went to Eustis, they won't find much there. Everything useful there was shipped north to the war."

"Thank heavens for small miracles, huh?"

"I don't know about miracles, but I think you killed that driver."

She had to admit, this Alma chick was pretty good. She didn't look like former military, but she knew her way with a gun.

"Good. Everyone one of them we kill now is one we don't have to face later," Alma said.

Shakti leaned over to be heard over the truck's annoyingly loud engine.

"I've been thinking. I see what you have here. It's pretty good. You got a small core of veterans that know what they're doing. I say, strike them now while they're not ready. Blow up their fuel storage. Sabotage their vehicles. Pipe bombs. Anything."

"I brought that idea up to Alex already. He wasn't a fan."

"Then we have to convince him. An alpha strike is the only way to even the field. If you make yourself too hard a target, they'll look elsewhere."

"You're preaching to the choir," Alma said.

She kept watch for any signs of a PG patrol as they made their way down the highway. There was nothing here to look at except fading traffic signs that told the distance to the next exit. She didn't recognize any of the names. All she knew of Virginia was Richmond and really just around the Virginia Commonwealth University campus.

After an hour she settled into her seat with her rifle propped between her knees, barrel down.

Alma's question filled her mind. Why had she survived? She wasn't the top of her field and she hadn't known a thing about nuclear reactors. When she survived the others didn't act surprised. It was like they had been expecting her so it was no accident that she got the vaccine.

They pulled into the town square just before sundown when the lights were coming on. The mechanics shop and blacksmith were illuminated in the blinding artificial light that used to be so common but was now like a rare treat.

The giant recovery vehicle rumbled to a stop behind them.

"That wasn't so bad," Alma said.

"Sure, next time you throw a party I'll be there."

"You did alright, Shakti."

Alma gave her a wink and then jumped out of the truck.

Shakti collected her stuff and walked back toward her new room that she hoped would become her home.

Miriam was there waiting for her on a bench. She jumped up and hurried over.

"How'd it go? You get what you went for?" Miriam asked.

"Yeah, we got it and a bunch of other stuff."

She pointed at the fat recovery vehicle.

"That thing's huge. What is it?"

"Just a glorified tow truck."

"You hungry? I got some apples for you. Dinner's in about an hour in the barn."

Dinner sounded pretty amazing.

She went to her room and dropped her stuff off. She looked over to Miriam who sat up on the top bunk, kicking her feet. Her antique pistol was still on her belt.

"Let's see about getting you updated," Shakti said and pointed to her pistol.

"It was my dad's."

"Great. Keep it, but carry something else to fight with."

"I'll give it consideration."

Shakti stripped off her tac-vest and opened her army-issued coat to let her breath a little. Back before the war and all of this, she would have been mortified to smell the way she did now.

"I think I'll go on a patrol tomorrow for some deodorant," Shakti said.

"Yeah, we can use a few things. Maybe a poster or a painting. Yeah, a beautiful painting would make this place real nice."

She had lived in an air conditioned trailer back at Ft. Knox. Now she was sharing a small wooden room with a woman she didn't understand.

Back in India her parents would never have let her talk to Miriam. Tensions between the Hindu and Muslim communities had gotten bad before they left. It was one of the things she liked best about America. The petty old world differences were meaningless.

Smores were the second best thing about America.

She went to the shared women's bathroom and washed herself down a little before drying off and getting her coat back on.

"Let's go. Time to eat," Miriam said and jumped down.

They walked down the stairs and out the door. Others were migrating in the same direction. Back with the PG it was always southern food. Beans, grits, gravy on toast, meatloaf. The same boring crap every day.

When she walked into the barn she smelled something that made her stop. The barn was already full of people and most of them were in line to the serving tables. Plastic tables were set up in rows like a cafeteria.

"What's up?" Miriam asked.

"Is that curry?"

She hurried over to the serving tables that already had a long line forming.

There was bread, boiled eggs, white rice and a big pot of curry.

"No way."

She looked up at the girl serving it and saw that she was Indian. She was maybe ten years old but she was unmistakably Indian.

"Hello there," Shakti said in Hindi.

"Hello, stranger. Where are you from?" The girl answered in Hindi with a huge smile.

"Philadelphia, but my family's from New Delhi."

"Mine's from Jaipur."

"It's probably crawling with nothing but monkeys now," she said in English. "Where'd you get the curry?"

"I got enough curry stashed away to last a few years."

"What's your name?"

"Rehka."

"I'm Shakti. Nice to meet you."

"Save me a seat, okay?"

"Will do."

She waved and then went to the back of the line where Miriam was.

"Met a friend, huh?" Miriam asked.

"What did you do all day?"

"They interviewed me and when I said I was a business major, they put me in inventory. I get to catalogue everything that comes in and out of our storehouses."

"Our?"

"I'm going to stay if they let me."

She looked over to a far corner of the barn and saw Alex talking to Alma. Alex had a notebook and was taking notes about something. The Chinese woman was right beside him. She stood perfectly still like a waiting eagle.

"If that woman isn't some kind of special forces I'll eat my shoe," Shakti whispered.

"Seems normal to me."

They waited in line and got their food. They found an empty spot at one of the long picnic tables near the rear of the barn.

The curry was amazing. It probably wasn't even that good but after two curry free years it tasted like it came from Ganesh himself.

"So, you're Hindu, right? You believe in hundreds of gods?" Miriam asked.

She'd had this conversation hundreds of times and it never got old.

"Not exactly. There is one god over all creation. Everything else is just a servant of that god. I do not worship Vishnu, Shiva, or Ganesh in their own right, but I honor what they do as a part of God's will."

"Wait, so you don't worship a bunch of gods?"

"Some Hindus do, but there is no one unified Hindu belief."

"I think I'm confused."

Then Rehka sat down next to her with her plate and cup of milk. She introduced them and asked about her life here. Rehka burst into a long story about how she was rescued from a bunch of rednecks and how nice everyone was here.

From the girl's account it really seemed that this place was legit. That meant it had to be defended. For that, they needed to strike first before the PG showed up on their doorstep.

Just a month ago she had been working with the PG to solve their human waste/fertilizer problem and now she was advocating a military strike against them. Life had a way of feeling absurd.

After dinner she left Miriam and Rehka to talk and found Alma standing off by herself.

"I've been thinking," Shakti said.

"I'm listening," Alma said but her eyes were on something else.

Shakti followed the gaze and saw that she was watching Jason.

"We need to talk to Alex and get him to send a strike team out to disrupt the PG."

Alma's eyes turned to her.

"You know the layout. You know where their soft spots are?"

"I do."

"Hold on."

Alma jogged over to Jason and pulled him by the arm back to where she was standing. The last thing she wanted was that merc standing near her. She hadn't known him personally but knew that everyone was afraid of him.

"Shakti says we need to send a team out to Ft. Knox and launch a raid to hit the PG where it hurts," Alma said.

"And she could walk us right into an ambush," Jason said without looking at her.

"I'm not with them," Shakti said.

"Of course not," Jason said.

"Would the two of you behave? Get over it and let's figure this thing out."

"We destroy their fuel, their vehicles and their armory," Shakti said.

Jason looked down at her like he was reading a report.

"Agreed," Jason said.

Shakti waited for the giant to say something else, but that was the end of his conversation.

"Let's go talk to Alex then."

The three of them walked over to where Alex and Lisa were.

"This looks serious," Alex said.

"We have to talk," Alma said.

"I'm all ears."

"We need to launch a strike against the PG and keep them from coming after us. They're getting too powerful and if we don't curb them now, it'll be too late. Shakti here knows the layout of the place. She knows where they keep things. If we strike at their weak spots we can keep them away."

"And start a war. Alma, I know war's coming but if we go off half cocked, that could get the PG coming down on us with everything they have. You want tanks rolling into town square? We're not prepared to fight them and until we are I'm not provoking them."

"You'd wait for them to come here?" Alma asked.

"I'm buying time to get ready. Once we have our outposts we'll know they're coming and can stop them from ever reaching here."

"And if they attack next week?" Jason asked.

"Then we'll do what we have to."

"Not good enough," Alma said. "We have to hit them now while they're weak or they'll grow too strong."

"No, we're not ready for a war. That's final."

Alma pointed a finger and made to say something else, but instead she stormed off with Jason close behind.

Shakti let out a short sigh and shook her head. The PG was coming after them no matter what. They weren't collecting military hardware for peace offerings.

She went back to the table and sat down.

"What's wrong?" Miriam asked.

"Nothing, just a disagreement with the boss."

"Shakti, I have my song book in my room. Can you read Sanskrit?" Rehka said.

"I can."

"Good. Let's go sing. I haven't sung in a long time."

She followed Rehka back to her room where she dug a small red book out of her backpack. Together they sung songs she remembered from the temples. They were songs she thought she'd never hear again.

The girl was smiling and her singing was pretty. This was a part of who she was and it was still alive. For the past four years she had buried it all under duty and then survival.

Rehka shared a room with another teenage girl but her side had a small shrine to Vishnu with flowers all over it.

When she got back to her room Miriam was there reading a book, a mystery judging by the generic yet ominous title. A lantern sat on top of the stove and she had her book angled to catch the light.

"It's cold in here. Let's get a fire going."

"Sure, but we'll have to go chop some wood first. Personal stoves are the responsibility of the individual. That's one of their rules."

"Never mind. I'll just zip up in my mummy bag."

She was about to take off her coat and boots when there was a knock at the door. She stifled a moan and went to the door. Alma stood there with intense eyes.

"I need to speak with you," Alma whispered and then motioned with her finger for her to follow.

"Alright."

She followed Alma out behind the blacksmith's tin-roofed shack. Jason was there.

"What's this about?" Shakti asked.

"Alex said no, but I'm going anyway. I want you two to come with me," Alma said.

She folded her arms and looked them each in the eye in turn.

"This will be very dangerous," Shakti said.

"Waiting around is more dangerous," Alma said.

"I meant with Alex. He won't be happy."

"I'm not doing it to make him happy. I'm doing it to save our town."

"Count me in," Shakti said.

"Three's not enough though. We need a few more," Alma said.

"I think I know a guy," Jason said.

The only person Shakti really knew was Miriam and she'd be more of a hindrance than a help.

"I might bring Rebekah and just not tell her we're going out against orders," Alma said.

"She's young," Jason said.

"We're not exactly holding try-outs here. We need whoever is willing," Alma said.

"Cassidy?" Jason asked.

"I don't think she'll go, but I'll try."

"I'll go talk to my guy," Jason said.

"Alright. I'll talk to Cass. What do we need?"

"Do we have any explosives?" Shakti asked.

"Grenades," Jason said. "The artillery shells would take time to set up."

"Incendiary?" Shakti asked.

"Yes," Jason said.

"We have some C-4, but it won't do much against armor from the outside," Jason said.

"Incendiaries in the engines, C-4 in the cabins," Shakti said.

"That means we'll have to get real close," Alma said.

"We need to plan this very well or it will fail," Jason said.

"Good call. We'll meet tomorrow at lunch."

Shakti went back to her room and laid there thinking about Ft. Knox. She knew where everything was, but she also knew how well guarded it was. The PG only used a small part of the base, so sneaking in wouldn't be a problem. Getting to the good stuff would be. And then there was the question of getting the right tools to destroy what they needed. If they didn't destroy enough they'd bring the entire PG down on their heads.

Planning a raid was a lot to think about. It wasn't the first night recently that she didn't get much sleep.

8

ALMA WOKE IN THE MORNING AND STRETCHED OUT IN HER bed. She had a good four blankets on because she didn't have a stove or fireplace in her room. She got up, got dressed and walked out into the hall. Both Cass's and Alex's doors were closed.

Of course they were. They had their precious loves of their lives so they could shut themselves away.

She sighed and put her hood up against the cold.

Alma went downstairs and got a fire going. She stayed there by the fire until she warmed a little and then went to the window.

The sun was coming up and only a few people were out and about. The mechanics were working on replacing tires on one of the trucks and the natural gas workers, all five of them, were heading out. Between them and Farmville, they had a lot of skilled people. A guy in Farmville knew how to make bullet casings and Promised Land had a chemist that could make the gunpowder. By this time next year they'd be making their own ammunition.

What knowledge did other settlements have? They needed to find others to open up trade and share knowledge.

She shook those thoughts out of her head. Those were thoughts for later, when they were safe. Now she had to think about war.

After breakfast she took the teenage group to the rifle range for practice. Rebekah was no longer in the teenager class and was in the advanced class with the rest of the adults that knew what they were doing. They all knew how to handle guns by now so she got them into the more advanced skills. She taught them how to do rapid reloads, how to clear jams faster and how to shoot with both eyes open.

The problem wasn't the students. They were amazing. They learned quick and jumped into the lessons headfirst. The problem was that they couldn't shoot enough. Due to ammo restrictions, they only got to fire four magazines each. It simply wasn't enough. She had gone through dozens of cases of ammo during her weekend practices for competition and war was far more important than a sporting event.

They broke for lunch and Alma went to the town square to look for Jason and Shakti. The new girl was proving useful. In better times they'd be using her chemical engineering skills instead of her trigger finger.

Jason and Shakti were already there waiting for her. The three of them walked off into the armory where they could talk in private.

The garage sized cement block building was one of the newer ones and was filled with racks of guns covering every wall and isle.

"I looked through what we have and I came up short. We don't have enough explosives to destroy what we need to. The 90mm, 105mm and 155mm are too big to carry with us," Jason said.

"So, it's over before it begins?" Alma asked.

"Not exactly," Shakti said.

The woman's already large eyes grew ridiculously big when she got excited. Coupled with her perfect raven hair and Alma had to admit that she was jealous. Her own hair was like dull straw in comparison.

"If we go to their armory first we can get C-4 there. Pop the hatches, drop in a brick and run," Shakti said.

"Do you guys know how to do it?" Alma asked.

"I do," Jason said.

"They also have AT-4s there. They won't scratch a tank but they'll hurt anything else," Shakti said.

"Alright, Shakti, Jason, draw out a map of everything you remember. I want it as detailed as you can make it. I want to know where guards are, where they walk, where they come from, everything," Alma said.

They agreed and then adjourned with a promise to meet after dinner.

When she walked into the barn for lunch, she saw Cass waving at her. After getting her one cucumber and spam sandwich she walked over and sat down next to Cass. Of course Chris was there too.

"What you been up to?" Cass asked.

Cass had on her cowboy hat and her red hair was tied back in a long pony tail. She had been getting some sun lately and her freckles were more prominent than usual.

"Just taught a marksmanship class to the teens."

"Oh, fun. I bet they liked that."

Cass went on about her day and how her and Chris had gone on a little patrol to Lexington for pregnancy tests for the community. It was Cass's not-to subtle hint that they were trying to have a baby.

"I know family stuff is kinda different now, but would you consider being our child's aunt?" Cass asked.

Alma almost choked on her food.

"What? Aunt?"

"We're family now. I mean the old families are gone, so we have to make new ones. A lot of others are doing it."

She hadn't noticed. Alma looked around the room and saw that people were in clumps and now that she really looked she saw that they were indeed in the same groups they always were in.

"Sounds great, Cass."

Cass wrapped her arms around Alma's shoulders.

"Thanks, Alma. We're now officially sisters, just not in the genetic sense. I mean...if my kid and your kid want to have a kid, they'd still be able to, right?"

"I think you've thought this through way too much," Alma said.

After dinner which she spent between Cass and Alex while they carried on conversations that did not include her, she met with Jason and Shakti.

"I talked to my guy," Jason said. "He'll go."

"I'll talk to Rebekah tonight. The less chance she has of finding anything out, the better," Alma said.

"I grabbed an M4 with a grenade launcher," Shakti said.

"I have some incendiary grenades," Jason said.

"Sounds like it's going to be a wild party then."

Then they poured over the map Shakti and Jason drew of Ft. Knox. There were three different ones. One showed the whole base, another showed the part the PG used and another showed the motor pool, fuel depot and armory in great detail. They went over plan after plan until they got a good idea what they had to do.

"If we're in agreement, we'll meet here at five in the morning," Alma said.

They agreed and Alma went to find Rebekah. She was in her room listening to her iPod.

She told Rebekah that they had a raid against the PG in the morning but no one was supposed to know.

"Tell no one, understand?" Alma asked.

"Understood. I'll be ready," Rebekah said.

"You can back out. This one's going to be dangerous."

"They're all dangerous," Rebekah smiled.

The grin on the girl's face was almost innocent, like a little girl that had just done her first backflip.

"Good girl," Alma said.

She patted Rebekah on the back and left her there to go back to the main house. A twinge of guilt ran through her stomach as she wondered if she was just using the poor girl or if she was just being a leader. Was there a difference?

Alex and Lisa were curled up on the couch with the fire roaring. They were reading a book about government together.

"How was your day?" Alex asked before she could slip past to the stairs.

"Fine. Taught a bunch of kids how to fight without enough live fire exercises to do much good. How about you?"

"Organizing a senate or community meeting."

"Fun."

She went up stairs without trying to continue the conversation.

Cass's room was closed but she saw light coming from under the door. She took a deep breath and knocked on the door. Cass told her to come in. She had been dreading this conversation all day.

Inside she found Cass and Chris sitting on the bed playing a board game. Seven Wonders or something.

"What's up, Alma?"

"Promise not to tell anyone what I'm about to tell you."

"Sounds interesting. I promise."

"I'm taking a small patrol to Ft. Knox. We're going to destroy their fuel, weapons and vehicles so they won't be able to hurt us."

Cass sat there for a few seconds and then looked at Chris.

"Wait…you're what? You're going on an unauthorized mission to do the very thing Alex told us not to do?"

"Yes."

"Alma, you shouldn't do this. I know you disagree with him, but he is our leader. We all agreed."

"This is about the safety of everyone here. We have to destroy their means of attacking us because if they come here, we won't have enough to stop them before they destroy this place or kill us."

Cass leaned back against the headboard and thought.

"I won't come with you, Alma, but I won't tell Alex."

That was as good as she had expected. She didn't know if it was Cass's religion or nature to cling to authority, but she had known Cass wouldn't come.

"It's the right thing to do, Cass."

"Says you. We voted on Alex."

"Doesn't mean we obey blindly. If he was doing something wrong, and I mean, morally wrong, wouldn't you try to stop him?"

"Well…"

"If you outlawed religion. You'd still pray, wouldn't you?"

"Yes, but this isn't the same."

"To me it is. If I obey him, we lose our homes and maybe our lives."

"Do what you must, but I'm telling you, you're wrong."

She thanked her and went back to her room.

There she got everything ready to go. She had her boots, tac-vest, weapons and ammo all lined up. She put the SAPI-plate in her vest, front and back.

Her backpack was ready to go and she'd wake up at four to gas up the truck.

On nights like this before a mission she seldom got much sleep. Plans and contingency plans swam through her head.

When the alarm went off she jolted awake. Good, that meant she had gotten some sleep. She turned off the old fashioned mechanical alarm clock and got up. She threw her clothes and gear on and went to the corner where her favorite guns were stacked. She chose her trusty competition AR because she was the most familiar with it. On a mission like this, she needed a gun she could trust.

Once she was ready she crept downstairs and outside. No one was awake and no lights were on anywhere. That wasn't good. The PG could sneak in here and kill them all in their sleep. When she returned she'd talk to Alex about posting all night guards.

If he was still talking to her at that point.

This was a risky mission, not just because she could get killed. She didn't know how Alex would react. He could get angry with her. Very angry. Maybe she'd lose his trust.

Is this mission worth that? Being impulsive has almost gotten me killed before.

She leaned on the hood of the truck as it fueled up.

This is the right thing to do. This is the right thing to do.

Then she heard heavy footfalls behind her. She turned to see Jason. He threw his pack in the back of the truck. Slung over his shoulder wasn't his "Lucy," but an RPK which was just a long barreled, full auto AK with a big ammo drum.

"You certainly have your type," Alma said.

"The Russians made good guns."

Next was Rebekah. She had her Tavor with the star of David painted on the side. Then came a man she had met but hadn't really talked to. He was a tall, lanky guy with an intense stare and unshaven face. It took her a few seconds to remember that his name was Todd.

The guy didn't look like prime spec-ops material, but she trusted Jason's judgment.

Then Shakti came with the M203 grenade launcher armed M4 she had taken from the armory. Her eyes were red and she seemed half asleep. She also had an air riffle and a box of pellets.

"Let's go," Alma said.

They loaded up into the modified Humvee and took off before anyone woke up.

No one spoke for several hours. Either they were too tired or they were thinking about what they were getting into.

She tried not to think at all. She handed Jason the map and told him to navigate. It was a long drive to Kentucky and she needed to concentrate on driving. The roads weren't what they used to be and there could be bandits with ambushes waiting for them.

****

Skyler Dullknife watched the single truck drive out of the settlement. The truck's lights in the pre-dawn darkness made it stand out in the lightless world. He sat huddled in his mummy bag with blankets below and over him.

Father had told him to watch the White People during the night. His sister watched them during the day.

At first they thought all the White People had gone away and wondered if their ancestor's prayers had finally been heard. But then they appeared again. A few here, a few there.

His tribe had killed a few wild men that had attacked a surviving White family. The tribe did not need people like that around them.

Bandits. That's all some of the people had become. Others were worse. The Appalachian Hunt Club had rounded up survivors like cattle. Father had feared that they would have to confront them.

But the new group of White People had done it for them and his tribe got to remain hidden in the mountains where they had always been. When the other Cherokee were forced west, his tribe stayed. They kept to themselves and remained where nobody would bother them.

It saved them then and it had saved them against the sickness that had killed the world. He hadn't seen a jet since that day they heard on the radio that people were dying.

Now something was different. The White People by the river were sending more trucks out with armed people. It was like watching animals. You could tell when a predator was around by the way the deer acted.

That was what he was watching. The River people were deer and there was a predator nearby.

Only he did not know what sort of predator could scare the River people. There were many of them and they had many weapons. Whatever was out there was a wolf and his tribe needed to know.

9

REBEKAH DIDN'T KNOW ALL THE DETAILS OF THE MISSION, BUT she knew Alma and Jason had a good plan. They always did. They had trusted her to come with them. Whatever it was, it was secret and they thought she was good enough to do it.

She put her earbuds in and listened to the "modern rock" list that Alex had made for her. Before she had met him, she listened to pop or whatever. But he had her listen to the rock songs and told stories about them so that they came alive in a way that Lady Gaga never did.

I wonder if Lady Gaga's still alive. I'd pay money to see a post apocalyptic Lady Gaga...if money still meant something.

Her mind was left to wander as Shakti and Todd were sleeping and Alma and Jason weren't talking.

She sat back and tried to get comfortable. Her trusty Tavor was propped against the door beside her. It was ready to go when she was.

What would mom think of me now? She wanted me to go to college. It didn't matter what I would study because I'd find a rich lawyer or doctor to marry and drive around in sports cars.

Mom didn't like violence or even raised voices. She never heard mom yell. When she was angry she would get very quiet. That was when her brothers and she knew they were in trouble.

She watched the road pass by as 'Shinedown' played in her ears.

Hours later they were heading west on 64 entering Kentucky. They still had a long way to go and they stopped at a trashed grocery store and picked up some canned food. Then they were back on the road.

Around noon Shakti had them pull into a side road that turned into a dirt path. Once they were well out of sight of the highway she told them to wait here until dark.

Alma pulled out the maps Shakti and Jason had drawn and went over the plan several times. She was paired with Shakti and the tall guy. Of course Alma and Jason were a pair.

She tried to look past their professionalism and see if there was something more, but neither of them gave anything away. That was no fun. It would be so cool if they got together. He saved her life, they both liked shooting things. It was perfect.

They took naps in shifts until night time came. Then Alma broke out the night vision goggles. She put hers on over her head and turned it on. The darkness exploded into bright green. The forest around which had been nothing but blackness was now as clear as noon day. She could see everything. Even the stars seemed so much brighter.

"Wow."

"Okay, everyone. We know what to do. Stay low, shoot first, shoot straight. We have to remain unseen for as long as possible," Alma said.

Only Alma's mouth was visible. Now she looked like a robot Cyclops in her NVGs.

Jason was holding a pair of wirecutters and Shakti had the air rifle. Todd had a bunch of smoke grenades strapped to his chest.

"Ready?" Alma asked.

"Ready," everyone said together.

She followed behind as they made their way through the woods. It was a long hike that seemed like it lasted hours.

Rebekah had no idea what time it was when they reached the fence. There was a field between the forest and the fence and they had to crawl on their bellies to reach it. She kept watch while Jason cut a small hole in the fence. Beyond was another open field with uniformed square buildings in the distance.

This was it. They were going into PG territory where they'd be surrounded, outgunned and outnumbered. She had trained for this. She knew what to do. Trust the others and she'd make it out.

After seeing that no one had spotted them they ran in a low crouch across the field to the closest building.

Shakti pressed up against the wall of the two story cement block building and peered around the corner.

"The motor pool is down that street. It'll curve past those buildings but we can cut through the grove of trees there," Shakti said.

They moved out.

The base was covered in empty buildings being overtaken by nature. It was just like everywhere else. Once spring hit, the old world would be swallowed by green plants.

Past the trees she saw a few distant lights.

"That's where we're going?" Rebekah asked.

"Yeah. Those are the guard towers. They have big spotlights, but that's why I have this," Shakti said and patted the air rifle.

They continued past apartments with rows of abandoned cars. She knew the story there. The people had gotten sick and stayed home. Inside were the skeletons or mummified bodies of the people that lived there. That was why they had stayed at Virginia Beach for so long, the breeze kept the stench at bay.

They came to a cluster of buildings that was clear of vines and weeds. Beyond a three story block building with small windows were the guard towers. This was the area that the PG lived in.

Alma motioned with her palm down and fingers spread out to stay low. They crept up to the wall and Alma looked around the corner.

Rebekah stayed as quiet as she could. She wasn't going to be the weak link in this mission. She was going to show Alma that she could trust her.

"It's the armory," Shakti said. "The door has a padlock. It's in full sight of the tower."

"If I'm fast enough, I can cut the lock before they see me," Jason said.

"Not likely," Shakti said.

Rebekah looked around. There was one window on the rear of the first floor and it was a small one.

"I bet I can fit through that window," Rebekah said.

"What are you talking…" Alma looked up at the window and then down at her.

After the world ended she had lost weight. She hadn't been overweight, but now she barely resembled the girl she used to be.

She stripped off her vest and gun belt and they hoisted her up. She used the cutters to remove the lock on the window and then squeezed in. It was slow and she had to get her arms in first and pull herself through.

Below was a cement floor and she was going through head first. She held on to the sill with one hand as she pulled her body through. Once her feet cleared she fell to the ground with a painful lack of grace. She stood up and rubbed her backside that had taken the brunt of the fall.

She was in a janitor's closet. There were metal shelves with cleaning supplies and buckets and mops everywhere. There was a small table that she pulled under the window to help her get out.

Then she went to the door. It was unlocked. She opened it a crack and looked out into the hall. There were metal doors running down each side of a long, cement hallway. She tried the doors but they were locked. The one door that led outside she unbolted and peeked out. There was a long gravel field where armored vehicles of all kinds sat in neat rows. Beyond that were three buildings which had lights on. One was a small one storey building like Pickett was covered in and the others were four storey buildings that she had no idea what they were. Everything on military bases looked the same.

Rebekah went back to the window and gave her report.

"Okay, we'll wait for the guard to turn around and sneak in one at a time," Alma said.

That didn't sound like a great plan, but they knew how to open locks and she didn't.

She waited inside as the others dashed inside one at a time. Each time they waited to make sure no alarm went off.

Jason went first and got started on the nearest lock. Then Todd. Todd was quiet and fast. Whoever he was he seemed to know what he was doing.

Rebekah didn't breathe until the last of them were inside. Alma stayed by the door with her rifle at the ready. She put her gear back on and slung her Tavor over her head and shoulder.

Jason unlocked the first door and found racks of pistols. Some of the racks were civilian pistols, evidence of the PG's foraging. Rebekah glanced in and looked around. A whole room of nothing but pistols. Alex would have loved this place.

It wouldn't hurt to take a souvenir.

Rebekah looked around while Jason was working on the other locks. There were all kinds but she wanted something special. There was a giant chrome revolver that was shiny and badass, but she doubted she had the strength to fire such a beast.

Then she saw a gun that didn't look like any other. It had a big box magazine in the front and a long skinny barrel. A red '9' was on the pistol grip. It was elegant and unique, everything she wanted a gun to be.

She slid it out of the rack and held it in her hands. It was heavier than she expected but it felt so right.

"What's this?" She asked when she went out into the hall where the others were.

"It's a Broomhandle Mauser," Todd said.

He held out his hand and she gave it to him.

"Oh, a Red Nine. Nice. You're in luck. This is chambered in 9mm so you'll actually get to shoot it."

"How do I get the magazine out?"

"You don't. It loads by stripper clips."

That doesn't sound like fun, but for this beauty, I'll figure it out.

He handed it back.

Jason had opened three other doors but so far, no explosives.

"It's already midnight," Alma said.

So far they had found hundreds of rifles and pistols. Nothing that went 'boom' though.

"Let's skip to the end," Shakti said.

They went to the last door and continued there.

When the door swung open she saw Jason and Alma's faces grow smiles.

Rebekah hurried over and looked in. There were several blocks of C-4. A quick count told her that there were ten. Boxes marked "detonators" sat on a nearby shelf.

Todd went in and loaded his backpack with the explosives. She knew from Alex that C-4 wouldn't go off without a specific charge so she didn't worry about it. Todd then gave them a brief class on how to arm the explosives. She was given two bricks with detonators.

One small mistake and she'd be missing an arm.

I can do this.

The next door had two AT-4s and a bunch of grenades.

"Alright, we got what we need," Alma said.

Jason and Shakti grabbed the AT-4s and they went to the door that led out to the motor pool.

"Alright," Shakti said. "I'm going to sneak over to the tower and try to take out the spotlight. When you see the light go out or hear shooting or whatever, start the attack. Alma, you know where the fuel is. The rest of you destroy their armor."

"Maybe I should go," Jason said.

"I'm not going to betray you."

"I'd rather not take the chance."

"Jason," Alma whispered. "She got us this far. It's time to trust her."

"Now's the time to catch us all in a trap," he said.

"Surrounded by all their guns and high explosives? No. Shakti, go for it."

With that, Shakti slipped out the door. Alma kept it open a sliver.

The minutes ticked by as they waited and her hands were sweaty on the grip of her Tavor. The only bomb they could spare was in the armory's grenade room and Todd hovered over it ready for the signal to start the count down.

Up till now they had avoided contact. Now they were heading into the jaws of the monster. The entire PG was outside those doors and they were about to waken the monster.

"Ready?" Alma whispered back.

"Ready," they said in unison.

Then the spotlight went out.

"Go," Alma said.

She took off through the door and Rebekah followed after her. She came out into the wide open space where the vehicles sat waiting for them. It was dark and all she saw were the dark shapes of the vehicles in front of her. The dim lights from the building across the way left her side in total shadow.

Jason was first. He ran up to a big tracked vehicle with a turret and climbed up. Jason ripped the hatch open and threw the C-4 down into the cabin.

Todd climbed up onto one that had a giant cannon of some kind.

The first one she saw was an eight wheeled vehicle that looked like the one they found at Pickett, only without the big gun. She found the steps and climbed up. One of the hatches was open and she pulled it up with both hands. She didn't bother looking inside as she armed the explosives and tossed it in.

She jumped down and ran to the next one.

Somewhere a shot rang out. She did a quick look around and didn't see anything so she ignored it and ran to the next vehicle.

Jason had already finished his two and got his big drum-fed AK ready as he took cover behind the tank he had just tossed a bomb into.

The timers were for five minutes. That didn't sound like a long time at all but when a firefight erupted one minute could feel like an hour or a second.

"This one," Jason said and pointed to a Stryker.

That was going to be their get-away car.

Then a siren went off somewhere and two men came running out of a door. They had vests on and carried M4s.

Jason opened fire with his giant gun. The muzzle flash lit up the surrounding area and sent brass flying against the tank he was next to. One of the men went down and the other dove for cover behind a Humvee. The man he had shot crawled back inside. He was wearing IBA armor and was probably more startled than injured.

She raised her gun and waited.

From other buildings more people came out. Most of them had body armor. She took aim and fired. It was dark and her red dot site was too bright. She didn't hit anything but they ducked down.

Todd started throwing smoke grenades all over the place to give them some cover.

Rebekah switched her site to the night time setting and took aim again. This time the dim red dot was perfect. She fired and struck the door where someone was peering out of.

Better.

Then a bullet struck the cement near her feet and she ducked back. More shots rang out and when she peeked she saw a muzzle flash coming from the third floor. Without waiting she raised her gun, put the red dot just below the window and fired.

Alex had shown her by shooting through a car door that just because she couldn't see the enemy didn't mean that she couldn't hit them.

She didn't know if she had killed the man but there wasn't any more shooting from that window.

From somewhere behind her Todd fired one of the AT-4 rockets and for a moment everything was illuminated like mid-day. The miniature sun streaked across the motor pool and exploded against an up-armored Humvee. A super nova of smoke and sparks covered the place where the Humvee used to be.

More muzzle flashes came from other windows and soon it was like it was raining from every angle. She couldn't peek out without exposing herself to someone.

Any second a bullet would bite into her and she'd be dead, just another casualty, a failure they'd bring home. Alex will see her lifeless body and say something like "she wasn't ready for combat." Maybe she wasn't but she was here and she was going to live, no matter what.

"Get inside the Stryker," Jason said without turning.

"Right."

Any excuse to get out of this mess.

She looked over to the bomb-free Stryker. There was a wide empty gap between her covering tank and the Stryker.

"Cover me," she called out to Jason.

"Covering," he said and let loose with his RPK. She heard the constant stream of gunfire behind her as she ran full speed to the Stryker. She climbed up the side faster than she had ever climbed anything.

She fell onto the bench and sat there panting. The gun was warm in her gloved hands and she could smell the gunpowder all over her. What she didn't see was blood. She checked herself all over in case she missed something in the rush of battle.

No matter what she did she couldn't get her heart rate back to normal. It was like there wasn't enough oxygen in the air.

Jason was next. He climbed in and started the vehicle up with a low roar that shook her in her seat. She noticed that his arm and leg were bleeding. It wasn't much, perhaps a ricochet or two.

Then Shakti jumped in and Rebekah gave her a quick pat on the butt.

"Good job," Rebekah said.

"Let's try to get out of here alive before we celebrate."

Todd got in last and sat down next to her.

"Let's go," Todd said.

"What about Alma?"

"We have to go pick her up," Jason said.

The Stryker lurched forward slamming her sideways onto the bench.

Todd manned the automated turret and fired using his small computer screen. It was like a video game. Using the .50 he fired on every vehicle that didn't get a bomb. Through the screen she saw Humvee's torn up and other army trucks shredded like paper.

Now she heard more gunfire through the open hatch. Wherever they were going, they were going fast. It was hitting the armored hull like hail now. They had woken the monster now and it was slashing at them with its claws.

The Stryker then slammed to a halt and threw her against Shakti. She heard the hollow metallic sounds of someone climbing up the Stryker.

Alma jumped in and crawled into the seat next to Jason. They both had computer screens in front of them instead of windows. It was better than having bullets flying at them through glass.

Todd sealed the hatch and they took off at full speed.

Then the sounds of muffled explosions shook the Stryker followed by a massive explosion that sounded like a deep *"FWOOOM!"* The Stryker lurched but kept going.

"The fuel," Alma said with a grin.

They tore out of Ft. Knox at full speed while flames erupted from burning buildings behind them.

Rebekah put her gun on 'safe' and leaned back against the bench. It was as if all the energy in her body left at once. Shakti must have felt the same because she slouched while rubbing her face and saying something in a strange language.

"That was wild," Rebekah said.

Jason patted her on the shoulder.

"You did good kid."

She managed a thumbs up.

10

ALEX SAT ON THE PORCH TAPPING HIS FINGERS ON THE ARM OF the rocking chair.

"She'll be back," Lisa said.

"I should have seen this coming. She never listens to me."

"You really think they went to Kentucky?"

"Where else?"

Lisa sat down in the rocking chair next to him and put her hand on his to stop the tapping.

"What are we going to do about her?" Lisa asked.

"Take away her position. She's no longer Head of Training."

"She's the best trainer we have."

"I can't give everyone the idea that they can go off doing whatever they want."

"We can keep her in her room for a while."

"House arrest?"

"Or something like that, yes."

He looked over to his beautiful wife. Sure, she was almost painfully beautiful and more dangerous than a laser guided bomb, but what he really needed from her was her brain. She was perhaps the smartest person he knew.

Alma had come across the entire post-apocalyptic United States to find him. The girl loved him more than he deserved and here he was thinking about throwing her in jail.

There has to be another way.

He got up and paced around while he thought.

It was getting near sundown and the work around the 'town square' was dying out. People were leaving their workshops, gardens and animal pens to get back to their rooms and clean up for dinner.

It couldn't last like this. These thrown together barracks were temporary. In the summer maybe they'd spread out. Each person with their own house, land and animals. They needed more horses and more cows. There were plenty of farm houses in the area to take over but he couldn't send them out until they knew they were safe from the Provisional Government.

Then he saw the new woman, Miriam, walking up to the porch. She was a small woman with dark eyes and dark brows. Individually all her pieces weren't attractive by artificial magazine standards. Her nose was too big, her lips were too round. But all together they created a face that was more beautiful than the sum of its parts.

"What can I do for you today?" Alex asked with his best "everything's alright" smile.

"I was wondering, can I join the shooting practice?"

"Of course. We want everyone to learn."

"Can I start tomorrow?"

"Our head trainer is away at the moment, but I'll see what I can do."

"I just think it's time I learn what to do."

"I wish I knew what to do," he said.

"Don't we all? Just let me know when and where and I'll be there."

Miriam laughed and walked off singing some pop song he didn't recognize.

"At least someone's happy," he said.

"You never know. Maybe Alma's little raid will be a good thing," Lisa said.

"Do you agree with her?"

"Going off without support was foolish. But maybe an alpha strike would work."

"So, I'm wrong now?"

"No, she's wrong for going off against orders and unprepared. The smart thing to do would have been to keep trying to convince you."

"Now I feel like some World War One general that refuses to see reason."

Later that night he sat reading a book about the Battle of the Bulge. Lisa was reading a spy novel and occasionally laughing out loud. Cass came in with a fantasy novel.

"I guess if Alma was back, I'd hear some yelling," Cass said.

"At the least," Alex said.

Cass took a look out the curtains before taking a seat.

"Stupid girl," Cass muttered.

Alex fully agreed.

The next day he spent choosing spots for their lookout posts. They needed to be hidden but offer a good view. They'd need food, water, guns and a good radio. That meant solar power and backup batteries.

It was a full day of riding around on horses because between the missions to Ft. Pickett and Alma taking the rest for her road trip to Kentucky they weren't left with much fuel at all.

Once the locations were chosen he and his three engineers rode back to Promised Land and arrived at sunset.

Alma's truck was there and there was a small crowd gathered around the main house.

His first instinct was to charge up the steps and rip her head off, metaphorically and literally.

But no one besides Lisa, Cass and Chris knew that Alma had gone off without orders. Keeping this quiet and dealing with it in private would be best for everyone.

He dismounted, gave the reins to the stable boy and walked to where Alma and her team were waiting. Alma was telling the details of their raid with one of her toothy smiles.

Alex took several deep breaths and walked up onto the porch where everyone fell silent. Lisa was standing in the doorway with her arms folded. She wasn't smiling.

"A successful raid, I take it?" Alex asked.

"We blew up their fuel, armory and their armor. It'll be a long time before they launch an attack on us," Alma said.

He turned to the crowd.

"Go get ready for dinner. I have to debrief Alma on the situation."

Alma kept her smile as she walked inside. He thought about bringing her team in with her but decided against it. He just wanted it to be him and her.

He took Alma up to her room and closed the door behind them.

"What the hell, Alma?"

"I did what I had to."

"You didn't have to go off on a suicidal raid against the PG."

"I did because you wouldn't."

"Do you have any idea how furious I am with you?"

"Probably very, but I did what was right."

"You went off on an insane mission against my orders."

"We did it though. We blew them up."

"And when they come for retaliation?"

"They won't have enough fuel and we'll beat them."

"You just pissed off the biggest hornets nest around. Whatever happens is on your head."

"I accept that. That's what responsibility means."

"Then you'll accept your punishment?"

"For what? For saving us from immanent invasion?"

"You went off on your own in an insane rush to get yourself killed."

Alma paused and looked him up and down.

"That's how I found you, remember."

He closed his mouth and rubbed his face with both hands. It was that very recklessness that led her back to him. The girl had crossed a continent for him but he couldn't let her get away. There was more going on here than the two of them.

"Alma, you're under house arrest until I think of what to do with you."

She froze.

"Are you serious?"

"Very. You endangered everyone here and you went against my direct orders. I can't let that slide."

"Wait, Alex…"

"Enough. You're confined to your room. Your meals will be brought to you until I can figure out what to do."

He then left before either of them said something they'd regret.

Alex closed the door behind him as a muffled stream of curses was launched at him.

He went down stairs and found Lisa and Cass waiting there.

"How'd it go?" Lisa asked.

The cursing and punches to the wall were clear.

"Judge for yourself."

"You can't keep her there. People will ask questions," Cass said.

"I know she's your friend."

"So? The people are cheering out there. If you take that away, they'll hate you for it."

"She has a point," Lisa said.

"So, I should let her off?"

"This time, yes," Cass said.

"I don't know anymore," Lisa said. "Back in China things were much simpler."

"We should let her go," Cass said.

"I don't think she wants to see me right now," Alex said.

"I'll let her out," Cass said.

Cass went up stairs and the cursing subsided.

"Let's go," Lisa said.

He took her hand and together they walked to dinner.

"I didn't know having a family was so difficult," Lisa said.

"It's not all bad."

"Speaking of which, I want a wedding. A real one."

"You think any of that still matters?"

"I want a wedding. Red lanterns, food, music, everything."

"Where's this coming from?"

"I want to see what a normal life is like."

"You came to the wrong place," he said with a forced laugh.

She hit him on the back of the head.

They took their usual spot at their usual table and people came up to tell them how glad they were that the PG had been crippled.

When Alma came into the barn, she cast him a quick glare and went over to stand next to Jason and that new woman, Shakti.

"I don't think she's going to talk to me for a long time," Alex said.

"She'll get over it," Lisa said.

"Alma tends to hold grudges."

He hoped this wouldn't be one of those times. He needed her. She was their best trainer, best shot and she was brutally honest.

An impromptu party broke out as they ate. People brought in guitars and basses and sung songs and danced.

Everyone around him relaxed and celebrated but Alex knew it wasn't over with the PG. This was a temporary victory at best.

Over the next week Alma continued to not even look at him. Alex did his best to act like he wasn't angry at her childishness.

He spent his energy on getting the lookout posts set up. Camouflaged bunkers were the design they settled on. Towers were too visible. The bunkers were set up on the sides of hills and mountains overlooking the most likely routes of invasion.

Everyone would rotate through shifts that lasted a week. A team of two would man each outpost. That meant at any given time, twenty people were out on watch. That was a lot but they were too spread out for constant back and forth shift changes. It wasn't ideal, but it was what they had to work with.

Once that was finished he turned his attention to Promised Land. The .50 cal was up in the attic window of the main house covering the one road in and out. Next he planned for some of the artillery shells to be turned into bombs and have the bridge rigged to explode.

By the end of the week, his plans were moving forward and Alma still refused to talk to him. She spent her time with Jason and Shakti.

"She'll calm down…eventually," Lisa said.

****

Miriam took aim with her old Mosin Nagant and put her finger on the trigger. The paper target zombie was two hundred yards away so she had to be completely still. She breathed out like Alma taught her and squeezed the trigger as smoothly as she could.

The gun kicked in her shoulder and the '*bang*' and smoke took her eyes off the target for a second. She lined the sights back up and tried to see if she had hit the target.

"Hit," Alma said. "Low and left."

Miriam racked the bolt and fired again.

"Hit. Looks like we might make something out of you yet."

She looked up to Alma who stood there with her pair of binoculars.

"Looks like tomorrow I can move you to the M4 and then the fun will start."

The other students with her were mostly teenagers. She was the only adult that seemed to have survived the apocalypse without learning how to shoot.

They walked back to the Town Square and she found Shakti working with another engineer over a table full of technical diagrams that she couldn't begin to understand.

"What's going on?" Miriam asked.

"We're trying to build a better refinery."

"Sounds fun."

It really didn't.

"How did practice go?" Shakti asked without taking her eyes off the diagram.

"Really well. I start on the M4 tomorrow."

"Another hit to our stockpile. We need to get ammo production up."

They already saved every spent brass casing for reloading, but it wouldn't be enough. Like any good business major she looked into the long term aspects of a problem. No matter how conservative they were with ammo, they would eventually run out. Then their ancestors would be down to spears and bows. They couldn't let it get that bad.

"Hey, Shakti," Alma said as she came up from behind.

"Teaching my friend to shoot straight?"

"She has the makings of a good sniper. She's patient and has a head for math."

"Maybe throw a scope on her Mosin," Shakti said.

Alma thought about it for a second.

"Not a bad idea. We have a mountain of 54r ammo she couldn't burn through in a hundred years."

"Sniper?" Miriam asked.

She had never thought about being a sniper. Back in Iraq she had heard people yell that word out and saw the fear in everyone's faces. She was meant to have a quiet job, and sit drinking tea while reading a good book in her expensive uptown apartment.

What would mom and dad think about me being feared? They hated violence and now their daughter was going right into the business that had chased them out of Iraq.

"What do you think?" Alma asked.

"Sounds good," Miriam said, not knowing what else to say.

"Great, let's go find our gunsmith."

They went to the armory where a man sat inside. He had a wide table covered in gun parts. Some kind of rifle she didn't recognize.

"Hey, Phil, we need to hook this woman up with a good sniper rifle that fires 54r. Think you can put a scope on her Mosin here?" Alma asked.

Phil was a large man with a larger beard that had gray streaks in it. The end of the world would put gray in anyone's beard.

"54r? Sure, I can put a scope on that Moz, but what about this?"

Phil got up and limped over to one of the weapons racks. He pulled out a rifle that looked like an AK-47 only longer. She recognized the weapon from her childhood. She had seen soldiers, good and bad carrying something similar. They were the snipers that people would shout about in fear.

"What is that?" Miriam asked.

"It's an actual Dragunov. Works good. I shot a magazine through it."

Alma took it and then handed it to Miriam.

"What do you think?" Alma asked.

It was heavier than the Mosin but it wasn't bolt action. It looked like a modern gun. The wood was beautiful but the gun was a terrible beast waiting to kill. She had seen what this gun could do. She watched Fatima, her neighbor's aunt gunned down by a sniper carrying one of these. She saw Fatima's head split open spreading dark red blood over the tan sand.

Now she had one in her hands.

At first she wanted to give it back and tell them it was all a mistake. But she remembered the fear and power the name "sniper" invoked. If she could use that power to protect her new home then maybe it was a good thing.

For the first time in a long time she wondered what Allah would have her do. If all was according to His will, then she had been put here in this situation to do this very thing.

"I'll take it," Miriam said.

"Sign for it and it's yours. You're responsible for it. Keep it oiled and clean," Alma said.

She signed for it and Phil handed her a canvas shoulder bag with pouches for magazines. Then he handed her several boxes of ammo.

"We'll get you working on your long range skills tomorrow," Alma said and patted her on the back.

As she walked back to her room she kept looking at the long rifle in her hands.

Sniper.

I'm going to become someone that kills people.

I don't have a choice. I have to protect my home.

She climbed up to her bunk and crossed her legs and she tried to take the gun apart. It took a long time of trying different things before she disassembled the thing. Then she had to put it back together which took much longer. Then she did it again and again.

She looked out the tiny window with her new scope. It looked like a mess of lines, dashes and even a big swooping line on the left side. Someone was going to have to explain all that to her because she couldn't make any sense out of it.

When she went to dinner she went with her new rifle slung over her shoulder and the magazine carrier slung across the opposite way. They were magazines, not clips. Alma got angry when she called them clips.

After getting her food she sat down next to Shakti and Rehka. Alma and Jason were there as well. Shakti had gotten close to those two ever since their raid on the PG. Her friend was a war hero now. Back in Philly her friend had been a co-worker at the bank. Rachel had been normal and boring.

Those memories didn't seem real anymore. They were more like half-forgotten dreams now. Now she was eating beans in a barn with a rifle on her back and wasn't even wearing the hijab.

She was used to being the only Muslim in a group. But now she could be the only Muslim in the Eastern United States. She was working hard to defend her new home and friends, but she was doing nothing for her faith.

Did Allah even care anymore?

"Something wrong, Miriam?" Shakti asked.

"You ever wonder if you're going down the wrong path?"

"I think the world went down the wrong path."

"Is any of this God's work or is it just man's?"

Alma leaned over.

"Sounds like you and Cass would get along. She's always talking about God's plans for us."

"What religion is she?"

"Mormon. They're the ones with seven wives," Alma said.

"Sounds like your two religions would get along," Shakti said.

11

ALMA SAT NEXT TO JASON AS THEY ATE. SHE TRIED TO THINK of something professional to say.

"I think training more snipers might be a good way to conserve ammo. Maybe make our enemies too afraid to come near us," Alma said.

"A Russian theory of combat, huh?"

"Yeah, just thinking of ways to maximize our resources."

"We'd need more people."

"Well, I'm not saying we're going to be like the Soviet army."

"I was teasing."

"He does have a point though," Miriam said. "We need more people. We have too few to maintain a healthy and sustainable population. I've been doing the math and if the population is going to increase without systematic inbreeding, we need to find more people and breed with the PG and Farmville."

"Breed with the PG? You're crazy," Shakti said.

"Why not? They're humans."

"Dating my cousin sounds better than that," Jason said.

"No thanks," Alma said. "I wouldn't want to have a kid with some PG turd. The kid will turn out to be some authoritarian jackass."

"That's one of the reasons the PG assemble survivors to a centralized location," Jason said.

"What do you mean?" Shakti asked.

"For population control. They've had this planned out for a while. That's why they kept you alive. You were useful and you were attractive breeding stock," Jason said.

Shakti's eyes went wide and she placed her fork and knife onto her plate.

"What the hell's that supposed to mean?" Shakti asked.

"I heard them talking about it. They were planning out their population for the next hundred years. They were joking about which one of them would get paired up with you. You were apparently very popular."

Shakti got up and stormed out of the barn. Miriam hurried off to catch up.

"What was that about?" Alma asked.

"It's true. They kept her to breed with her. Alex is thinking too short term. If the Promised Land is to have a chance of lasting, we need a wider gene pool."

This was a topic she really wanted to talk to him about, but not like this, not like some clinical exercise for a statistics class.

But thoughts of the PG deciding who married who placed the PG even lower in her esteem. And it had already been low.

"I think I've lost my appetite," Alma said.

"They have it wrong."

"Huh?"

"The PG. They have it wrong. It's not about breeding like animals. Humans don't work like that."

"Darn straight I don't. But why did you tell Shakti?"

"To make sure she understood what was at stake."

"You don't trust her?"

"I want to."

"You saw what she did against the PG."

"I didn't say she was with the PG."

He wasn't making any sense and the subject needed to be changed immediately before she said something she would regret. Probably something about not minding being forced to mate with him. Duty to country and all that.

"So, what are you doing tomorrow?"

"I was thinking of planning out a long range patrol, maybe all the way down to Florida."

"What for?"

"To find other settlements like ours. They have to be out there."

"I want to go," she said without thinking.

All she knew was that if she went, she'd be with him doing something important.

"I was counting on you going," he said.

A warm rush swept through her body.

"Then I'm going, whether you want me or not."

"You're a good shot and you won't hesitate."

That's all? That's kind of a let down. Oh well, gotta take what I can get.

The next day she spent with Miriam and her new Dragunov. Miriam was good. Not the fastest, but she was improving. The entire time she had to fight to keep her mind focused. Her thoughts kept going to images of her and Jason stuck in a tent during a rain storm. He'd say something about having to remain warm.

"Alma," Miriam said.

"Huh?"

"Look."

Miriam pointed her gloved hand at someone coming up the hill. It was Alex. *Fantastic.* Just the person she didn't want to see.

"Alma, got to talk to you," he said.

She stood up from the blanket they were lying on and straightened her clothes out. She hadn't spoken to Alex in over two weeks. What did he want to talk about now? Did he want to throw her in jail or say how horrible she was for saving their people?

"Is this important?" Alma asked.

"Jason just talked to me about a long range patrol."

"Yeah? So?"

"He said you were going."

"You going to stop me again? Lock me in my room?"

"Alma, please don't be like that."

"Like what? A useless third wheel to you? Now that you have Lisa, you don't need me. I'm just in the way. I should have stayed in Vegas, right?"

"What? No. What are you talking about?"

"Screw you, Alex. I came across the country to find you and now that I'm here, you don't even care."

"Of course I care."

"When was the last time we hung out, just me and you?"

We haven't. Not once.

"That's right," Alma said. "I'm going with Jason where I can be useful to someone."

"Alma, stop acting so psycho. I'm just trying to tell you that I think the patrol is a good idea."

"Oh, thank you for your permission, master. May I sleep tonight or eat or does that go against your plans?"

"You're being unreasonable and there's no point talking to you when you're like this."

"I guess there's never a point to talk to me, is there?" She shouted at Alex's back as he walked away.

She stood there watching him walk away. For a moment she wanted to run after him and apologize, but the moment passed and she turned back to Miriam.

"Keep practicing," she said to Miriam and walked down the hill toward Town Square.

She found Jason in the barn with a dozen maps spread out over the tables.

"You talked to Alex?" Alma asked.

"Yeah," he said without looking up.

"What did he say?"

"He said we have the green light. We can take two others."

"This is your show. When are we leaving?"

"Soon. Maybe three days."

That was soon. It was getting warmer but it was still cold at night.

"How long will it take?" She asked.

"It would take about a month to reach St. Augustine, but we're also taking a lot of detours to the most likely place for surviving settlements. Maybe two months there, another month to come back."

Three months on the road away from warm food, warm bed and all the people here.

It would also be three months away from Alex.

"Who should we take?" Alma asked.

"Shakti has to stay here. She's more useful as a chemical engineer."

"I'll need Cass to take over the training classes."

"Rebekah's too young," Jason said.

"She did good in Kentucky."

"That was luck."

"Lucky in Kentucky. Sorry. She's good and she's eager."

"It's my patrol and I say she's too young."

Stupid male pride got in the way of seeing Rebekah's real skill. Rebekah was becoming one of the most skilled shooters they had.

"She's good. Really good," Alma said.

"I know she is. But she's too valuable to risk."

"Valuable?"

"She's one of the people we're protecting and I don't want to put her in more danger than we have to."

So, that was it. He wasn't being a pig, he was actually showing his soft inner core.

That just made him much more handsome.

"I think we need someone more personable on our trip," Jason said.

"I'm personable."

"Then someone personable and even tempered."

He suddenly became much less handsome.

"Whatever. Jen is good, but she's getting up there in age," Alma said.

"And she's needed in the gardens."

"Adam?"

"He's the cook here and he won't leave Jen."

"What about Todd?"

"Maybe. He'd be good but I don't know if he'd come."

"Ask anyway. Who else?"

"I have no idea."

He threw his hands up.

"Alright, I'll announce it at dinner then and ask for volunteers."

Rebekah would be one of them of course so she hoped others stepped up.

She went to her room and cleaned up before dinner. She listened to her iPod until the dinner bell rang. Then she went down to the barn and looked around. It was full of people, people who were alive and happy. She intended to keep them that way no matter what it took.

Alma raised her hands and shouted.

"Hey! Listen up." She waited for the crowd to calm down. "Me and Jason are putting a long range patrol together. We're going down south all the way to Florida looking for settlements like ours. We need two more volunteers."

Several hands shot up. One of them was a former journalist that loved to talk. Perfect. He was about thirty and very smart. He wasn't the best with a gun, but that's why she and Jason were going.

Rebekah's hand was up but she skimmed over it. She wanted Rebekah but this was Jason's show. The next good one she saw was a man she knew could shoot. He was one of their hunters. He could track and skin deer since he was nine.

She whispered her selections to Jason and he agreed.

"Tom and Dave. You're it," Alma said. "Get your food and come see us."

Over dinner Jason gave the two men the outline of the plan and went over the possible areas to look for. It should be near a river and somewhat remote.

Then they went over the boring parts of everything they needed to bring with them. She tried act like she was paying attention. She had been on enough patrols to know what she needed. She also let them calculate how much food they'd need. Details were boring.

"We leave in three days," Jason said.

"So get ready. Bring your ammo and your game face," Alma said.

During the next three days she didn't talk to Alex. He made some half hearted attempts to talk to her but she ignored him. If he really cared about her he'd spend time with her and not leave her with the leftovers.

The night before they left Jen knocked on her door.

"What's up?" Alma asked.

She was wearing her Hunger Games PJs and Flyleaf hoodie. Jen was wearing something that looked like a South American poncho with more colors than any one item of clothing should ever have.

"Dave broke his foot," Jen said.

"What? How bad?"

"He'll be fine. We reset the bone and it's going to heal good."

"But he won't be able to go with us tomorrow," Alma said.

"Can you do it with three?" Jen asked.

"Maybe, but four's better in case we run into trouble."

"Anyone else you know that would go on such short notice?"

There was one name she could think of.

"I better get my shoes on," Alma said.

She walked over to the barracks where Rebekah stayed and knocked on her door. Rebekah answered the door with wet hair and a towel around her shoulders.

"Hey, Alma. Need anything?"

"Actually, yes. Dave broke his foot and can't go with me tomorrow," Alma said. Rebekah was already smiling and jumping up and down. "So we need a last minute-"

"I'll go! I'll go! Just let me get ready. When and where do we meet? What do I need to bring?"

"Everything's already packed. Bring what you would for a long patrol, but bring anything else you can fit in your backpack, especially food."

"Absolutely."

"Be there tomorrow at seven."

"Will be there."

Jason wasn't going to be happy about this.

She went to his room and found him resting on his bed with his feet up on his fully packed backpack. A giant book was in his hands but she didn't see the title.

"I asked Rebekah to come along to replace Dave."

"What happened to Dave?"

She explained everything.

"You got to be kidding me," he said.

"I'll keep her safe."

"It's not always up to us."

"I know, but who else?"

He let out a long breath.

"Alright. She goes."

"Thank you, Jason. I'll make it up to you."

"Of course, now get out of here."

As she walked back to the main house in her jammies and winter coat she thought about everything that could go wrong. What if someone broke a leg out there? What if they got sick? Shot? Captured? There would be no help for them.

Maybe this whole thing was a bad idea.

She went to her room and plopped down on her bed. All her things were ready to go in the corner.

Alma slept very little and in the morning she got dressed, shouldered her pack, grabbed her rifle and went down stairs. Cass and Chris were there eating breakfast.

Cass ran over and threw her arms around her.

"You be careful out there. I'll be praying for you," Cass said.

"You know me, nothing but careful."

"I'm serious. Don't take any risks and come back. Okay?"

"I got it, Cass."

She patted Cass on the cheek and went outside. Most of the town had gathered around. This was their first patrol out to see the rest of the world and she couldn't blame them for being curious. It wasn't like big news happened every day here.

Jason was talking to Tom and going over the map for the hundredth time. Rebekah was there with that old Broomhandle Mauser in a holster that looked custom made out of leather.

"Nice holster," Alma said.

"Made it myself."

"What's with the antique?"

"I like it."

Alma ignored the weak reasoning and went over to Jason.

"We ready?" Alma asked.

"When you are."

"Then let's go."

Their group walked to the stable where their horses and pack mules waited. Alex was standing there.

"Good luck ladies and gentlemen," Alex said.

"We'll come back with a full report," Jason said.

"Stay safe, stay out of trouble," Alex said.

Then Alex walked over to her.

"You especially. Don't give them a hard time," he said.

"I never would."

"Of course not."

Then before she could react he picked her up in a tight embrace like he used to do when she was a kid.

She buried her face in his shoulder and hugged back.

"I'll be back," she said.

"You better or I'll come get you."

"That's my job."

Then before she knew it, they were off and all she could hear was the clopping of the horse hooves. She looked back and saw Promised Land disappear behind the trees along the river. Her last glimpse of it was from the hill by the Walmart. Three months was a long time, especially if things didn't go according to plan and lasted four or even five months. A lot could happen in a few months. It only took a week for the world to end.

12

MIRIAM LET HER BREATH OUT AND HELD IT WHILE SHE squeezed the trigger. The SVD Dragunov bucked in her hand with the sound of thunder, less than a second later the distant pumpkin exploded in an orange mess.

Behind her Rehka cheered and clapped.

"That was...six hundred yards," Rehka said.

"Not bad, huh?"

"That was awesome."

She took out the magazine and racked the bolt to get the round out.

"I think that's enough for today."

"You're getting good."

"That's what I'm afraid of."

Miriam stood up and cracked her back.

Down below the hill was Promised Land and the river which looked crystal blue from the cloudless sky.

It was the first day she didn't have to wear a full winter coat outside. Instead, she wore a cute little jacket she had found in a boutique store in Lexington. It had pockets on the upper arms and was some kind of faux military jacket. She liked the dark gray color. It made her look tougher than she was.

She looked down at Town Square. Still no sign of Alma and the others. It had been three months and they were due back any day now.

"You think the PG will come back?" Rehka asked.

"Eventually."

"You think Alma will come back?"

"Definitely."

Then something caught her eye. It was someplace she hadn't looked in a long time. The sky.

High above was a tiny speck and a thin white line.

"Rehka, are you seeing that?"

"Is that a…"

It was a jet and it didn't look like a passenger liner.

"It looks military," Miriam said.

Before the virus hit, she was used to the sight of military jets flying overhead. She knew what one looked like.

It was soon out of sight but the contrail it left behind went from one side of the empty sky to the other. Everyone had to have seen it.

"Let's go."

When they got back down to Town Square, the jet was all everyone was talking about.

"Where did it come from?" Someone asked.

"Maybe an aircraft carrier. They could have escaped the virus," Alex said.

She turned to see Alex looking at the contrail while holding up a compass. It came from the east and was headed west.

"Think its looking for us?"

"I hope so," Rehka said.

"You think it saw us?"

"No telling."

"Where's it going?"

The questions didn't stop and had only increased by dinner time. By then people were making up all kinds of stories, especially the kids.

The other topic of conversation was the planting. Everyone that didn't have a vital job was in the fields. There were going to be fields of squash, yams, pumpkins, potatoes and a few other things that she never dealt with. She was in charge of supplies because she kept good records.

They had to make the planting work because their supply of canned food wouldn't last through fall, let alone winter.

Shakti sat down next to her with her plate. Their usual place was next to the double side doors that were now open because it wasn't so freezing out as it had been.

"How goes the target practice?"

"It's coming along. How goes the refinery?"

"Not as exciting as the plane."

"I didn't think I'd ever see a plane again."

"What about the…"

Then Miriam heard something. No one else reacted so maybe she didn't hear it.

94

It sounded like a scream though.

"Did anyone hear that?" Miriam asked.

"Hear what?"

"I thought I heard something."

Miriam got up and walked outside. Town Square was empty and the few lights left on showed nothing. She stopped moving and listened and watched.

Nothing.

Then she heard something soft padding up behind her. She turned to see Caesar with his short little legs and floppy ears come up and stand beside her.

"You smell something, boy?"

Caesar let out a few barks towards one of the barracks.

Miriam unshouldered her rifle and moved forward. Caesar stayed where he was and barked a few more times, sad eyes fixated on the building.

Something moved; a dark shape ran out from the doorway to the next barracks.

She turned back to Shakti and waved her forward. Shakti jumped up and hurried over.

"I saw something by the houses," Miriam said and pointed.

"Intruder?"

"I think so."

"Follow."

Shakti ran off to the side behind a storage shed. Together they made their way in the shadows to the barracks.

Gunfire erupted from the second floor and they ducked back behind the shed.

Another figure ran from the woods and into the first barracks. The figures were just shadows, like they were wearing all black.

Behind her she heard people running and yelling. In front of her she heard a crash coming from inside the building, like someone had pushed over a desk or threw a table on its side.

"PG?" Miriam asked.

"Who else?" Shakti said.

Alex and Lisa came up behind them in low crouches.

"Report?" Alex asked.

"At least two men in there. One of them saw us and opened fire," Shakti said.

"I heard a scream. Sounded male," Miriam said.

Alex turned back to the others and used his hands to tell them to surround the house.

Once their people were in place Alex shouted out to whoever was in the house.

"We have you surrounded. Come out with your hands up and I promise we won't hurt you."

"Where's the boy?" A man shouted back.

"What boy?"

"Alex Attaway? You're a lying backstabber. Give us back the boy or we'll never stop killing you."

"Fred? That you? What's going on?"

"You took John. We want him back. Now."

"I didn't take anyone."

Miriam saw something move in the top window. She took aim through her scope and waited. It was too dark in there so see much at all.

"Sandra Gibson saw you and your men take John. Don't try to deny it."

"I didn't take anyone. No one's taken anyone. Come out and let's talk about this. You can search every building here."

"You're a liar. You came to us with promises of peace and now this."

Shakti then tapped Alex on the shoulder.

"It could be the PG," Shakti said.

"What do you mean?"

"They could have taken the boy."

"But their witness said she saw me."

Shakti thought for a moment.

"When did this Sandra come to them? Is she new?"

Alex nodded.

"Fred, when did Sandra join Farmville?"

"Don't change the subject, liar."

"When did Sandra come to you? Was it after the PG made contact?"

Fred didn't answer for a few moments.

"Sandra came to us four months ago," Fred called out.

"And she was the only witness?"

"Yes."

"Fred, what reason would I have to kidnap anyone?"

"The Provisionals set us up," Shakti said. "Sandra's a spy sent by the PG to make us turn on ourselves. I know their methods."

"You're lying," Fred yelled.

This wasn't working. If they couldn't trust each other then nothing would ever get done. Since no one else was doing anything, it was up to her. It was risky but it beat shooting each other.

Whatever happened, it couldn't come down to bloodshed. There were far too few people to waste lives on stupidity like this.

Miriam put her rifle down and with hands in the air, she walked out. Alex and Shakti whisper-yelled for her to get back behind cover. She didn't listen.

"Sir, we didn't take the boy," Miriam said.

"We're supposed to believe the PG framed you?"

"They did. I'll be your hostage. Search through everything here. We have nothing to hide."

"Don't move. If anyone tries anything, you're dead."

A man dressed all in black with a baklava on his head came out. He came up to her and pressed the barrel of his M4 to her stomach.

"Come with me," the man said and lead her back inside the barracks.

There were three men there, all similarly dressed and armed. One of them stood in front of her and removed his baklava. He had bushy red hair and a bushier red goatee.

"Mighty brave, girl. But if you're lying, you're the first to die."

"We're not lying."

Her eyes didn't leave the gun. These men would kill her in an instant if she tried anything. To them she could be plotting to take one of their weapons and kill them or even setting them up for some kind of trap.

That wasn't why she was there. She could have fired and the entire Promised Land would have fired with her. They would have torn the barracks to shreds along with the people inside.

She had seen what violence did and it had to be avoided if possible. She didn't want this new world to end up like Iraq.

With a gun pressed against her head, they searched every room and then went outside. The entire Promised Land was waiting for them with guns. But the guns weren't pointed at them. Alex stood in the front with his hands out to the side.

"Check the main house next," Fred said.

"There's nothing there," Alex said. "I swear we didn't take anything. Use our radio. Call back to Farmville and ask if Sandra is there."

"Why?"

"Tell your people to arrest her and tell her they know she's a PG agent."

"Don't be ridiculous."

"It's true," Miriam said. "A couple of months back we did a raid against them and blew up their fuel and vehicles. They're out to pay us back."

The gun pressed harder against her head and she closed her mouth.

The men lead her inside the main house where they searched around. After making sure the boy wasn't there, they got on the radio to Farmville.

Fred asked where Sandra was and they said she had disappeared after they left.

"What do you mean?" Fred asked.

"We gathered for lunch the morning you left and she wasn't there. We looked for her but her stuff was gone."

"She went back to the PG," Miriam said. "She couldn't risk staying in case you found out."

The gun lowered from her head.

"Damn it all, we've been had," Fred said.

"They couldn't strike at us directly, so they tried to have you do it." She took a deep breath and swallowed before continuing. "I don't want to ask, but what was that scream?"

"A man. He's unconscious in one of the rooms."

She let her breath out. Good. There hadn't been any deaths.

"We're about to have dinner. Hungry? It's always better to talk over food," Miriam said.

Fred gave her a brief and sad smile.

They went out with their hands raised and weapons put away.

Alex walked up the steps to the porch and held out his hand.

"We're friends," Alex said.

Fred took his hand and together they went into the barn.

Shakti and Rehka came up and covered her in tight hugs.

"Don't do that again," Shakti said.

They went inside and saw that the Farmville people were being given food. Yes, they had come in, knocked out one of their people and accused them of kidnapping, but that had to be forgiven. The alternative was far worse.

"So, the PG has the boy?" Fred asked.

"They must," Alex said.

"They use children for basic chores and cleaning," Shakti said.

"How do you know?" Fred asked.

"I used to be with them."

Fred looked to Alex.

"We trust her," Alex said.

Fred then pointed to Miriam.

"You got a brave young woman there," Fred said.

"We have the best," Alex said.

"I'm not. I just didn't want anyone getting shot," Miriam said.

That night she got to sit next to Alex and Lisa as they talked about ways to find John and get him back. It sounded like there would be another patrol. Alma and Jason were already gone, that was two of their veterans. Cass was left along with Adam, Todd and a few others. The rest were still in training or hadn't seen combat.

The Farmville men were put up for the night in one of the barracks and everything went back to normal.

She began walking back to her room when Alex stopped her.

"Thank you for stepping up like that," Alex said.

"I just did what I had to do."

"It was very brave and you probably saved several lives today."

"No problem."

She gave him a big smile and continued to her room. Inside she leaned the SVD up in the corner and took her gear off. Shakti still wasn't back yet, probably reading a story to Rehka. They'd been reading Stephen King together or some other scary book.

When she lay down, she replayed the events in her head again. Looking back on it, it really did seem crazy and stupid. She had stepped out in front of people that were willing to shoot her.

Shakti was right. She really shouldn't do that again.

Maybe it was the Will of Allah, blessed be His name that I was sent here to help these people. Everyone was so quick to pull the trigger. It's like they didn't even realize that there were solutions other than fighting. They talked about making a new world, but they did everything just like the old one.

Miriam reached in her pack and for the first time in two years, read from the Quran.

13

ALMA HAD HER HORSE PACKED UP AND READY TO GO BEFORE anyone else. She was ready to get out of there and get on the road back home. They should have left weeks ago but Jason wanted to check out the rumors of a settlement in Baker's County Florida.

Five settlements found in total. Not bad. Regular trade was out of the question for now, but at least they knew each other were there and that they weren't alone.

The Baker County settlement had about eighty people spread between four clusters of houses. It was by far the largest but least organized group they found. They did however keep an outpost at the fort in St. Augustine on the coast.

Jason was still talking to them about sending boats down for trade and news as she tried not to act too eager to leave. The people had been nice enough, but she had already spent three months away from home and it was at least a three weeks trip back.

The old man in charge of this place came out and shook everyone's hand. He had a long white beard and wore jeans and a Lynyrd Skynyrd shirt.

The houses were open with little more than screen doors and screen windows. Chickens ran around all over the place while pens of horses, cows and hogs outnumbered the houses. The stoves were needed only for cooking. The other people wore little more than cut off shorts and tank tops.

Winters here were probably a cake walk compared to Virginia. Dang. What did they do up in Canada? Screw that. I don't want to know.

They made their final handshakes before leaving to lots of waving and the sounds of goodbyes.

"We're the most exciting thing to happen to them in two years," Alma said once they were out of earshot.

"They don't have the PG threatening their existence either," Jason said.

She looked back at their entourage. Tom and Rebekah were behind her and behind them were two new pick ups. They had found them wandering down I-95 looking for a place to stay. Brent and his daughter, Abigail. Brent was a dark skinned black man but Abigail was much paler with giant frizzy hair that looked softer than a pillow. Abigail was his actual daughter so it strengthened the theory that immunity from the virus was a genetic trait that could be passed down.

No way to test it though, not that she wanted to. The virus was gone and wasn't coming back.

Only one settlement had turned them away. The rest had been more than happy to see them. One place had an actual doctor that was training others. That was marked as a high priority town.

"Not bad work," Jason said. "Now let's get home."

They rode all day up the cracking highway and camped out at a rest area along the side of the road. They had canned food and didn't bother with a fire. They were hot and sweaty enough as it was.

As usual they sat in a circle as they ate and talked. They liked hearing about her adventures going across the country. Good thing Cass wasn't there because she exaggerated the stories to the breaking point.

Their group moved up I-95 day after day. They passed the exits that lead off to the remote areas where they found other people. A few of them hadn't even known about their nearest neighbors.

Jason and she found them, but it was up to the leaders to figure out where to go from there. It wasn't her problem. She was a trigger puller. Let the brains figure out the rest.

The cities they saw from the interstate looked normal from a distance. It wasn't until they got close that they showed the signs of neglect. But from a distance she could almost pretend that the world hadn't ended.

They set up camp along the road next to a pulled over semi trailer filled with furniture.

"Anyone need any expensive Swedish furniture?" Alma asked.

"I think there's a stream down that way. I'm going to go take a look," Rebekah said.

"Be careful. It's getting dark," Alma said.

"Yes, mom."

Rebekah marched off into the forest and disappeared.

"She's a good kid," Jason said.

"You glad we brought her along?"

"Yeah, she did alright."

That was as much of a compliment as she'd get from him so she took it as a victory.

"We have the beef jerky those guys in Camden County gave us," Brent said.

"As good as anything else," Jason said.

"I can't wait to get back for some of Adam's barbeque," Alma said.

"Y'all keep talking about Adam's barbeque. There's no way it's as good as you say it is," Brent said.

"After this trip, it'll probably taste even better," Alma said.

"Adam knows how to throw down a good steak," Tom said.

Then in an instant a ragged man jumped out from behind the semi truck like a startled deer. He wore jeans and a sleeveless shirt opened to show a scrawny chest. The barrel of a twelve gauge shotgun aimed right at them.

"Hold it right there," the man said.

Another man came out from behind the other end of the semi. He had an AR-15 with an extra magazine sticking out of his cut-off shorts. A third man appeared behind the first one. He smiled with a mouth missing a few teeth. He had a chrome revolver. Another man came out carrying an old M1 carbine and a baseball cap with grease stains.

"Look what we got here," one of them said. "If it ain't them idgets from up north."

Alma recognized one of them. They were from the town that didn't want to talk to them. They had turned their party away with threats of violence for trespassing.

"Look at all the free stuff," the second man said.

"Where you folk heading?" The first man asked.

"Back home," Alma said.

"And here I was hoping that I'd never have to see another damn Mexican again," First Man said.

"I guess they're crossing our border now," Second Man said.

"And we got a pair of darkies," the carbine man said as he eyed up Brent and Abigail.

Alma's rifle was lying beside her and she had a pistol on her hip, but they had guns pointed right at her. Anything she attempted would just get her shot.

She looked over to Jason whose eyes were fixated on the man's shotgun. He was looking for an opening to attack.

While the rednecks went off about how they had hoped to never see another minority, she watched the Second Man's gun. If she could grab it, the shotgun guy couldn't shoot her and she could use his body for cover.

The problem was that she had never tried anything like that before. Chances were that she'd just get shot without accomplishing much at all. She was a good trigger puller, not an MMA fighter.

"Look at their horses. I could use a horse," Third Man said.

"Maybe I can make some horse stew."

They needed an opening or these redneck scums were going to steal everything they had and worse.

"For a Mexican, she's kind of pretty. Maybe we should take her back as well," First Man said.

"I'm sure we could find something useful for her to do."

"No you won't," Rebekah shouted.

Alma turned to see Rebekah coming out of the woods. She aimed her old Broom handle Mauser with both hands and fired. Her bullet struck First Man square in the chest. He staggered backwards and looked down at his chest. She fired again, hitting just an inch above the first hole. He fell backwards with blood gushing out of his chest.

The Second Man behind Alma yelled something unintelligible and raised his AR.

Now!

Alma lurched backwards, ramming her elbow into his stomach and then reached up to grab the barrel. He tried to pull away from her but she pushed forward knocking them both to the ground. She fell on top of him and she heard the hollow sound of his skull hitting the pavement. Alma smashed him in the face with her fist and tore the AR out of his grip.

She then bashed him in the face with the butt of the rifle before turning around to see what was happening.

Jason was holding on to the shotgun with both hands while head-butting the man. The man with the carbine was backing up and taking aim at Brent and Abigail.

Alma took aim but before she could fire, a bullet struck the man's head and he jerked back and fell to the ground, twitching. Tom lowered his pistol.

Brent ran over and snatched up the carbine.

Jason gave the man another head-butt and he fell to the ground. Jason pointed the shotgun at his head.

"Give me one reason I shouldn't kill you," Jason said.

The man didn't answer and only spat blood.

Alma looked down to her unconscious redneck. He was out and probably would be out for a while. His face was little more than a messy smear of blood but he was still breathing.

Rebekah came up with both hands still on her pistol.

"Is he dead?" Rebekah asked.

"No, but he will be," Alma said.

"Why did you attack us?" Jason asked.

"I got nothing to say," the surviving redneck said.

"I say we shoot him," Brent said.

"They're from that town, right?" Abigail asked.

"Yeah," Alma said.

Abigail's tall, lanky form stepped up to the man and she crouched down in front of her. She was only sixteen but had the mind of someone far older. Her Glock was in her hand.

"Tell me, what were you going to do to us?" Abigail asked him.

The man's answer was curse words mixed with racial slurs. Abigail nodded.

"I see. From where I'm standing I think we have a chance to help the future. The new world doesn't need people like this. If we lesson their gene pool, they'll inbreed themselves out of existence."

"Abby, don't" Brent said.

"He has to die, dad. He will continue harming people and if we don't stop him now all those future deaths will be on our hands."

Abigail put her gun up to the man's forehead.

"We all have to do our part, dad."

She pulled the trigger and the contents of the man's skull spread out across the side of the semi.

Abigail stood up and wiped a splatter of blood off her face without flinching.

Brent stood there looking back and forth between his daughter and the man she had just killed.

"Let's pack up and go. There could be more of them," Jason said.

Brent didn't move for several minutes. Abby went on like nothing happened. Alma wanted to ask if Abigail was out of her mind, she wanted to thank her, hold her and ask if she was alright.

She didn't know which one to choose so she did none of the things and got busy packing.

No one spoke as they left the side of the road. They took the rednecks' weapons to make sure their people wouldn't get them. The sun had gone down but there was enough moonlight to see.

Alma moved her horse closer to Rebekah.

"You did good back there," Alma said.

"Yeah."

"You okay?"

"I'm fine. Just a little shaken, I guess."

"Was that your first kill?"

Rebekah nodded.

Alma remembered her first kill. Cass had been captured and she did what she had to do. This was the world they lived in now. There was no SWAT team and no court. If they wanted justice, they had to do it themselves.

"You did the right thing. You saved us. Keep that in mind."

"I'll try."

Rebekah even managed a smile. It was forced and weak, but it was a smile. Even more than that was the look in Rebekah's eyes. They weren't the eyes of an innocent child. They were the eyes of a tired survivor that didn't sit well on such a young face.

They stopped for the night much further down the road. They went off into the woods where they'd be out of sight in case more rednecks came looking for them. They were in a small clearing in the woods. There was no fire and no stream, but it was safe.

Brent was whispering to his daughter about how he didn't want her fighting.

He could talk all he wanted but she knew that Abigail was different. She wasn't going to sit back and do nothing.

She laid her sleeping bag next to Jason's and climbed in. Everyone else fell asleep but Jason was still reading with his flashlight. She was on her side with her head propped up by her arm. He was on his back with a book on his chest.

"One heck of a day, huh?" She whispered.

"Brent told me that Abigail has an IQ of over one eighty."

"She's a good find."

"So is Rebekah. She did good today."

"How many 'told-you-so's' do you need from me before you start to trust my opinions?"

"I do trust your opinions. You're probably the only person's opinion I do listen to."

What did he mean by that? Did he actually listen to me? He always seemed to ignore me.

"Jason, you saved my life and I've never properly thanked you."

"You're welcome."

105

"Just a second, I'm trying to be nice."

"Then be nice."

"Forget I said anything," she said and flipped around to face away.

She then felt his strong hand on her shoulder. He pulled her over to face him.

Alma wanted to ask what he was doing but couldn't form the words. She knew what she wanted him to do.

He then pulled her in to him and kissed her. She had never kissed anyone before and it was like being struck by lighting. Her whole body surged with raw energy. Everything she imagined was nothing compared to the reality. There were so many sensations at once that she couldn't tell them apart.

When he finally pulled away she gasped for breath.

"Wow," was the only thing she could think of to say.

She wrapped her arms around his neck and pulled him in again. It was even better this time.

When they finished she pulled away and lay on her back staring up at the stars.

"Does this mean you like me?" He asked.

"I guess so."

"Good."

This was everything she wanted. She had someone to care for and would care for her. She had thought that person would be Alex, but now she knew better. Here was a man that would give her the love and attention she needed, not just scraps from his table.

"Before the world ended, I never paid much attention to the stars," he said.

"Me neither."

"But now look. When the artificial lights died, the lights in the heavens came back out. I never saw the Milky Way before. Not for real."

"Cass is good with the stars. She can point out all the constellations and specific stars. She even told me that one of the stars I was looking at was actually two stars."

"A binary system."

"Yeah, that's what she called it. I never learned astronomy. I spent my time learning to shoot."

"A wise investment in hindsight."

"Yeah, but I want to learn more." She then turned to him. "I want to kiss more."

"That, I can help with."

They kissed until they both grew too sleepy and finally drifted into slumber with a smile on her face larger than it had been in a long time.

14

SHAKTI TIGHTENED THE SCREW INTO PLACE AND STEPPED BACK. The well pump was completed. It was a small project compared to the oil refinery they were working on, but it made getting water so much easier than dragging it from the river and running it through several filters.

Her engineering partners were out doing their shifts at one of the look out bunkers. So, while she couldn't work on the refinery, she did something else useful.

The well pump was just off to the side of the barracks, across from the main house which some people were calling "the White House."

She didn't like that name because every time she heard it she thought of the real White House that was now a radioactive burnt ruin.

The Library of Congress might still be there. All the books and important documents were kept deep underground. Maybe one day their grand children would go there and find the Declaration of Independence.

For now, they needed water and fuel more than the original copy of a document.

She heard shouting coming from Town Square and she turned away from her creation to see what was going on. People were pointing and one girl was jumping up and down.

She put down her wrench and greasy rag and walked over. They were all looking down the road where several people on horseback were riding toward them.

"It's Alma," someone said.

The patrol was back and they brought more people with them. As they got closer, she saw the sunglasses wearing Alma, the ex-mercenary Jason, Rebekah, the other Tom guy and three new people.

People ran to meet them like conquering heroes. Maybe they were. They had traveled for months to get information on the world outside the Shenandoah

Valley. What used to be a nine hour drive was now a dangerous journey of a month.

Miriam came up beside her wearing a pink t-shirt with a cartoon turtle on it. She had her clipboard with her that she now carried with her as much as her rifle.

"What's going on?" Miriam asked.

"Alma and the patrol are back."

"Think they found anything new out there?"

She could imagine what they saw. They saw vacant cities, empty houses and skeleton filled cars. Sure, there were other communities out there, but they wouldn't be much of any use.

Alex came out of the White House with his hand around Lisa's hip.

Jane came out with her accordion and began playing "When Johnny Comes Marching Home." She was a red head with short hair, glasses and an annoying habit of finding any excuse to play that horrible instrument.

The patrol came into Town Square amidst cheering and music. They dismounted and Alex was the first to greet them.

He threw his arms around Alma who gave him a quick hug and then turned to the crowd. For being gone so long, she thought it would have been a more tearful reunion.

"We have so much to tell you all," Alma said. "Let's get something to eat first."

Sandwiches were brought out and everyone gathered in the barn where Alma sat up on the table. She noticed that Alma kept patting Jason on the shoulder and speaking in his comfort zone which he didn't seem to mind.

Something had happened between those two. Something good.

Alma introduced them to the three new people, a father and daughter and a teenage boy they found wandering on his own. He looked only about fifteen or so. Still, there were more girls here than boys so he was probably a very welcomed addition.

Alma told about the different small settlements they found along the way and how they promised to send letters every year and create a chain of communication.

Shakti sat in the back and thought about the people of the other settlements. She wondered if there were more Hindus nearby. She wanted to hear the music, dance, watch some Bollywood movies, eat curry and be with her people.

Here, all she had was Rehka. Rehka had had an uncle but he died before Miriam and she arrived.

Rehka came over and sat next to her.

"This is so cool. There are others out there," Rehka said.

"I wonder if they found any other Hindus."

"I'm sure they're out there. Besides, if only one percent of one billion Hindus survived, that's still, what…ten million?"

"That does make it sound better, but it doesn't help us here," Rehka said.

"Well, we can keep our ways alive. Why don't we throw a Festival of India? They used to have one in Richmond every year."

"Like what?"

"We cook, dance and tell them about our culture."

That sounded like a lot of fun. She hadn't danced since college four years ago.

"We'd need the right clothes," Shakti said.

"There's a store in Lexington where we keep all the cloth we find in plastic bins."

"Alright, tomorrow we're doing a cloth patrol. I need a sari in my life."

"Several."

"You are correct."

The thought of wearing a loose, brightly colored sari or Ghagra Choli made her want to jump on a horse and rush out to Lexington now. She needed long flowing scarves again.

She focused back on Alma where she was talking about a violent group of rednecks that didn't want to communicate with anyone else.

Alex declared it a holiday and everyone got the rest of the day off. The planting was done and except for pest control and watering, there wasn't much left to do. The real work would come during harvest time.

During dinner, Alma came over and sat next to her.

"Welcome back. I imagine the bath felt good after so long," Shakti said.

Alma smiled that enormous toothy smile of hers.

"That it did. Listen, I need to talk to you in private. Would you follow me?"

"Sure."

She left Miriam and Rehka and followed Alma outside the barn.

"Tomorrow, me and Jason are going to ask for a vote that the two of us become head of a new military. Not just police, hunting or self defense, but I mean a real military. Alex said he would follow the will of the people and we need this."

"Will the people vote for it?"

"I think so. I'm more popular than Alex right now and everyone's scared of the PG. They will come back and when they do we need an actual trained army, not whatever we have."

"Alex won't like this. It'll look like you're questioning his authority."

Alma looked to the ground with eyes that were looking at something no one else saw.

Then her face scrunched up into a scowl.

"I don't care what he thinks. We need this," she whispered.

"You don't mean that."

"Will you help?"

"I'll talk to who I can."

"Thanks for having my back."

"No problem."

"Also, I want you as one of my lieutenants."

Shakti folded her arms and thought.

"They need me to finish the refinery. That's more than important to the future of the Promised Land."

"I know, and you can keep doing that. It'll be a long while before our army is trained up. You don't need the help with training, but once we're ready I'll need you as one of my officers. Will you do that?"

"Only after the refinery is up and going."

"Deal."

She watched Alma walk back inside and wondered if a new army would be enough. Their raid at Ft. Knox had been successful, but it would only delay the PG and when they came it would be with their full fury.

Ideas of dancing fled and were replaced by thoughts of war. Rehka and Miriam asked what was wrong and Miriam said something about going back to her "grumpy old self," but Shakti pushed them out of her mind and focused on the bigger problems.

That night she read "Salem's Lot" to Rehka and went back to her room. It had been an odd day. Aside from the excitement Alma's return brought, it had felt like one of those days that just weren't right. Something was about to change and she didn't know what it was.

The next day she took two horses and with Rehka went down to Lexington to the old boutique store they used to store their scavenged cloth. Together they picked out the brightest colors and patterns and took it back to Rehka's room to get to work. It was going to take a while but they'd eventually have clothes worthy of a movie.

They didn't quit until dinner time when they met up with Miriam and took their usual spot in the barn. Everyone had their usual spots and she could tell who was late or missing by which spots were empty.

Miriam was wearing a shoulder bag now and took it everywhere she went. This was recent. She had yet to see Miriam put anything in or take anything out of it.

In the middle of dinner, Alma rang a small cowbell and stood up on top of a table.

"I have a proposal that I wanted to bring before everyone here so we can vote on it," Alma said.

"What proposal?" Alex asked.

"I propose that we start an actual army with ranks, including daily individual and unit training. We have our militia right now and that's good. Everyone will need to learn to fight. But what I'm proposing is that we have full time soldiers whose job of fighting is their first and only responsibility."

Alex stood up.

"I don't want a military caste that can take power and dictate what civilians should do."

"That's not what I'm saying. It'll be a job just like any other. The military will be completely subject to yours and the Council's leadership, but we need to step up our game before the Provisional Government returns. Alex, can you honestly say that we're ready to face them tomorrow?"

"We have to look at the future. What kind of future will we have under a military dictatorship?"

"One that's better than a future under the PG."

"We won't be any different than them if this gets out of hand."

"It won't. America didn't have a coup and neither will we."

"You need to be careful with this," Alex said.

"Let's put it to a vote," Alma said. "All in favor raise your hand."

Almost everyone raised their hand, even Lisa.

"Tomorrow morning, after breakfast, if you're interested in joining, come to the target range at seven in the morning."

Alex then motioned with a nod of his head and took Alma out and to the main house. He wasn't smiling. She assumed it was going to be a rather long conversation.

"I wonder how old you have to be," Rehka said.

"You're too young," Shakti said.

"What about you, Miriam?" Rehka said.

"I don't know."

Miriam's gaze was far off somewhere else.

"You've gotten good with your SVD. You might want to join up."

"I like working in the storehouse."

"Of course, but is that what you really want?"

"Nothing has turned out how I wanted."

That was true enough. If she had her way, she'd be in a lab with a white coat talking to the head of a petroleum company about their newest project.

At six thirty in the morning she was awakened by Miriam. She was getting her boots on.

"You decided to join?" Shakti asked.

"I want to see what it's like."

Miriam wanted to or she wouldn't be going. She just didn't realize it yet.

She wished Miriam good luck and went back to sleep.

****

The weeks passed and soon they were down to t-shirts and shorts. People were out plowing a new field for next year's crops. It turned out that Rockbridge County had a lot of rocks and the plowing was slow. Her team continued to work on the refinery while the fifteen professional soldiers continued to train almost every day. Rebekah was technically too young but she was allowed in as Alma's assistant and messenger.

Every night, Miriam would come in to dinner dragging her feet and complaining about sore muscles or feet.

At night, Rehka and she would practice their dancing to Punjabi music. Jane saw them practicing and joined in. So there were three of them now and thankfully Jane left her accordion in her room.

Eventually the batteries on the iPods would go bad and soon they would have no more music except what they could perform themselves. She needed to learn an instrument while she could still listen to her music.

It was decided that she'd play the drums and Rehka would learn acoustic guitar.

Shakti walked out into a hot July morning and looked around Promised Land. The Town Square was dry and dusty and everywhere people were at work, while the children sat in the barn listening to Jen teach them about history.

She could smell the flowers and hear the birds chirping in the nearby trees. The animal pens were gone. They were all moved up to the emptied out Walmart on the hill across the river. The fields were growing and would be ready for harvest in the fall.

The refinery was almost finished and soon they'd be making their own gasoline.

There was a sign posted on the bulletin board. It was from Jared Bowman, one of the farmers. It was a sign saying that the militarization has left too few people to do the necessary work.

She read it and dismissed it. There was a shortage of people everywhere. Everyone had two or three jobs to do. During the day, she worked on the refinery and at night she met with Alma and Jason to work out who would be in what squad and who would drive their armored vehicles.

The recovery vehicle was currently being worked on and as she passed by she saw that they were mounting the pack howitzer on top. She didn't know whose idea it was, but it was brilliant.

It was another quiet day. She went to the refinery workshop where Eric and Michael were already at work. It wasn't a big refinery at all and they'd only be able to keep one or two vehicles going on a regular basis.

It was out away from the town in an empty field. It was in a thrown together barn to keep PG prying eyes off of it.

"How goes the work, gentlemen?" She asked.

"I don't like Eric's day for music," Michael said.

Michael had a shaved head and a braided goatee. His heavy metal music days weren't the best, but she couldn't stand Eric's country music either.

"Very well, then it's my day for music."

She took out Michael's iPod from the speakers and put in her own. Punjabi music played in the wooden barn that seemed to let more sunlight in than kept out.

"Another emergency?" Eric asked. "Can't we go just one day without an emergency?"

As she was about to get to work she noticed what Eric was referring to. It was Alma riding a horse full gallop towards them. She went out to meet Alma who didn't dismount.

"What's going on?" Shakti asked.

"One of our outposts didn't answer the hourly check-in and when we went to find him we found his body. Shot in the head."

"Who?"

"Kyle."

"Any signs on who did it?"

"None. We're going out on four man patrols."

'I'm on the way."

"I need you to stay here and organize the security here. I'm leaving you Miriam and Rebekah and whoever in the militia that can be spared."

Then Alma rode off sending clumps of dirt flying in her wake.

"Kyle's dead?" Michael asked.

"I'm sorry. Stay here. One of you keeps watch until I send someone back to guard you."

"Got it," Michael said and tapped the 1911 on his hip.

She ran off back to Town Square where she saw patrols mounting up. She found Rebekah and Miriam by the armory. They both had their IBA vests on but neither of them wore helmets.

She sent two of the armed teenagers to help guard the refinery. She gave them a flare gun in case anything happened.

"Think it's the PG?" Rebekah asked.

"Could be anyone," Miriam said.

"Don't worry about that. Right now we capture anyone we don't recognize and figure out the rest later," Shakti said.

The rest of the day was spent patrolling around Promised Land.

Maybe it wasn't the PG, but someone had killed Kyle. She didn't know him personally but she knew that he always sat on the far side of the barn during dinner and was always talking to the same group of soldiers.

That night, Alex gave everyone a full report on what happened and promised a funeral first thing in the morning.

This was her first funeral since coming here, every death was one less person they needed and loved. Despite the deaths of everyone she knew, she still found herself crying when she got back to her bunk. Her heart should be stone to such things. She should have built up immunity to death by now.

But, it turned out that the world still had the capacity to be cruel.

15

ALEX SAT ON THE PORCH ON A LAZY SUNDAY MORNING AND sipped his hot chocolate. Unless they found a cocoa plant, they'd eventually run out of chocolate. He hoped that didn't happen until after he died.

Maybe one of those southern settlements has some cocoa. He'd trade half their fuel for some cocoa seeds.

It was a cold October morning and the fields were almost ready for harvest. When that happened, almost everyone would drop what they were doing to harvest by hand. Like the old days, they would make it a time of festival.

Lisa stood next to him drinking her tea. For some strange reason, she loved tea more than any other edible food or drink out there.

Lisa paused with her tea cup half way to her mouth.

"Lisa?"

"Shhh."

He froze and listened.

Then he heard it. It was a faint '*bop bop bop bop*" sound.

"Helicopter," she said.

He ran up to his room, grab his scoped M-14 and hurried outside. Others had heard it too. They had stopped what they were doing and were looking up at the sky.

Over the tree line, the black shape of a distant helicopter came into view. It was one of the twin rotor transport copters.

"A Chinook," he said.

Whoever was in the helicopter had to see them because the chopper was flying right at them.

"Lisa, go get on the fifty cal."

She took off running up the stairs where they kept the .50 cal machine gun. If the helicopter was there to cause trouble, they would find it.

The Chinook came closer and he saw that it was definitely an old army helicopter with the white letters "US" on the side.

Cassidy came running up to him.

"Cass, get your broadsword aimed at that thing,"

"Right."

She unslung her rifle and took aim.

The chopper flew over Town Square with an almost deafening sound. He couldn't tell if it was coming in for a dramatic landing or something else.

It flew past them and toward the fields. The chopper came to a halt and hovered there. The wash of the rotors created ripples in the fields like a rock thrown into a pond.

The back cargo hatch opened and he saw men moving around inside. They pushed something out, something big.

Alex raised his scope to take a closer look. The men were in army uniforms and whatever they were pushing had five barrels tied together in a pyramid on a wooden pallet.

The tied up barrels fell off the back and landed in the fields. A second later there was a giant '*fwoom*' as it exploded into a fireball that engulfed half the field. Within moments, their entire wheat and corn fields were covered in flames.

And just like that all their work was gone. Their food for the coming year was all destroyed. Even as the flames rushed into the air, his mind asked what they were going to do. Feeding sixty people for a year was huge. It was more food than people realized. Their meager stockpile of canned food would last a few months at most. His mind continued to race as the faint wave of heat hit his face.

He didn't have to give the order. Lisa opened up with the fifty and she tore into the Chinook like it was wet tissue paper. He saw the engine houses get shredded in seconds.

Other people were firing their rifles while others ran for cover.

The Chinook's rear engine exploded into black smoke and the chopper veered out of control. The rear end swung in a wide circle as it made high pitch grinding noises.

Lisa let out another burst that struck the cockpit, tearing it up into metallic and glass splinters.

The helicopter then took a sharp dive and piled dived straight into the ground next to the burning fields. It crushed into the ground before exploding into another fireball.

The fire was spreading to the other fields and already people were getting buckets of water from the well and river but he knew it was too late. Their entire harvest was gone. In one stroke, the PG had destroyed their food for the coming winter.

Already his mind was running through what was going to happen.

"Freaking wonderful," Cassidy said. "What are we going to do now?"

Lisa came running down the stairs and looked around.

"No," was all she said.

Alma ran up to the porch.

"The PG will die for this," Alma said.

"Why do you think they did this? Huh? This is retaliation for what you did."

"They were going to attack us anyway, moron. Only, they did this instead of rolling into Town Square with tanks."

"Shut up, both of you," Cass said. "We have to go help."

For the next hour, they made a line while passing buckets back and forth. They wetted the houses in case the fire came too close. The crops were almost a complete loss. Only a few corners were spared, not enough to make any kind of significant difference this winter. And the canned food wouldn't see them through.

The entire time he worked, Alex tried to think of what to do. Nothing came to mind.

The faces around him were covered in sweat and ash and they were all looking at him. They needed something to do, they needed guidance and they needed hope.

"Alma, Cass, get patrols out there immediately. Search every house and store for canned food. You'll have to go to Roanoke and Staunton, Lynchburg, Blacksburg and maybe Richmond. Search every pantry and garage. We're going to need it all."

"Right," Alma said and ran off.

"What do you need me to do?" Lisa asked.

"Get the militia together and have them patrol the immediate area."

"You think the PG is around?"

"I'm sure they have eyes on us somehow."

Lisa hurried off.

Within the hour patrols were riding out. They were kitted up to be gone for a long time. They had donkeys with empty saddle bags. A team also rolled out in a truck heading to Richmond. He hoped it would return with the bed full of food.

That night at dinner, the people left were silent except for a few whispered conversations. He saw the fear and despair on their ash covered faces.

These were his people and they had just seen months of hard work go up in flames. He could see their questions about the future in their eyes. They were wondering something his people should never have to wonder.

How are we going to eat?

Alex stood up.

"Listen, everyone. I know we were hit hard today, but we'll make it through. Our people will return with enough food to see us through. Don't worry about that."

"We need to kill them for this," someone yelled out.

"Hold on. I know that we all want revenge. That won't help us right now. We need to focus on what we can do to make sure we get through the winter."

"We won't make it, if we keep getting attacked by the PG," a woman said.

Lisa whispered in his ear.

"Dear, we need to do something about the PG. They won't be satisfied until there's a plan."

He nodded and faced the audience again.

"We're working on a plan to strike back against the PG. It will have to wait until our people come back. Then, I promise that we'll do something to make sure this never happens again."

He sat back down, clueless as what to do about the Provisional Government.

"We need to strike them while they think we're down," Lisa whispered.

"How? A full assault on Ft. Knox?"

"Yes."

"We're outgunned and out manned."

"Get Farmville."

"Even with them, it's still too dangerous. Do you know how many of us will die? Too many."

"Alex, as your advisor, I have to insist you do this. This needs a military response."

"I don't like it, but I'll see if Farmville would even be willing."

Lisa nodded and said no more.

After dinner, he went to the White House and got on the radio to Farmville.

"Alex, what can I do for you today?" Mayor Stevens asked.

"Stevens, we got a big problem. The PG came with a helicopter and dropped a fire bomb on our fields."

"What's the damage?"

"We lost our entire crop."

"Heaven help us, but we won't have enough crops to share."

"That's not what I'm asking."

"Then what are you asking?"

"I propose a joint strike on Ft. Knox. Together we have enough to destroy them as a threat."

"At what cost?"

"I don't know, but we can't keep living under the threat of invasion or bombings. What if they get their hands on an actual attack helicopter? You were in the Air Force. You know what they could get in the air."

"Alex, I know you're angry, but are you suggesting we send all our forces out to Kentucky for some final battle?"

"We won't have to worry about them ever again."

"I'll have to talk to my people about that, Alex."

"Stevens, you know they want to take us over."

"But attacking them in their stronghold is suicidal. I'm glad to help but I won't commit suicide for you."

"What if we had a solid plan?"

"It better be rock of Gibraltar solid."

He hung up the receiver and leaned back in the office chair.

"He has a point," Lisa said.

"We have to do something, but I can't think of anything."

"If it were me, I'd set a trap for them."

"What kind of trap?"

"We go to Kentucky. We have two forces. One is quiet and remains unseen. They plant bombs and ambush sites. The other force is big and loud. We make a show that we're coming to fight them. We stop at a certain place, set up a cannon like we plan to camp there and drop shells on them from a distance. They will see the main force and move in to destroy them, but they fall into the ambush they did not see."

"But do we have enough people to do that?"

"The big force only needs enough to look big."

"Start drawing up plans."

"Will do."

The next day, attacking the PG was all the people could think about. He ignored that the best he could as he walked past the burnt reminders of his failure.

Michael was there at the refinery working on it alone.

"Hey, boss," he said.

"How long until this thing is working?"

"Not long. A few days at most. Our drill is already working."

"How long would it take to make enough fuel to get our tanks and all our trucks out to Kentucky?"

His eyes went wide and he put his torque wrench down.

"Boss, this thing isn't going to be producing a lot of gasoline or diesel. We're talking small amounts here. What you're asking for could take a while."

"How long?"

"Three, maybe four months."

"Then get busy. We're going to need all the fuel we can get."

Over the next few days the patrols trickled back in. They carried a lot of food with them but he didn't know if it would be enough.

When Alma and the rest came back, he called for a war council meeting. Alma was there along with Cassidy, Chris, Jason, Shakti, Lisa and Adam. Lisa proposed her plan and set out maps showing the potential ambush sights. They'd need all their vehicles, an artillery piece and trained soldiers.

Alex noticed that Alma had her hand on Jason's knee.

When did that happen? She got a boyfriend and she hasn't said anything. How far apart have we become?

Jason and Shakti approved the plan immediately. Alma asked a lot more questions about potential casualties. Good. That meant she was concerned about not losing people they couldn't afford to lose.

"When will we be ready?" Shakti asked.

"Not till February," Alex said.

"So we wait around all winter?" Alma asked.

"Do we have a choice?"

"They could attack us at any time."

"We have Farmville to help us."

"They didn't offer any help after our crops got torched," Shakti said.

"They'll come because it's in their best interest to," Alex said.

When the meeting adjourned, he pulled Alma off to the side.

"Are you and Jason a thing now?"

"Why? You don't approve?"

"No, I was just wondering. I thought you would have mentioned it at least."

"You're not jealous, are you?"

"Jealous? What are you talking about?"

"Of course you're not. I'm just one of your people to you."

"You're my sister, the only family I have left."

"Then why don't you ever act like it?"

She turned and walked off before he could say anything more.

October passed and Alma moved out of her room and into Jason's. That was as official as it got around here. Cass and Chris had Alex officiate their wedding. They had engineers, a nurse, a chemist and even a computer tech, but not a single clergyman, priest, imam or rabbi.

"I think she felt ignored," Lisa said from behind him.

He was staring into Alma's now empty room.

"When did she become a stranger?"

"I'm the last person to ask about family relationships."

He'd have to ask Cass about it. But even those two had drifted apart. Alma was now a different person and not all of it could be blamed on the knife attack by the psycho.

****

Skyler Dullknife looked through the scope of his rifle at the burnt fields. The White People were having a bad time. His sister had seen the helicopter come in and drop fire onto their crops.

It was an army helicopter with army soldiers inside. When she told his father about it, he had not been happy.

"That could mean that the government is still out there and will return one day to take back our lands."

"Should we find them, father?"

"We are too few. We will do as we've always done. We will stay hidden where they cannot find us."

When the Cherokee were rounded up and led out west, his tribe had stayed hidden deep in the Appalachians. There they stayed and there they would always stay.

At least that is what father said.

Skyler saw that the White People had an enemy and that enemy was more powerful than his tribe. They had helicopters and he wondered what else they had.

He watched as they sent out more horse patrols for food. His sister followed one patrol all the way to Staunton and they only brought back food.

Did they not know how to hunt? The past two and a half years lead to an explosion in the deer population. Father said to not hunt them until next year. By then, there will be more than enough.

He saw the cute girl again. She was pale with black shoulder-length hair that she usually kept in a ponytail. She carried a gun he did not recognize, one with the magazine behind the pistol grip. There was a name for guns like that but he couldn't remember it. He read it in a gun magazine a long time ago. The whole issue was about those guns but he hadn't paid much attention because they didn't look like good hunting guns.

He watched her through his scope as she walked across the open area to the big white house.

When she disappeared inside, he sat back from his Remington 700 VTR and chewed on his dried apples.

Something was going on down there and he wanted to know what it was. It was like they were all preparing for something, like to move, but it wasn't to move.

He remembered seeing in movies, back when they still had movies, the CIA or FBI would use these microphones that could pick up sounds long way away. He wished he had one of those.

Lizzy came up and lay down next to him.

"What are you looking at down there, bro?"

Her hair was in two long braids and she wore a pair of aviator sunglasses she insisted were cool.

"Something's going on. They're preparing for something."

"Maybe they're leaving."

"We're not that lucky."

She handed him a plastic bag with a thermos of tomato soup.

"From mom," Lizzy said.

She put down her identical 700 and looked through her scope. Unlike his though, hers was only .223 and his was .308.

"Think they're going to go use those tanks on the army guys?" Lizzy asked.

"Something's going on."

She let out a long sigh and rolled onto her back.

"I'm going to take a nap. Wake me if anything happens."

"I think we should talk to them."

"Because that's always worked for our people in the past."

"We might have the same enemy."

"And once that enemy is gone, they'll turn on us."

"It could be different this time."

"Our people say that every time and it never is. It's always the same."

She yawned and rolled over.

16

CAESAR WALKED OUTSIDE INTO THE NIGHT AS THE HUMANS finished eating. He was full from the food the humans gave him under the table. He would go to the human that looked at him the most and wait. It worked most of the time.

He padded over to the big white house and curled up on his favorite rug on the porch.

Lisa came up and petted him before continuing inside. Alex talked to other humans for a long while and when he failed to come over and pay attention to him, Caesar was forced to get up and walk over to him.

A woman with brown skin and black hair kneeled down and petted him as she continued to talk. Her hands were soft and slow and scratched his neck how he liked it. He licked her hand to let her know that he liked her.

When they were finished, Alex walked inside without paying him any attention and the other humans left. He barked once to tell them that he wasn't pleased with that. No one had scratched his belly yet.

Humans. They were always running around doing stupid things instead of petting him and giving him treats.

Caesar started walking back to the porch but he smelled something. He knew everyone's smell here. After a while of eating the same food, all the humans here smelled similar. But this was a different person he didn't recognize.

Caesar sniffed the air a few more times to make sure which direction the new human was.

He padded past the big white house and toward the stream where the big bunch of trees began. It was dark but the moon was out, so he could see just fine.

Caesar wondered if the new human was here to pet him or if he came with treats.

He sniffed again. It was a male, healthy and had something that smelled like the liquid the humans put on their metal things that made noise like thunder.

The man came out of the trees. He was in all black so he was hard to see. Stupid human, how was he supposed to find them if they wore all black?

But then he smelled something else. Adrenaline. This man was ready for a fight. He carried one of the metal thunder things in his hands and Caesar knew those things could hurt others.

He barked and the man ignored him. He walked slowly to the barracks. Then another man came out and followed the first one.

Alex had to know that there were strangers here that wanted to fight.

He galloped back to the house and ran inside to where Alex, Lisa, Cass and Cass's mate were.

He barked to get their attention and when they didn't move he kept barking. Lisa tried to pet him but he wasn't here for attention.

"What's wrong?" Lisa asked.

He went to the door, faced it and kept barking.

Stupid humans didn't understand anything.

Alex grabbed a thunder thing from the wall and Lisa followed with another thunder thing. Good, Alex did understand. Now he had to show them.

Caesar rushed out and led the way.

He was faster than Alex and when he went behind the house, he saw that the men were still there. He kept barking until Alex and Lisa arrived.

Then thunder surrounded him and Caesar ran back inside the house to get away until the thunder stopped. He had done his job. The humans knew the strangers were there.

Now, he needed a treat.

****

Alma jumped up from the bed and threw on a t-shirt. There were gunshots, a lot of them.

"Hurry," she said to Jason and she grabbed her vest.

With her vest and ammo on, she ran downstairs and stopped at the door. Out behind the other barracks, she saw muzzle flashes. He heard the crack of Alex's M-14 and the sharp sounds of M4's.

Whoever Alex and Lisa was shooting at was in the tree line.

At a crouch, she rushed to the next barracks and made her way to get a good flanking line of sight.

There were three, maybe four people in the trees trading shots with Alex and Lisa. All she saw of them were dark shapes, but that was all she needed.

She turned her red dot site down to night time settings and took aim.

She breathed out and squeezed the trigger just like she had done back in the competitions.

Her gun was an extension of who she was and when she fired, she knew where her shot was going.

Her target went down and one of the other men in black turned her way. She fired again but he got behind a tree.

But now they were being fired out from two different angles.

Jason came up behind her; leveled his Saiga shotgun and fired. The buckshot ripped through the leaves, dropping another shadowy figure.

Muzzle flashes now burst into life and bullets flew past her head.

Something bit into her left arm, like a hot knife.

Alma ducked back next to Jason.

"You're bleeding," he said and bent over to get a look at it.

She glanced down and saw it wasn't anything serious.

"I'm fine."

He kissed her on the lips and moved out again to fire at the intruders. His giant gun blasted away like a jackhammer.

She ignored the pain, ducked down below Jason's arms and fired from a kneeling position.

Another figure went down, thanks to Alex's M-14.

More people were coming and she saw Cass with her Broadsword take aim.

The woods erupted in shredding leaves and a second later the figures were still.

Todd came up beside her with a pair of NVGs. His tall lanky form hid the experience of an Army Ranger.

"They're not moving," Todd said.

He took aim and fired four times to make sure. Then they walked forward with guns at the ready.

They found the dead bodies with multiple bullet holes in each one.

Jason knelt down next to one and removed the NVG's.

"I know this man," he said.

"Who?" Alma asked.

"PG."

Alex came up with his M-14 down but stock still to his shoulder.

"They're PG," Alma said.

"What is this? An assassination team?" Alex asked.

"Scouts. I think they were coming to take you out or blow up whatever they could before the main strike," Jason said.

126

"Main strike?"

"We should expect company soon," Jason said.

Alex cursed and then fell silent as he thought.

That was a skill she had yet to learn. She acted and thought later. Alex always took the time to try to get it right.

That was why he was the leader.

"Listen up, everyone," Alex said. "Go wake everyone up as quietly as you can. Go fast but don't sound any alarm bells. Get into your positions and prepare to receive enemy contact."

That was her cue.

"All officers, assemble on the White House's porch."

She went to the porch and waited for her officers. She had Jason, Shakti, Cass and Adam.

Adam had his IBA, helmet and NVG's on and ready.

"Alright, we've trained for this," Alma said. "Send our demolitions guys to the road. As soon as the PG are in the kill zone, set it off."

"Right," Adam said and ran off to get his demolitions team going.

"Jason, Shakti, Cass, get your men ready. You know what your sectors are. Draw the big guns from the armory. Go."

They ran off to gather their teams.

She stood there on the porch and wondered how it had gotten to this point. They had survived the end of the world. They deserved a friggin' break.

But they had this. They'd beat back those PG barbarians and make them run home to mama.

Somewhere in the night was a force of trained people coming to kill her. Unlike her raid, not everyone was going to live through this night.

The half trained militia were taking their positions and setting up pre-made sandbags.

She hit the support column and tried to get her mind in the moment like she did before a competition.

This wouldn't be her first fight.

She watched the crews jump in the Stryker and recovery vehicle. The recovery vehicle had extra armor welded on and the 75mm pack howitzer on top. It was attached by a rugged swivel mount like pirates used to have; only this was much bigger. Their one AT-4 team ran off to take position in the woods and she saw three people leave the armory with M203 grenade launchers. The .50 cal was up in the attic and the Barrett 50 was also taking position up in woods.

127

Lisa came out wearing her body armor and her FS2000 slung on her chest.

"Are we ready?" Lisa asked.

"We're getting there."

Out in the night, she saw a flare shoot up. It was far in the distance and was only a speck of light.

"Orange. That means outpost six," Alma said.

"At least we know which way they're coming from," Lisa said.

She went in and got on the radio. Lisa followed close behind.

"Outpost six, what do you see?"

"Three troop trucks with two Bradley's and two Strykers."

She knew the Bradleys. Alex told her all about them. They had an automatic cannon, two big missiles and were immune to small arms. Their grenades wouldn't scratch them. All they had were the road bombs, the Stryker's cannon and two shots with an AT-4. Then, there were the Strykers. They weren't armed with cannons like theirs were, but their .50 cals would do a lot of damage. There wasn't much they could hide behind that would stop a .50 cal.

"Alright, get out of there and come straight here."

"Roger."

She called all outposts and told them to come back at once. There were only six people, but six might be enough to make a difference.

"Tonight's the night," Lisa said.

"I hoped this day wouldn't come."

"We both knew it would."

Lisa had her faults, but knowing how to fight wasn't one of them.

She got up from the radio and went back outside.

Out there along the road, her people were setting the bombs to go off. If they took out even one of the APCs, that would be a blessing.

Jason came up to the porch with his giant AK-shotgun held in both hands.

"We're ready, Alma."

"Are we?"

"We're going to win. This is our turf. We have the advantage."

"Then why are they coming, unless they think they have the advantage?"

"Arrogance," he said. "That will be their downfall."

She wanted to kiss him at that moment but held back. She was the leader and had to act professional.

"You ready to do this, handsome?" She asked.

"I've been ready for a long time."

They met Alex in the middle of Town Square. Sand bag positions were in place at strategic spots, and 155mm artillery bombs were placed on the edges of the town in case the PG tried to outflank them. Their back was to a river. They were as set as they were going to be.

The rumbling was growing louder and as it did, her heart beat faster. She checked her gear and made sure her Aimpoint was on. Weapon loaded, round in the chamber.

I'm ready for this. I got this. They aren't going to kill us.

"Too bad they're not coming over the bridge," Alex said.

"Life isn't that simple," Alma said.

Alex turned to her and started to say something but stopped himself.

"What?" She asked.

"Nothing. Get into position everyone."

Alma went into the Main House and took her position by the window. Teenagers were still putting sandbags in front of the windows.

"Hurry and get in the basement," Alma said.

On the other side of the house were Cass and Chris. Jason went out and took his position in the motor pool with the AT-4 team.

She saw Alex standing in the middle of Town Square. He looked around one last time and then took his position behind sandbags between the Main House and the machine shop.

There was a sudden light over the tree tops, a flash in the distance and a few seconds later they heard the '*thwump*' of an explosion.

"I hope that took out a bunch of them," Cass said.

"I hope you're praying your heart out."

"Don't worry about that. I got it covered."

"God seems to like you, so maybe he'll listen."

"He likes you too, Alma. Kind of."

Whatever happened, at least she had Cass with her. It felt right that if she died, Cass would be at her side.

Another explosion erupted through the trees but it was closer this time. The windows rattled from the concussion.

"There aren't any lights," Cass said.

"They're probably using night vision," Alma said.

She got on her walkie talkie.

"Team, three, when they're in sight, send up the flares. Light this place up like noon day."

"Roger that, Bandita actual."

When did they start calling her that?

Alma propped her AR on the window sill and waited.

Then, much too soon, a Bradley rumbled into view. It came around a bend in the woods coming right down the road at them. All she saw of it was a dark shape.

The turret turned toward Town Square.

She gripped her AR tighter and prayed that it was the only Bradley left.

The cannon opened up. She heard the shells screaming through the air toward her.

Above her on the second floor the shells tore through the walls sending splinters down in front of the porch. She heard the destruction and felt the blasts in her teeth.

Good thing I don't live up there any more. Sucks to be Alex though.

Then their Stryker named "*Grease Thunder*" roared forward and came within line of sight. It leveled its cannon and fired. A split second later there was an explosion of smoke and sparks from the side of the Bradley's turret. The cannon flew high into the air and landed a ways away in the fields near the river.

The two PG Strykers burst out of the woods behind the wounded Bradley. Their eight tires tore up the grassy field like red necks on a Friday night. Small arms fire from her people '*pinged*' off the Stryker's armor. Their automated turrets took aim and opened up on *Grease Thunder.*

The .50 cal machine guns poured fire onto their Stryker. Most of the shots deflected off the angled armor but she saw the sparks of some penetrating hits.

Grease Thunder fired again, hitting one of the Strykers in the side near the rear. The back tires went flying and the vehicle skidded to a stop as black smoke poured out of the flaming hole.

The other Stryker rode around and fired. Its .50 cal tore into Grease Thunder's side. Sparks and flames erupted from inside the vehicle and she knew the crew was dead inside.

Then the recovery vehicle they named "*Big Country*" lumbered out of the garage. The 75mm pack howitzer didn't have the hi-tech targeting system the Stryker did. It had a man on top aiming the small howitzer with crude iron sights.

The Stryker was zipping around while its automated turret stayed locked on. There was no way the howitzer was going to get a direct hit.

The enemy Stryker opened up with its machine gun but its rounds bounced off *Big Country's* armored hull. It was slow and weak, but it was built off of a tank chassis so a .50 wasn't going to scratch it.

It was a draw. Any moment the Stryker's deadly machine gun would be turned on her people.

Men climbed out of the back of the smoking Bradley and an army duce and a half rolled in to a stop as a dozen men jumped out of the back. The Promised Land erupted into a storm of gun fire as muzzle flashes lit up the night.

She aimed at the men climbing out of the ruined Bradley. They were in a field and exposed. Alma fired and hit one of them on the first try. He fell over but she had no way of knowing if he was alive or dead. They were most likely wearing full body armor.

A rocket shot out from behind a parked Humvee in the motor pool and struck the enemy Stryker. There was a deafening explosion as the Stryker burst into flames and continued on its course straight into the river.

That was my man's team that did that.

The .50 cal from the attic opened up on the men in the field and grenades soared in the air toward them.

Then she heard the "*thwump thwump thwump*" of an approaching helicopter.

"How much more do they have?" Alma cried out.

She looked over to Cass who gave her a thumbs up. Her stupid optimism usually grated on her thin nerves, but not this time. She could use some optimism, even if it was a lie.

If Cass said it would be alright, it would be alright.

Her eyes went to the motor pool where Jason was. Now was too late to start praying, but she hoped Cass was asking for every favor she could.

17

MIRIAM TOOK AIM AT A FIGURE DUCKING BEHIND ONE OF THE big army trucks and fired. She saw the man's arm jerk and he fell over. Looked like a shoulder hit.

She raised her head from the scope and looked for another target. She was in the second floor of one her barracks and had a good view of the battle.

The battle between the armored vehicles was unlike anything she had ever seen. The fire power those things had been unbelievable. If a sniper was terrifying then a tank was a thing of pure nightmare.

But now the APCs were smoking wrecks and only *Big Country* was left. It fired its old cannon and hit one of the trucks where several PG soldiers were hiding behind. She saw one body fly in the air.

That was when she heard the sound of an approaching helicopter.

There was no one around her to turn to for comfort or encouragement. She only had her rifle and her duty. And her God.

She took aim at another group of soldiers that were running for cover behind the garage. She fired but didn't see anyone go down.

The helicopter came into view high above Town Square. It was a Black Hawk. She remembered it from Alma's lessons.

She had no idea of whether it was bullet proof or not.

Machine gun fire erupted from the side door of the helicopter and she didn't want to know who its target was.

She took aim at where she thought the pilot would be and fired.

She hit but she didn't notice any noticeable difference until the copter turned bringing the machine gun to bear on her.

Miriam almost cursed and took aim again. She fired at the cockpit and this time there was a sudden turn to the side that made the machine gun point almost skyward before it corrected itself.

She let out a breath she didn't know she had held and took aim again.

This time at the engine, because she couldn't see the pilot or the door gunner anymore. She fired and heard the sound of her bullet striking metal. She was using Old Russian surplus with the steel core penetrators, but she might have missed everything important.

She changed mags and aimed through her scope.

The door gunner fired down at the house's attic and tore the roof to pieces.

Miriam fired again and again.

Smoke poured out of the engine and the copter started making strange sounds. She fired two more times before the copter started tilting like a top losing its balance.

It was going down, but not like the Chinook that had burned their crops. This seemed much more in control.

It went down out of sight past the woods. But it was out of action and that was all she cared about. She didn't bother watching where it crashed.

That might have been her first kill. She had killed another human being. Her parents would be more disappointed than she had ever seen.

I have no idea what, Allah, praised be His name, thinks of me.

She scanned the battle for more targets.

Big Country fired its howitzer again at an unlucky target behind the garage.

She saw a man with a machine gun peek out from behind a shed and take aim at some people behind sandbags.

Miriam aimed and fired. His head jerked back and fell in place to the ground.

A bullet tore through the wood near her head; she felt splinters dig into her face. She ducked down as more bullets sailed through the thin wooden walls.

Time to relocate.

She grabbed her things and crawled to the room furthest down the hall, the bathroom.

She only had five magazines, so she took the time to reload her two empty ones before looking out of the small bathroom window.

Miriam scanned for a target as she tried to ignore that she was standing in a tub.

There was a full on firefight going on in Town Square and she had to do her part or more of her people would die. Muzzle flashes marked people's locations and the fire from the ruined vehicles lit Town Square up like it was a celebration. Her people were in and beside the Main House with their backs to the river. The PG was shooting from the work shops and the woods near the road.

She took aim at a moving figure and fired. She saw the man's knee collapse out form under him.

She scanned for another target.

She had to. She didn't want to kill anyone but if she didn't, then her new friends would be killed.

Miriam wiped a tear from her eye and kept firing.

Another bullet tore through the wood near the window. This time it was below the sill and hit her canteen, spilling water all over the floor.

"Crap!"

She ducked down and tried to breath.

This was not what she was meant to do. She wasn't cut out to be a warrior. Allah had chosen the wrong person, if this was indeed what she was supposed to be doing.

Miriam moved again to a different window and stood way back from it to avoid being seen. Alma had said that only in the movies did snipers frame themselves right in the windows for all to see.

She looked through her scope for whoever spotted her.

The PG soldiers were on one side of Town Square and her friends were on the other. But she didn't see anyone looking her way.

Patience, Miriam. There could be an enemy sniper out there.

She watched as the gunfire down below came and went in sporadic bursts of intensity.

Then she saw him. He was the only one not looking towards the White House. He was walking toward her position while keeping his gun pointed up at the windows.

Before she could take aim, he ducked behind the barn.

He had been looking up.

So she went downstairs and from the darkest corner she could find, waited for the enemy.

The man poked out from behind the barn, still looking up at the window. He dashed from the barn to the seed shed. When he came out again, he was aiming his rifle with one hand and carried a grenade with the other. He was going to try to blast her out.

I have a surprise for you, sadiqi.

But this guy wasn't her friend. He was here to kill her and her friends.

Miriam crept down the hall and out the door. She went behind the barracks and walked, with her rifle up and ready, to the corner.

She peeked out and there he was. He was walking up to the window with his grenade.

Miriam stepped out with her rifle trained right on him.

All she had to do was pull the trigger.

The man's eyes turned to her and went wide. He lowered both his arms.

He was a young man about her age. He had a clean shaven face and he was gorgeous.

"Drop your weapons," she said.

He did and then put his hands up.

"I don't want to hurt you so please don't do anything stupid."

Enough people had died tonight. She didn't need to waste another life.

After picking up his grenade she walked him back to friendly lines where the militia handcuffed him and took him away.

Miriam turned back to the battle. She had killed tonight and she was about to kill more, but at least she had spared one life. Perhaps it was a tiny bit of mercy from God.

Father always said that it was God that led them out of Iraq and to America. He would agree that it was God that led her here and guided her to save who she could. There were no coincidences, only the will of Allah.

Miriam shouldered her SVD and ran back to the barracks to get a good view of the battle. There were more lives to take and more to save.

****

Shakti fired a few rapid shots to keep their heads down as Rebekah ran to another set of sandbags. The girl had energy to spare and didn't seem tired or worried at all.

Rebekah let loose a fast but constant stream of bullets at the men behind the tin roofed garage. They couldn't see them but their bullets tore through the garage and with luck, the soldiers as well.

She looked around but didn't see any targets.

Big Country drove around blasting away with its pack howitzer. When it was reloaded, it was angled up. The gunner ducked down inside and reloaded it in safety. When he popped back up, she made sure to try to keep the PG's heads down.

She heard a sound she didn't recognize until they came into view. Two up-armored Humvees raced into Promised Land with machine guns firing from the top.

From somewhere behind her, she heard what sounded like a gunshot, only louder. A burst of sparks hit the hood of the Humvee and the engine ground to a halt. It was their .50 cal sniper in the woods. The machine gun on top of the

Humvee continued to open fire so she kept her head down. Thank goodness it wasn't another .50 cal. The sandbags wouldn't be much use against them.

She peeked out when she thought it was safe and saw the other Humvee racing behind the White House to come up behind their positions.

A rocket shot out from the Motor Pool area and hit the Humvee in the back. It exploded, sending the gunner flying out the top. The Humvee tumbled onto its side and skidded to a halt through Jen's garden, tearing it up in the process.

She suspected that the PG didn't know how heavily armed they were or they would have chosen a different way to attack. Maybe they expected them to roll over like the others.

A machine gun opened up from across Town Square and she ducked back again. Someone over there had a SAW.

Off to the right, she saw someone go down. She glanced over and saw it was Robert, one of the farmers. She didn't know if he was alive or dead.

Something heavy landed in front of her sandbags.

"Grenade!" She shouted and tucked her head down.

The explosion shook the ground and sent dirt from the torn sandbags all over. Her ears rang and drowned out all the gunfire. For a moment, the Promised Land seemed peaceful except a painful ringing.

She looked over and saw that Rebekah was giving her a thumbs up. She returned the gesture, unsure if it was true or not because she didn't feel 'okay.'

A blast from *Big Country's* howitzer hit the top of the remaining Humvee and in a flash of smoke and fire erased the man and the machine gun that had been there.

That recovery vehicle had definitely earned its money back.

Then gunfire focused on it and the gunner ducked down. Without the gunner, it was big and scary but couldn't do much else. Still, that was gunfire not directed at her.

All she saw of the PG soldiers were dark shapes darting from cover to cover so she couldn't recognize any of them. She had probably had coffee with the people now trying to kill her.

Up in the White House, she heard a steady stream of fire pouring out. She knew Cass and Alma were in there, their two best shooters. Off to her left, on the other side of the White House, she saw Jason and his squad of three moving into the woods. With their AT-4s spent, they were now going after the troops by sneaking into the woods and coming in behind the PG. Assuming the PG didn't have any more surprises, it would be a good move.

She thought they had destroyed enough of the PG's assets in the raid, but when she saw the Bradley and the Strykers, she knew they had to have had more somewhere else.

All she could do was hope that this was the last of it.

She glanced over to the barracks in hopes of seeing Miriam. That was stupid though. If Miriam was doing her job, she wouldn't be seen.

Then a girl crawled up to her. It was the new girl, Abigail, and she had a bag full of flares.

"Throw these over there. It'll make them easier to see," Abigail said.

"Brilliant."

"Thanks."

Abigail and her poofy hair crawled down the line, handing out flares and water.

Shakti lit her flare and tossed it behind the shack. The red light lit the wood line up making the enemy soldiers easy to see like silhouette targets at the gun range.

She fired and hit one of them. He went down and she laid the fire on until the SAW opened up again, strafing bullets across their sandbags and over their heads.

There were fewer PG soldiers, but they were better trained. The PG was losing but how many would they take out with them?

Not even in New York, had she been in a firefight this intense.

****

Rebekah fired off her magazine, hoping to hit the soldiers ducking behind the garage. There were also soldiers behind the smoking Bradley, the empty stables and the blacksmith's, but she was focused on what was in front of her.

They needed something, maybe grenades.

She looked back to the armory.

"Shakti, cover me."

"Covering."

"Moving."

Shakti emptied her magazine to keep the PG's heads down as Rebekah ran to the cement block armory and ducked inside. She took out her small but powerful flashlight and looked for anything.

There were no grenades.

What else?

There had to be something else. God was cruel enough to lead her here only to have everything taken away. He tried His people under the hottest fires. But there had to be a way. If they had the .50 in the attic up and running, but the helicopter took it out.

Maybe the .50 was still working though?

She ran out and sprinted to the Main House's back door. She saw Alma and Cass firing away as she got to the stairs. Piles of empty brass lay around their feet.

The attic was a total mess. The front half was shredded wood and Arthur's body lay in a bloody heap by the .50 cal.

Rebekah hurried over and checked the weapon.

There was a gash on the side where a bullet grazed it and the ammo chain had been severed in one place, but it looked good to go. She opened the top, removed the shortened belt and loaded in the rest.

She gripped the handles and took aim at the garage. Then she pressed down the trigger with her thumbs and the fifty rocked and hurt her ears even through her ear plugs.

A stream of fifty caliber death tore the garage to pieces in an explosion of torn metal and dirt. She saw someone running out from behind the garage to get away and she led her stream of death over to him. The man burst in half like ripe fruit. Both halves fell to the ground.

She kept her vomit down and looked for another target.

A group of soldiers from behind the Bradley opened fire and bullets tore through the wood around her.

A blinding pain like a white hot poker pierced her eye and she fell down, clutching her face. Warm liquid gushed over her hands as she cried out.

When she tried to sit up, a wave of nausea swept over her and she found herself on the ground again.

She had to stand. Her people were counting on her.

Rebekah took a deep breath and sat up. Pain filled her body with every movement.

Down below, the remaining PG soldiers had gathered in the wood line. They could be preparing for an assault. She had to get back on the fifty. The ammo chain was out and she had to reload it.

With a grunt, she flipped open the feed tray cover with a hand that was covered in her own blood. Rebekah tried not to think of that as she struggled to load the fresh ammo chain. Her hands were shaking and the dizziness didn't help. When she tried to pull the charging handle, her hands slipped. She tried again and her body wouldn't do it.

Her people were counting on her and she failed.

138

A shot rang out from the left near the river. She looked over with her one good eye and saw five people coming across the bridge. From up there, she couldn't see much but she saw that they had hunting rifles.

They fired on the PG troops as Jason and his squad attacked from the rear.

Within moments the soldiers' hands were up and the gunfire ceased. People came out and covered the prisoners while others tied them up with zip ties.

Boots stomped up the stairs and the next thing she knew she was being carried down stairs to the couch in the living room.

Alma and Cass hovered over her while Doctor Parker looked her over. Their worried faces told her that whatever they were looking at wasn't good. Frank took a long time looking her over and checking everything.

It gave her too much time to think. She thought about infections like they had in the Civil War. She thought about not being able to be a soldier anymore.

What if it was worse than they were telling me? What if it made me ugly?

"How is it?" Rebekah asked as he put a bandage over her eye and wrapped her head.

"It could have been worse," Frank said.

"Details?" Rebekah asked.

"You've lost the eye. Nothing I can do about that. But the bullet only grazed the eye socket so there's no other serious damage. You'll have a scar on your cheek and brow."

"Will I get a cool eye patch?"

"If you want."

Frank made a smile she knew was forced. She had seen that smile before. When Rehka's uncle grew sick, he smiled like that while he was powerless to do anything.

"You're going to look badass, *chica*," Alma said.

Again, the forced smile.

The doctor gave her three injections and a bottle of pills.

"Take those every five hours."

He explained why but her head swam with nausea and it went right by her.

One of those injections had to have been morphine or something like it because the pain receded into the background.

Shakti came in and knelt down beside her.

"How are you feeling?" Shakti asked.

"Not so bad at the moment. I bet that won't last," she laughed.

"Drink and eat as much as you can," he said, patted her on the head and left.

Rebekah sat up despite everyone telling her not to. After the vertigo passed she stood up. Her hands were still a little shaky, but she walked out onto the bullet torn front porch.

The PG prisoners were huddled in the middle of Town Square. Burning vehicles were everywhere and it looked like a tornado had passed through. The smell of gunpowder, smoke and coppery blood filled her nostrils.

Alex and Lisa were talking to the people that had come across the bridge. Their hunting rifles were slung over their shoulders.

"Who are they?" Rebekah asked.

"No clue," Shakti said.

She walked over to them on weak knees to get a better look. They looked like Native Americans and a few of them even had the long braids.

Where the heck did they come from? Is this some hallucination from the morphine? Indians, to the rescue!

One of them was a young man and looked her way.

She was covered in blood and bandages. Not her best day. She looked away and hid behind Alex.

All around her people were looking around, expecting more trouble and wondering what came next.

The Promised Land was torn to shreds. The Main House was a wreck and most of the smaller buildings were completely demolished. Her home was destroyed and she didn't know if it could be fixed.

She didn't know if she could be fixed either.

18

A LEX HAD TOO MUCH TO DEAL WITH. THE PROMISED LAND was in smoking ruins, there were PG prisoners, possibly friendly Indians that came out of nowhere and then there were the wounded and dead.

"Lisa, deal with the prisoners. Get information and put them somewhere for now. Jason, deal with security. I don't want any more surprises. Cass, deal with the wounded. Alma, organize the people and get them…doing something. Anything."

They all rushed off and he turned back to face the five Indians.

"I'm Alex Attaway."

"Gary Dullknife."

"Where did you all come from?" He asked.

"We live nearby," the oldest one said.

He was a middle aged man that looked like the teenage girl and boy. They were probably family. The other two were large males that didn't have the same family resemblance.

And somehow they were living nearby and I didn't have a clue. Fantastic. What else don't I know about?

"Why haven't you contacted us before?"

"Didn't need to. We stay where we are and you stay where you are."

"Then why help us now?"

"The army here was a bigger problem."

"Alright, I thank you for helping us. I appreciate your need for privacy. Sure. I won't ask where your home is. But if we can help each other, we should stay in communication."

"I will discuss it with our council."

"Please do. Tell them that we only want to live in peace."

"We've heard that before."

"Things are different now," Alex said. "This is our chance to do things right this time."

"I will discuss it with our council."

He reached out with his hand.

"Again, thank you all," Alex said.

Gary shook his hand with a strong grip.

He watched the Indians go. He had a ton more questions but there wasn't time for that. They were the least of his concerns now.

He turned back to Town square that had burning vehicles, debris and wounded people all over.

His people were doing their job. A casualty collection point was set up in the middle of Town Square as a patrol went out to secure the perimeter.

He checked his watch. It was two thirty. No one was going to get any sleep this night.

He found Lisa leading the prisoners into the former cattle pens. Four armed guards were posted around them.

"How's it going here?" He asked.

"I will start interrogations. I'll take them to the seed shack and question them one at a time."

"Don't be cruel."

"They deserve it."

"Maybe, but we're not that kind of people."

She looked at him for a moment before nodding.

He then went to check on the wounded. Doc Frank was busy and his nurses in training were helping. They had bottles of rubbing alcohol, bandages and medicines on a fold out table. There were twenty people with wounds from small cuts to bullet holes. Some of them looked bad.

His eyes went to the area beside the Main House where the dead were laid. There were seven of them there and three in the Stryker. Ten of his people weren't coming back.

The teenagers and children that had hidden in the Main House's basement came out to help out with the clean up. They picked up the broken pieces of the workshops and the metal from the destroyed vehicles.

Inside, the Main House was a wreck. Bullet holes were everywhere and the second floor and attic were gone beyond repair. His room was a mess and opened to the sky thanks to the spiteful cannon of the Bradley. His stuff and his personal arsenal were still there but he'd need a new place to live.

When the sun came up, he looked through the gaping hole in the attic. Promised Land was gone. Some of it like the machine shop could be fixed soon. But the Main House and other buildings were destroyed. Smoking wrecks of large armored vehicles littered the area.

A year and a half of work and it was in ruins.

Lisa came up behind him and put an arm around him while she rested her head on his shoulder.

"Are they saying they need a new leader yet?" Alex asked.

"Nothing like that. We did well. It could have been a lot worse."

It could have been a lot worse, but that didn't make this situation good.

"And the prisoners?" He asked.

"This seemed to be their swan song. I don't think they have anything left."

"Neither do we."

"We've got a lot left."

"But how much have we lost, Lisa? Can we save Promised Land? Should we?"

"I think we all knew it was temporary. We need more room. Let people have their own farms."

"But fall's coming and it's too late to plant." He sat down with his legs dangling over the jagged edge. "I don't want to be leader anymore."

"Too bad. You are the leader."

"What would you do?"

"Regroup for the winter and in spring we spread out."

He thought about it for a while.

"Why do you believe in me?"

"Because I know you can do it."

"How?"

"Because you always do."

It didn't feel like that at all. He looked down at all the debris and ruins of their home and saw failure.

"It's time to move to our fallback position," he said.

"The castle."

The VMI barracks would be their new castle. The animals would be moved to the football field and the parade ground would become their field for crops. Others would stay here and man the refinery and try to replant when the time came.

Plans moved through his head. Yes, they had been struck a blow, but they would recover. The PG was no longer a threat and now all they had to do was rebuild.

"Lisa, gather everyone that can be spared. Meet me in the barn."

He waited in the destroyed attic and thought as the people that weren't helping the wounded or guarding the prisoners began to gather in the now bullet ridden barn.

He scribbled notes on the small notebook he kept in a back pocket, where his wallet used to be.

When he was ready, he went down stairs. He took his time to gather his thoughts as he walked to the barn. Alex looked at the pale faces and red eyes of his people. They were tired and heartbroken. He had seen these faces on TV when they showed survivors of a hurricane looking at the ruins of their houses.

He stood up on one of the tables and cleared his throat. Lisa and Alma were standing right below him.

"Alright everyone, we just went through a terrible trial, but I'm afraid we have more hard times ahead of us. As of now, we only have enough canned food to get us halfway through winter. Also, the main house is destroyed and a few other buildings. One of the barracks took a few grenades. Maybe we can fix the house and barracks. But here's my suggestion.

"I propose that we move our operations to the VMI campus. The barracks there will be much easier to defend. We'll have the high ground and lots of empty space for crops and animals. However, it's a short term solution. As we grow, we'll outgrow that area. There are plenty of farmhouses around the area. We can spread out and each family group gets their own farm.

"Some will need to stay here and man the new refinery. Others will replant in the spring. Also, we'll need teams to go out and look for more food."

Alma raised her hand.

"So, you're saying we need to split into three separate groups?" Alma asked.

"I am. But we need to vote on it. All in favor of splitting into three groups raise your hand."

Almost everyone raised their hand. At this point, he wasn't sure if they voted because they liked the idea or just didn't know what else to do.

Either way, the idea was passed.

"Alright, we know the people working on the refinery. They'll be staying here. Also, we need farmers and the mechanics because the motor pool is staying here. Volunteers?"

Several people raised their hands; they were in the same unofficial "family." Most of the new army was the same family, and the farmers had grouped together as well. Machinists, farmers and soldiers.

"Alma, take your trained soldiers and get them out there looking for food again. That's their permanent duty until we're sure we can make it through the winter."

"Understood." Alma said.

That left about twenty people with him to go to the VMI barracks and get them ready.

The fourth group, the government.

He jumped down to talk to Alma, Lisa, Jason and Cass in private.

"I'll be in charge of the VMI group, Alma; you're in charge of the soldiers. They'll stay at VMI as well. We need someone in charge of the Promised Land."

"How about Shakti?" Alma asked.

"She's too new."

"Adam and Jen?" Alma said.

"Alright. They're in charge."

Cass took off her cowboy hat and looked around.

"So, this is the end of our town," Cass said.

"Not the end, just a change," Alex said.

"It feels like the end," Cass said.

"We need to pay the PG back for this," Alma said.

"And what good would that do?" Alex asked.

"Keep them from coming back at us again."

"And what should we do with the prisoners? Execute them in cold blood? You want that, Alma?"

She met his gaze before looking down and shaking her head.

"We're not going to execute anyone and we're not going to attack Ft. Knox. We have wounded and we need to concentrate on our survival. Revenge is a luxury we can't afford."

The crowd assembled into their three groups. He saw the new head of the refinery, Shakti, talking to Miriam. Figured they'd be together. Jason was with Alma. Jen and Adam were together."

"How's Rebekah?" He asked, Lisa.

"She's passed out on our couch."

"I want her with our group when she wakes. I don't want her going out on raids. She suffered enough. Tell her I want her as my personal assistant or something else that sounds important."

"But what should we do with the prisoners?"

He had no clue what to do with them.

"I'll have to think about it."

She nodded and went off to organize the VMI group.

He sat there and wrote more notes in his little book. He did the math to figure out if his numbers for the three groups were correct. Then he tried to figure out how much food they'd need for basic survival.

He hated math.

By noon, the people that were leaving were packing their things up in trucks. Lisa had loaded one truck with the spare solar panels they had collected. She and a few others would get to work getting power on at VMI.

All of these new changes were going to take a while.

By three in the afternoon, he was at the Castle with his people choosing rooms and figuring out where to put everything. There was already a small armory and storehouse from when they had set it up as a fallback position. That had just been a vague idea though; now, it was real.

By five, he was standing in the courtyard looking everything over and trying to figure out how to make this all work.

The new girl that Alma had found approached him. Alma had told him that Abigail was very intelligent and if she spoke, he should pay attention.

"Alex, may I talk to you?"

"Of course."

"I've been thinking. VMI and the neighboring campus of Washington and Lee have huge libraries. We can't let that go to waste. I suggest we move all books into one place and spare the power to maintain climate control."

"Why's that?"

"We can't afford to lose all of that knowledge. Generations from now, they'll need that knowledge when the stories from elders no longer mean anything."

That was a good reason.

"You think it'll get that bad?"

"I'm trying to make sure it doesn't."

"Alright, you're in charge."

He tore out a page from his notebook and wrote her a quick note.

"Give this to Lisa. Tell her you need solar panels for the library. The W&L one is larger. Use that one."

"Thank you Alex."

"No problem. So, what do you think of all this?"

She looked around the courtyard before answering.

"I think we're doing the best we can with what we have. But this is a temporary solution at best."

"Have you made any friends here?"

"Everyone here is my friend. They're not going to shoot me and will fight to protect me. Right now, that's as good as I can expect."

She nodded and left with her note.

The work wasn't nearly finished by the time night fell. He curled up under several blankets with Lisa in their new room, a simple barracks room on the third floor.

"Did we fail?" He asked her in the silence of the dark.

"No. We did good."

"Then why do I feel that we failed?"

"Why do you doubt yourself now?"

"I didn't save Promised Land."

"We're not the Promised Land. That's just a place."

"Maybe its time we hold another election."

She sat up and looked down at him. She then pushed her finger at his face.

"Don't you dare give up now. Not after everything we've been through."

"What if Alma's right?"

"She's not. I've seen what useless hatred causes. I killed the last of my team because he wanted to continue a useless war."

He pulled her into his arms and kissed her.

"I knew I kept you around for something."

"And what would that something be?"

"I'll let you use your imagination."

In the morning, he stood out on the balcony of the third floor and scanned what looked like the courtyard of a medieval castle. The stables would fit in there, maybe a few workshops as well.

Lisa was on the roof with her team putting the solar panels up. Others were bringing in the iron stoves to put in the inhabited rooms. Their carpenter was looking over the work and figuring out what else needed be done. There was a kitchen in the nearby mess hall, but it was too modern. They needed something simpler.

Alma walked up to him from the side.

"Well, my lord, you have your castle," Alma said.

"Is your team ready?"

"Shakti says she doesn't have any fuel to spare."

"We don't. We have to save all our fuel to go get more military vehicles."

"So, you are planning to strike back at the PG."

"No, I'm preparing to defend again."

"You can't really be that thick. They're weak. Strike now."

"With our one recovery vehicle?"

"It's more than they have. With Farmville, we can take them over."

"What good would that do?"

"You don't think they don't have stockpiles of food? You wanted a solution, that's it. We take their food."

"That's not a solution."

"I swear; you're so stupid sometimes."

"Thank you, Alma. That'll be all for now."

"For now."

She glared at him and left.

Another failing. He had saved his people but lost his sister. Dad wouldn't be very happy with this situation.

He grabbed a horse and rode back to Promised Land to see how they were doing. The garage and machine shop were back up and running though some of their equipment was destroyed. He'd add that to Alma's list of necessities.

"Hey, boss," he heard a voice say.

It was Rebekah. Half her head was covered in a giant bandage. She looked paler than usual which contrasted with her raven hair to make her look more like a walking corpse than the young girl he knew.

"How are you feeling?" He asked.

She shouldn't have to suffer like this. He wanted her safe and for that he needed her to stay home. He needed a position that would tempt her to stay.

"Like I've been shot. Doc says I shouldn't handle any guns right now because I'm as high as a kite. His words."

"Rebekah, I want you to be my personal aide. Help me run things here."

"Wait…what?"

"I need you here to help me keep everything organized. Food, defense, training, everything."

"But I'm too young."

"Neither of us believes that anymore."

"Are you sure?"

"I'm sure. Get our people ready to defend themselves."

"Of course."

"After you're healed up though."

"You won't regret this."

He put his arm around her and drew in her close.

"It's been a crazy time, hasn't it?" He asked.

"Yeah…crazy."

He then looked over at the animal pen where they used to keep the cow and bison. The prisoners were there. Eleven of them. He couldn't keep them here but if he let them go that would be eleven trained soldiers added back to the Provisional Government's strength.

Maybe I should hold an election and let someone else deal with all this crap.

19

MIRIAM WOKE UP TO THE COLD OCTOBER MORNING. THE trees outside were gold, red and orange and the sky was a cool gray. It had that feeling in the air that it would rain later. She liked that feeling. In Iraq, she had loved the rainy season because it was a break from the painful heat. Now when she woke up and saw gray clouds, she knew it would be a good day.

She opened the small door to her iron stove and stoked the coals again before adding in a few pieces of wood.

Shakti was gone. She was probably already off working.

She wondered what her parents would say about their daughter being a farmer. They'd be happy that she was alive, but before the world ended, they wanted her to be something more.

Now, there was nothing more important than making the food that would keep them alive.

There wasn't much farming to be done at the moment. They had a lazy schedule of clearing other fields for plowing. It was simple but hard work.

Up at VMI, they were transforming the parade field into a plowed field. They had more work up there. They were making stables in the barracks, turning the football field into a pasture and making the W&L library a school.

Sounded like fun, but she would rather wake up late, work at her own pace and enjoy life.

Rehka was with Shakti. She always was now. It was like they had adopted each other. There was a lot of that going around. The people here had grouped together into families. It was all unofficial but she wondered how long it would be until they were official. Houses, clans, tribes were all good names.

Aside from Shakti and Rehka, no one had adopted her. She was friends with everyone, but not close with anyone. A part of her wondered if it was because they still feared Muslims. But no one had even mentioned it yet. Perhaps this was a new world after all.

She got dressed in her bomber jacket that made her look tough and went outside. The mechanics were working on some kind of pump system to bring water up to VMI from the Maury River while the machine shop was working on a press to make the brass shells for ammunition.

It was growing fast. Sure, they were hungry most of the time, but they didn't have to look over their shoulders for the PG anymore.

Well, at least not for the time being.

Alex sent the prisoners back with a warning that further aggression would not be tolerated and with the promise that they'd send back the kidnapped boy. He made them swear. That seemed a little too lenient for people that had tried to kill them but the alternatives were far worse.

She waved at Jack, who was under the hood of a classic truck as she walked up to the refinery where they were processing a fresh batch of crude. Shakti was walking Rehka through the process step by step.

Shakti looked up when Miriam entered the barn.

"Taking a break from your vigorous schedule?" Shakti asked.

"You know me. Those naps won't take themselves."

"You poor thing."

This was her family now. Shakti and Rehka. It was a small family for now, but she knew it would grow.

Then they heard the sounds of hooves charging up to the barn.

Her hand went to the Nagant revolver on her hip as she walked out. Shakti told her to get rid of it at least once a week, but she just couldn't do it. It was the last piece of her father she had left.

It was only Lisa. Her hand came off the gun. Lisa reined her horse in and came to a stop in front of her.

"Miriam, you're not busy, right?" Lisa asked.

"That's right."

"We need a volunteer to come with us to Farmville."

"What for?"

"Not sure. They invited us to some kind of meeting. They said it's important."

"When are we leaving?"

"As soon as you get your stuff."

"I'll be right there."

"Meet us at the motor pool."

She waved to Shakti and Rehka and ran back to her room. She got her pack, threw some things in, put on her ammo vest and grabbed her SVD.

There were two Humvees with Alex, Lisa, Alma, Jason and a few others. She jumped in the one empty seat and they were off without further ceremony.

Alma and Jason were up front and a soldier named Jim was across from her. He had in his earbuds since the Humvee was too loud to hold much of a conversation.

She got out her book and continued reading. One of the raids from Roanoke had brought back tubs of books from bookstores there. They already had plenty of educational books that would help civilization get back on its feet, but what they got in the raid were novels. Entertainment kept people sane. There wouldn't be any new movies for a very long time, but there were books people hadn't read.

It seemed as if everyone had suggested a book. Cass offered "Dune," Jason gave her "Carnage and culture," and Alex suggested "Monster Hunter International."

She had a lot of reading to do.

Miriam had never been to Farmville and wasn't sure what to expect. She had heard it was smaller with about thirty five people and that they were pretty good people.

It took two hours to get there, two hours of empty houses and crumbling roads.

When they finally came to a stop, they were near a lake. There were several nice houses around the lake that had clothes hanging out to dry and outdoor barbeque pits. A few children came out to see them with young women standing over them with guns on their hips.

She couldn't tell if they were looking at her. They probably wondered if she was a Muslim. They also probably wondered if she was a terrorist. Not every American thought like that, but enough of them did. The people of the Promised Land didn't look at her like that. To them she was just one of the family. They didn't care what religion she was.

But now she was in Farmville and she didn't know what these people thought. It was like old times again.

"They've got a nice set up here." Miriam said.

"There's a hospital just over there along with several creeks running through town." Jason said.

"Yes, yes, they're doing very well. Pat them on the back later." Alma said.

They got out and she stretched her back and legs. She tossed the novel on her seat and put her sunglasses up on her head.

A group of armed men and women came out. They had guns but they were smiling.

"Alex. So good to see you again." a man said with what sounded like a New York accent.

He had black hair, a large nose and a huge smile.

"Hey, Frank, how's it going?"

The man took Alex's hand in his own bear paw and shook.

"Glad you could make it. We got a lot to talk about, buddy."

"What's this all about Frank?"

"Come inside and we'll get started."

They went into a building that looked like it used to be a club house. The main room's far wall was nothing but glass that looked out over the lake. There were docks and boats out there and a few boats on the water. Looked like they were fishing. In the middle of the room were several leather sofas arranged in a circle.

"Have a seat. Can I get you something?" Frank asked.

"Sure, anything would be nice." Alex said.

They all sat down across from eight Farmville people. A teenage girl brought out a tray of small sandwiches and juice.

"You're not trying to bribe me, are you?" Alex asked as he took a sandwich.

"Kind of." Frank leaned forward and clasped his hands together. "Important stuff first. We've looked over the reports about the other settlements to the south. Some of them are too small to maintain a stable population. We want to send delegates down there and ask them to join us up here. Together we'll be much stronger than scattered groups."

"Sounds logical. I've thought about something similar but I've been rather busy lately."

"Yes, about that. We also want to launch a joint attack on the Provisional Government and make sure they'll never threaten us again."

"Attack Ft. Knox?"

"Yes."

"We still haven't recovered from the last battle."

"Exactly. I'm sure they haven't either. We got some army hardware. You have some. Together we can take the PG. I said we'd wait for a good plan, this is it."

"I don't want another battle. At least not until we're ready for one."

"Better now than later when they get back on their feet. We have some self propelled artillery here. We can blast them off the map."

"They have civilians."

"We'll try to target the military stuff. Tell me, did they ask about your civilians?"

"No, but they're not us. We need to be better."

"We need to survive."

"Then let's talk about these smaller southern groups."

Miriam listened as they talked about sending groups down to convince and bribe the smaller groups into coming up and joining with Farmville or Promised Land. They spoke a lot about population growth while avoiding inbreeding.

"Fifty three people for us, thirty five from you...that's still too few," Alex said.

"We need more bodies. One hundred and fifty is about right," Frank said.

"One group in North Carolina has fifteen and one near Charlotte has about twenty."

"That's still not enough."

"How many does the PG have?" Miriam asked.

They both looked up at her.

"We're not breeding with them," Frank said.

"We might have to unless we want our first cousins to marry. I can't say that I do. Alex said.

"They have a lot of civilians." Jason said.

"How many?" Alex asked.

"Maybe sixty."

"That's our solution." Alex said.

"No, we'll intermarry with the groups further south then. They need us and we need them."

"We're talking about the human race. We need the PG." Alex said.

"The human race will be better off without them." Alma said.

She noticed the glare Alma gave him and wondered what that was about.

"We'll come up with another plan. We're going to attack the PG with or without you." Frank said.

"Can we at least put that off until we talk to these smaller settlements?"

"We can wait, but only until spring."

"Deal." Alex said.

"Now, who do we send?"

"Me and Jason will go," Alma said.

"Good. They know you." Alex said.

"I'll go." Miriam said.

"They might need someone friendly." Alex said with a nod.

"I'm friendly." Jason said.

"Of course you are, dear." Alma said.

They formed a group of four, each from Farmville and Promised Land and decided on next month. They'd pony up for fuel for a truck. That was good because she didn't feel like riding a horse for several weeks. She barely knew how to ride the dumb things. For some reason, the beasts just didn't like her.

"Now that that's settled, let's not decide on anything about the PG until they return." Alex said.

"Agreed, but after that we have to decide. I don't want to wait too long and watch them come at us with tanks and more helicopters."

Alex better find a way out of this. There doesn't need to be any more death. There has been far too much of that already. It's like everyone's crazy except me. Can't they see that we need to work together? The fate of the human race is in question and here they sit talking about killing each other.

They talked about forming groups of eligible singles to meet and greet singles from the other town. They needed to start making babies if the population was to grow. But they weren't animals to be bred. All they could do was arrange the best situations for the young people to meet someone.

She hated dating before and this new "meat market" approach didn't sound much better. Before she had only dated Muslims. Her parents didn't let her date anyone else and she agreed with them. She didn't want to marry an unbeliever.

Before, she would have just refused to marry. But now if she didn't marry and have kids, her blood lines would be extinct forever. There would be no one to pass down the stories of her and her family.

"We'll give our people more time off to mingle," Alex said.

"Never thought I'd be playing match maker. It's *amore*! Right?" Frank said.

They fleshed out the details of the ambassadorial delegation and then worked out opportunities to exchange people.

Once they were finished, Frank gave them all big hugs and thanked them for coming. Then they were back on the road to Lexington.

She thought about looking for someone but no one had interested her or shown interest in her. Of course, her former roommate said that she was always clueless about such things.

"That guy was totally into you." was a common Michelle saying.

Maybe she just needed a good wing woman.

She went through the list of eligible bachelors in her mind. Some were cute and a few were downright handsome, but she didn't know any of them enough to make a judgment about liking them.

And if she did find one she liked, the chances of him letting her raise their children as Muslims were slim to none.

What would Allah have me do?

As far as she knew, Shakti didn't have eyes on anyone. She was always so busy with the refinery and Rehka, that she didn't have time for men.

Now was the time to make time though. They had to start thinking about the future and not just their immediate survival.

It was more than that though.

"What kind of future are we making?" Miriam asked as she leaned forward so Alma and Jason could hear her.

"A safe one, I hope." Alma said.

"But that can't be all. We want freedom and tolerance, right?"

"Of course," Alma said.

"We need to plan what our future will be now or it'll get out of control."

"And what do you suggest?" Jason asked.

"As a people, we need to decide on what we want to be."

"We're not going to make some peaceful utopia," Alma said. "People will continue to be people."

"Why? If there was ever a time to change, now is it."

"You sound like Alex." Alma said.

When they got back, she went to her room and took out her diary. She had started it in September. It wasn't for posterity; it was for her to keep her thoughts straight.

She settled in her bunk and wrote down what she thought the future should be.

There needed to be respect for people that don't believe the same things. America, before the war was tearing itself apart as the political parties polarized further and further from each other. There has to be the desire for compromise. In Iraq, it was the uncompromising men that couldn't tolerate any other way of thinking but their own, that had massacred thousands of people in her home town.

People needed to learn compassion and charity for others. That was the first thing.

She put her pencil down and wondered how she was going to teach people something like that. Her first thought was religion, but they had Jews, Hindus, atheists and Christians. Too potentially divisive.

Shakti came in and dumped her gear in the corner.

"How was Farmville?"

"Very nice. They got a lake there. Cool, huh?"

"Great, but what was the meeting about?"

"Breeding."

"What?"

"Yeah, breeding. We did the math and figured out how many people we needed for a viable population. It turns out that us and Farmville isn't enough."

"You mean, we don't want babies with two heads, right?"

"We need about fifty more people."

"Freak, what are we supposed to do?"

"We're sending a group down south to talk to those small settlements they found. Also try to talk to that small group up north."

"Will that be enough?"

"If they agree to move up here it might be. Either way, we got to start having babies."

"Whoa, I'm not ready for that. Not at all."

"We can't force anyone, but basically we have to really start thinking about it."

"I did think about it and I say I'm not ready. Not even close."

"Even more important, think about what kind of world you want to create and how we can make it."

"I don't have time for philosophy."

"It's not philosophy. I'm talking about setting the direction of future generations."

"I'm more worried about getting enough fuel and electricity. One day those solar panels are going to break and wear out. When that happens, we'll need something else in place. I want a world where we don't have to fear the dark or die of common colds. The rest can figure itself out."

Shakti wasn't being much help. She doubted Alma would be much help either. Jason was always reading, maybe he would? Alex, definitely. Lisa.... she had no idea. The woman was a total mystery.

Again, she felt like she was the only sane one in a mad world.

20

ALMA LAY IN JASON'S ARMS AS HE READ ALOUD FROM THE book he was reading, "Heart of Darkness."

She liked listening to his voice as he read. It became softer and she could feel his words in his chest.

If she had known that having someone was so good, she would have found a boyfriend long ago. She didn't need anyone else as long as she had him. The world could burn for all she cared.

Their tiny room was all they needed. The wardrobes didn't have doors and all her clothes hung in a scrunched up mess. Jason had fewer clothes that were in neat order. His boots were all in a perfect row.

"We should stop here and get some sleep," he said.

"I want to keep reading."

"I know but we have to get up early tomorrow."

"You're no fun."

"I know. Now shut up and go to sleep."

He kissed her on the top of her head and turned out the lantern.

She lay there wondering what she had done in a past life to deserve Jason. He was everything she had always wanted, and needed. Maybe everyone felt like that when they were in love, but he understood her more than even her own brother.

In the morning, they gathered with all their things in front of the barracks where their Humvee waited. Some of the teenagers had made bowls of oatmeal for their breakfast. She scarfed hers down while she looked at the map one of the drivers had.

Miriam came up with her SVD over her shoulder and smiled like they were going on vacation.

"I'm ready to go." Miriam said.

Rebekah was there in her new eye patch with a skull on it. She looked much older than her fourteen years. The good eye that looked out at them had seen more death than a girl should ever see.

"Double check everything before you leave." Rebekah said to the other volunteer, one of the soldiers in training.

"Where's Alex?" Alma asked.

"There was a problem with the water pipe down by the river. It was leaking out all over." Rebekah said.

"Too busy to see his sister off."

"Let's mount up." Jason said after they all went through their check lists.

They got into the Humvee and took off for Farmville.

Cass would have been a good choice. She was friendly and was a good shot. Two things this mission needed. Also, Cass was great for a road trip.

It had kind of sucked, but going across country with Cass had been a ton of fun. No speed limit, no worry about food, just driving and seeing what was left of America.

The long drives were like an old friend wrapping its arms around her. She could relax and just watch the world go by. The old gas stations covered in ivy and weeds now seemed less like gravestones and more like life returning to a dead world.

Farmville was a small town inside a cute historic district with brick buildings and colonial architecture. The windows were cracked in places and a stop light dangled from the pole overhead, like it was ready to fall off any second.

They pulled into the parking lot of the lake's club house and found a truck of Farmville men waiting. Frank was there and shook all their hands with his giant mitts. Then they were on their way, a heavily armed two truck convoy.

It was a five hour drive to the first of the small settlements. Five hours of empty highway and no signs of life. She listened to music and did her best to pretend everything was normal.

She mostly listened to music and went over her "road trip with Cass" mix. Some of it was more Cass's music than hers, but they had good memories attached to them.

The settlement was a quiet little farm where everyone lived cramped up in the farmhouse. They had cows, chickens and everything else a farm needed, including a lot of horses. Alex was very interested in the horses and wanted to eventually start trading with them.

They pulled up to the fence that led to the long dirt road to the farm and honked. A few minutes later a teenage boy on a horse rode up. He had a scoped lever action rifle and a cowboy hat. He held the gun in both hands, ready to fire.

Alma got out slowly with her hands away from her guns.

"Hey there, remember us?"

"Yeah," the boy said.

"We brought some friends. We came to talk about something important."

"Hold on."

He took out a walkie talkie.

"Hey, it's those guys from Virginia. They say they want to talk." He listened to the response and then put the radio away. "Follow me."

He led the way as they drove behind him.

They pulled up to the gravel driveway of the farm house, where all twelve of the people waited for them. They were all armed except the small kids. Four children from eight to twelve, two teenagers, two old people and the rest between the ages of twenty to thirty. She saw one tall woman that the younger ones kept looking to.

Their leader was a tall, thin man with a balding head and wire glasses. His name was Charles and he had been a cop before all of this. He looked more like an accountant than a cop.

He didn't smile but he walked out with his hand extended out for a shake.

Jason shook his hand first and then she did.

"Well, this is an unexpected surprise." Charles said.

"We came with a proposal." Alma said.

Charles waved them forward and they sat down on the chairs on the front porch. From the number of chairs, it seemed that this group spent a lot of time there.

Like usual, Miriam was all bright eyes and large smile. Her natural levity seemed to put the people at ease.

"Sir, my name's Miriam and our group here represents Lexington and Farmville. We came to offer more than an alliance. We invite you to come live with us."

"Why would we do that?" Charles asked.

"Because there are only twelve of you here," Alma said. "You're vulnerable."

"Twelve crack shots is nothing to laugh at." Charles said.

"It is when your enemy has tanks," Miriam said.

"A few months ago we were attacked by the Provisional Government. They brought APCs and helicopters. We fought them off but came out with more than a bloody nose." Alma said.

"We're too far south for them. Besides, we have nothing they want."

"You have your cows. You have your people. That's what they want." Alma said.

"There's something more," Miriam said. "We've been thinking about the future and doing the math. We need a wider gene pool than our two towns offer. You twelve by yourselves will eventually die out. To avoid that, we need you all. We invite you to come live with us, pool our resources to be more efficient and restart civilization."

"You want us to give up everything we have here?" Charles asked.

This man wasn't getting it.

"Sir, there's nothing here but extinction. Unless we unite together, our population won't rebound and we'll become extinct. If the PG attacks again, we need everyone. Also, farming is much more efficient when you have more people. We can have normal lives again instead of scrapping by." Alma said.

"And we have electricity." Miriam said.

She saw the younger people look at each other and whisper.

"We have lights, heating and a river." Alma said.

"We'll have to think about it. Can you wait till tomorrow for an answer?"

"Of course." Jason said.

"Until then, please be our guests."

That night, they had fried chicken and mashed potatoes as they sat around a big dinning room table. Lanterns and candles lit the scene and it seemed quiet comfortable. She doubted it would be this homey in Lexington, but there were more important issues than a house that belonged on the cover of "Country Home and Living."

After dinner, the twelve locals retreated out to a bonfire where they talked the issue over. They were there late into the night while she lay on the couch and tried to get some sleep. Miriam and John were already passed out. Miriam was on a love seat and John was on a big cushioned chair.

She could see them out the back porch French window. They were all gathered in a circle around the roaring fire. She saw lots of hand gestures and moving around.

"Think they'll accept?" She asked.

"If they do, great. If not, then we'll move to the next one."

"Yeah, but could you read anything from them?"

"The older ones want to stay, the younger ones want to leave. I guess it depends on how much they listen to their young."

"I hope it's more than my parents listened to me." Alma said.

"How well did you listen to your parents?" Jason asked.

"Totally irrelevant."

"You're avoiding the question." he said.

"It's distracting from the issue at hand."

That wasn't as helpful as she had hoped.

She tried to get comfortable in his arms but she lay awake long after he had drifted off. She knew the sounds of his breathing when he slept and could feel the now familiar rise and fall of his chest.

In the morning, they woke up to find breakfast ready for them. Eggs and bacon. It smelled amazing and she was hungry. Lately, she was always hungry.

Charles sat at the head of the table while they ate.

"So, Charles, what has your group decided?" Jason asked.

"We decided to send some people to inspect the two towns. We'll wait for their report before making a final decision."

"That's fair," Miriam said. "Take your time."

"We'll send them in the spring."

"Then it's settled for now."

After breakfast, they thanked everyone and were on their way to the next town.

The next town was a small sixteen person settlement along the coast living in fancy beach houses. They were much more receptive of the offer and said that they'd pack up as soon as they could. Apparently last year's hurricane season had been trouble and they had lost someone. Also, they were much lonelier than the other group and were excited to meet new people.

"Maybe the others will go that well." Alma said as they climbed back into their trucks.

"Not likely. Once comfortable, people tend to stay there even if there's something better."

Jason started the truck as they waited for the Farmville guys to get in their truck.

Then they were on the road again.

"That's one 'maybe' and one 'yes.' Not so bad." Alma said.

"We can make two more stops before we have to go back."

"What's the matter? You don't want to walk home?"

"Not really."

She tried to laugh as other thoughts clouded her mind.

"So, Jason. What do you think about all this?"

"I don't think these other groups will be inclined to move. Especially when we're at war."

"No, I mean, about this whole…survival of the species thing."

"This virus could be an extinction level event if we let it."

"But what about you?"

He turned to her with a half grin.

"I'll do my part. For the good of the species of course."

"You're so selfless."

"I'll close my eyes and think of England."

"What does that even mean?"

"It means, if choosing between making love to you and the death of the human race, I suppose I'll choose making love to you."

She hit him on the shoulder and tried to act angry.

It didn't work and she let out a snort which only made her laugh even more.

Jason's predictions proved correct when the other two settlements rejected their offer. They wanted to trade and even send delegations, but moving was out of the question for now. Like Jason said, they were comfortable.

With just enough gas to make it home, they turned back.

She knew what it was like to be stranded without gas and knew that she didn't want that happening again.

The drive back was long and they took turns. When she drove, Jason stayed silent with his eyes glued on his book. She had never been much of a reader but Jason and Cass were always reading so there had to be something more to it. In high school, the books they made her read were always so boring that she just looked up the summaries online. Life was too short to be bored.

When it was his turn to drive, she curled up in the passenger seat and pulled out the book Jason had given her. He said it was more her style than what he usually read. The title was "Starship Troopers."

She opened the book and began to read. When it turned dark she took out her flashlight and continued reading.

They arrived in Lexington sometime after midnight. It was hard to tell because she didn't wear a watch anymore. They drove up the hill to the VMI campus and came to a stop in front of the barracks castle. The fuel gauge was on 'empty.'

Alma climbed out and stretched her back. Jason cracked his neck and popped his shoulder.

But the castle just wasn't the Promised Land. This place wasn't a home. It was just a place to live for now.

"I'm going straight to bed," Jason said.

"Leave the report and inventory for tomorrow."

"I like the way you think."

Together, they climbed the stairs to the second floor where their room was. The guard on duty greeted them and said it was nice to have them back.

They crawled into bed and Jason began snoring almost at once. He had a remarkable ability to fall asleep anywhere, under any circumstances. The frustrating part was when she didn't realize he was asleep and turned to find that the entire conversation had been a monologue.

If that was his biggest problem, she could live with it.

She was going to read some more, but when she lay on the bed to get comfortable she went right to sleep like someone had flipped a switch.

Alma woke in the morning with all her clothes and boots still on. She groaned and crawled out of bed. Jason was gone. His collection of Russian firearms was stacked in the corner and his footlocker of magazines and parts sat at the end of the bed. She had all her rifles on racks hanging over the bed. Her old competition rifle was in its place of honor. They were all different versions of AR-15s and Glocks. It was what she knew and could run them on pure muscle memory.

She slid a Glock 22 into her holster and walked out onto the balcony walkway that encircled the courtyard. Down below, she saw people erecting a new stable and blacksmith's.

Despite the activity, the place was empty. There were people going around doing their work, but it wasn't how it used to be. She didn't see Adam, Jen, Miriam or anyone else she recognized. These people weren't strangers, but she didn't know them.

Alma walked down to the courtyard. After a while, she found Rebekah sitting on the tailgate of a truck outside the entrance. She sat there with several maps around her. She looked up at Alma and gave a weak smile.

"I saw that you were back. How'd it go?"

"We got one group and a 'maybe' from another."

"That's... better than nothing."

"It's not enough."

"We'll make it work. Luray has ten," Rebekah said and looked at a pad with a bunch of numbers scribbled on it.

"They already said they didn't want to join." Alma said.

"Yeah, but they'll need to marry their children to someone, so they'll have to intermarry with us. Also, there's no one near my age."

"You got a couple of years before you need to worry about that."

"No, we need to worry about the future now. That's why the Old World died, they only thought about the present. They weren't thinking of the future when they released that virus."

"I suppose not."

"Miriam's been telling everyone that we need to have a meeting to decide who we want to be."

"Sounds like a good idea."

"I want a place where the government can't murder its own people. We can't have another holocaust, not even a small one."

"I want a place where the government doesn't tell me what to do."

"I want a government with free ice cream Fridays."

"Even in winter?" Alma asked.

"Yes, even in winter."

"What about pizza Tuesdays?"

"I like that. Tuesdays are boring. It needs a boost. You should write this down."

"And siestas."

"Absolutely. An hour at noon for siestas."

Rebekah smiled. Even that faint smile was an improvement.

Then she spotted Jason. He was walking with Alex and talking while Alex nodded his head. She waited until they split up. Alex went into the stone church while Jason walked back to the castle. When he spotted her, he picked up his pace.

"I didn't expect you up." Jason said when he reached the truck.

"You were going to say because it's before noon."

"You stole my thunder."

"I just know you."

She patted him on the cheek.

Rebekah cleared her throat.

"Enough flirting. A delegation from Farmville is coming down today to discuss the attack on Ft. Knox."

Alma rubbed her hands together.

"Finally, someone's doing something about this mess." Alma said.

"I'm not sure a direct assault is a good idea." Jason said.

"What do you mean? They can't have much left."

"They're a wounded animal. They're still dangerous and many will die."

She looked around and saw that they didn't have a lot of spare people. A big fight wouldn't be fun, but if it came down to it, they'd do what they had to do.

"We'll stop them, Jason. No matter what."

21

ALEX WAITED IN FRONT OF THE STONE CHAPEL FOR THE TWO delegations to arrive. He knew one would be there but didn't have a clue on the other. The two trucks from Farmville were already in Lexington and headed their way.

The other delegation was a mystery. He didn't even know if they had received his invitation. The Cherokee hadn't made contact with him and he had no idea where they were, but he suspected that they had their look outs. So he had posted signs inviting them to the meeting about "mutually beneficial agreements."

He heard the truck engines before seeing them. A few moments later, two pickup trucks drove into view from the W&L side of the old campus. He recognized Frank waving from the open window.

Alex waved back and waited. Next to him were Cassidy, Rebekah, Adam, Jen, Shakti and Lisa. Alma was supposed to be there but was probably still sleeping. Shakti was their expert on the PG and the rest were there because he trusted them.

The trucks came to a stop and the eight men and women from Farmville got out. Instead of a handshake, Frank gave him a chest crushing hug.

"Glad to see you, buddy." Frank said.

"Good to see you too. We got a lot to talk about."

"We're getting John back. That's first priority. The PG didn't return him like they promised."

"We'll talk about that inside."

"You're not going to try to talk me out of it, are you?"

"Depends on what you're planning."

Frank laughed and went inside.

"The PG could use the boy as a hostage." Lisa whispered.

"Believe me, I've thought about it."

He was about to say more about how low the PG would go when he saw a group of people emerge from the woods across the parade field. By their black hair and hunting rifles, he guessed it was the Cherokee. At least they had gotten his invitation.

Alex smiled and walked toward them with his hand out. Gary Dullknife didn't smile but he did take his hand. That was a good start.

"We got the memo. You said it was important." Gary said.

"Very. It's about our future."

"You are going to promise that we can keep our land as long as the river runs?"

He knew that was a reference to the many treaties the US made and broke with the Indian nations.

"This isn't the nineteenth century." Alex said.

"Or the seventeenth, or the twentieth?"

"It's a new age for all of us. Let's start over and do it right this time."

"Our council says we cannot trust you."

He knew that was coming. They had no reason to trust them. He had rehearsed all the arguments in his head many times over.

"And what do you say?" Alex asked.

"I don't trust you, but I will give you a chance to earn that trust."

"That's all I ask for."

He shook his hand and watched his delegation go into the chapel. He had the teenage boy and girl with him again along with the same two large men. The two large guys carried a FAL and an AK-47 instead of the hunting rifles of the others.

"I'm going inside and see if our guests are comfortable." Rebekah said.

"Good idea."

He didn't look at Rebekah when he spoke. His eyes were on Alma and Jason who had just left the barracks. He waited outside for them.

"You're late." Alex said.

"I figured you'd survive a few minutes without me." Alma said.

"That's not a good habit to get into, especially when dealing with guests."

"I was drawing up a complete list of all our military assets."

She handed him the notebook and folded her arms in that pose she always did when she knew she had won.

"Right. I'll take a look at this later. Now get inside and make them feel at ease."

"Yes, sir." she said and saluted.

She was being sarcastic and condescending again. Something he didn't have time to deal with right now.

He went inside and saw his people sitting in the pews. The Cherokee on one side and Farmville on the other. His own people were sitting up on the platform up front.

The chapel was white with stained wood. It looked like something from a medieval movie set, like it was made to look old but didn't have the age to make it believable.

He went to the podium and cleared his throat. He looked at each face in the audience while he thought about what to say. Hopefully it would come off as solemn and thoughtful and not desperate and clueless.

"Thank you all for coming here. We have delegations from Farmville and the Appalachian Cherokee. I welcome you all. There are many reasons I asked for this meeting. Mainly, we have to discuss the survival of our species. For the Cherokee, what I'm talking about is how many people we need to breed to maintain a viable population."

"How many people?" Gary asked.

"Around a hundred and fifty."

"And how many do you have?" Gary asked.

"A little more than ninety. Ten more up north and another dozen coming."

"Let me stop you right there," Gary said. "Right now our council is trying to decide if we stay here or go out west to look for our fellow Cherokee. If we stay, yes, we will intermarry with you."

"When will they decide?" Alex asked.

"Soon."

"We don't need them," Frank said.

"Why not?" Alex asked.

"We're going to have the people from Kentucky once we take Ft. Knox."

"I thought you didn't want to breed with them."

"The PG leaders, no, but the civilians shouldn't be held accountable for the actions of their leaders."

"What's he talking about?" Gary asked.

"There's a plan to attack the Provisional Government in Ft. Knox. They attacked us and kidnapped a boy from Farmville," Alex said.

"The world was destroyed because of a war and now you wish to start another one?" Gary asked.

"We didn't start this war, but we have to finish it or they will continue to come after us."

"They probably say the same about you," Gary said.

"I'm not playing this game. They kidnapped one of ours and given the chance, they'll attack us. We're going after them with everything we have." Frank said.

Alma stood up and walked over beside Alex.

"I know we can't afford to lose anyone else. Life is more precious now than it ever was, but if we don't do anything about the PG, they will continue to attack us and there will be more lives lost."

"We will have no part in this." Gary said.

"What about staying here and forging a new nation? Now's the time to decide our future." Frank said.

"We don't want a future with people that will choose war as a means of solving problems when other solutions still exist." Gary stood up along with the other Indians. "Show us that you can work in peace and we will stay."

With that, the Cherokee walked out.

As he watched them go, he knew that he had failed somehow. Perhaps he could get them back but he'd need to stop this war first.

"Fantastic," Jen said. "All our talk about not making the same mistakes and here we are, making the same mistakes."

"The mistake was to take one of our children. It would be a mistake to let that go unpunished." Frank said.

"We have to get the boy back, but let's send a delegation first." Alex said.

"What? They destroyed Promised Land and you want to talk to them?" Alma asked.

"I want payback as much as you do, but I also don't want to lose anymore of our people. Every death is a loss we can't get back."

"You expect us to sit back and have the PG come after us in the night like they did with you?" Frank asked.

"I'm saying we should talk to them first. If war becomes necessary, then I'll fight without reservations, but I want to at least speak to them first."

"Alex, go look at our home. The war's already started."

"Then let's see if we can end it." Alex said.

"Agreed on that. We have two Paladin self propelled howitzers. We also have a Bradley. With your forces we have enough to take them down and take them over," Frank said.

"We'll take a vote." Alex said.

"You know where we all stand. Everyone wants to see the PG destroyed for what they did." Alma said.

She was right about that. He knew what his people thought and knew that they wanted to fight. He also knew what Farmville would vote. It was like asking the sun to not set.

"All in favor of an attack on the PG, raise your hands," Alex said.

Almost everyone raised their hand.

"All in favor of negotiation first."

Only Jen, Cass and one Farmville person raised their hand.

His second and bigger failure of the day. Things were turning out as he had expected but not, how he had hoped. He cast a quick glance at Lisa, who gave him a small nod of encouragement.

"Very well, that settles it." Frank said.

Now his mission was to plan this war to avoid as many casualties as possible. Damage control.

"We begin preparing then," Alex said. "We have a map room in the barracks. Let's adjourn for lunch and then get started."

As everyone filed out of the chapel, Alma came up and stood next to him with folded arms and a wild grin.

"We're going after those bastards." Alma said.

"And we'll have more funerals."

"It'll be less death if we do this now rather than wait."

"It'll be less death if we sign some kind of peace treaty."

Alma laughed.

"Yeah, because asking them politely to stop killing us will work."

It probably wouldn't work. Whoever was in charge of the PG had shown themselves to be ruthless and uncaring to the needs of people. They had wanted to take all their supplies, kidnapped a child just to split Promised Land and Farmville and then burnt their entire crop to let them starve in winter.

Maybe they aren't rational and do need to be destroyed. I'd still like to know for sure first.

He followed them out and to the cafeteria, where his people had homemade bread with melted cheese on top. He got his plate and sat down next to Frank.

"So, we're going to attack Ft. Knox. Let's make sure we do this right." Alex said.

"We don't have as many veterans as you do. We need your help on this." Frank said.

"We have a man and woman who used to be with the PG. They can help us plan. But whatever happens, Frank, we're going to lose people and any death will affect your group more than mine. You only have thirty five."

"We have ten fighters. You have twenty. How many could they possibly have left?"

Not many. They had killed a good number of PG soldiers. Whatever they had left couldn't be enough to stop their combined army. They would win, he just didn't know if it was worth the cost.

"We have one recovery vehicle with a small cannon. That's all."

"We provide the tanks, you provide the manpower."

"At least we know what we're working with."

He took out Alma's notebook and together they went over everything. He wrote down what Farmville had and added it all together. They could, in addition to the two Paladins, Bradley and recovery vehicle; arm two Humvees with .50 cals.

It didn't look so dire. With that force, they could take on the PG if they did it right.

He called Lisa, Shakti and Jason over to sit with them. Of course Alma came too.

"Help us come up with a plan of attack. Where are they weakest and what should we avoid?" Alex asked.

"Send in one or two people to disrupt them before the assault. Cut off power, communications." Lisa said.

"I like the way your wife thinks," Frank said.

"Do you have someone in mind?" Alex asked.

"Me and you."

"We tow some 155mm howitzers out and set up a camp there," Frank said. "They come out to destroy them and we drop an ambush on them."

"We don't have enough 155mm for four guns," Lisa said.

"It's just a diversion." Frank said.

"And if they don't fall for it?" Alex asked.

"Then we drop artillery shells on them until they're all dead."

"It's a good plan," Lisa said. "But it could use some refining."

"We've been thinking about it for a long while, Alex."

They spent the rest of the day organizing their people into squads and teams. Alma, Shakti and Jason knew their people well and knew who would work more efficiently with whom. Most of Frank's people were in the armored vehicles. But Promised Land had their demolition teams and snipers.

Shakti and Jason drew up a detailed map of Ft. Knox and together with Alex and Frank, they planned out the assault.

As he planned it out, he knew it was stupid. People would die and they couldn't afford to lose anyone. It was like he was planning his own execution and there was nothing he could do to stop it.

The Farmville delegation stayed the night and left in the morning. They were going back to assemble their people and equipment. In two days they would be back. Together they would roll out and go to Kentucky.

Two days before war.

"Something's troubling you." Lisa said.

"This shouldn't be happening."

"We don't have a choice. It's simple. If we don't kill them, they will continue to kill us. Even if it takes them a generation to get up to strength, they will come."

"It shouldn't be like this."

"You're wasting time worrying about how things shouldn't be. Accept it and focus on the problems we can deal with now."

"Do you believe our people are ready?"

"They're as ready as they're ever going to be."

There still had to be a way to stop this.

At night he lay next to Lisa, going over the plan of attack in his head. Perhaps the PG would call for a truce when they saw how outgunned they were. Winning without firing a shot was too much to hope for though.

"Miriam's been asking for a meeting." Lisa said.

"Ah, yes, her Constitutional Convention."

"Her what?"

"She wants to set out a list of our freedoms and values. It's actually not a bad idea at all."

"Once the current problem is over, then I'll worry about the future."

"That's her point though. We have to choose our future now."

And what future am I creating? One of unnecessary war and violence. If Miriam is correct, then there was no bright future of progress and peace, only more of the same.

The next morning he saw the Farmville delegation off and then turned back to "The Castle" as people were calling it.

In a few days, his people would be in another fire fight. He saw Rebekah walk by with a notebook and a gun on her hip. The eye patch glared at him in accusation.

How many others will I fail to protect?

22

SHAKTI SAT ON THE HOOD OF THE HUMVEE AS SHE OILED HER gun and slapped the upper receiver closed.

All around her people were getting ready to leave. Goodbyes were being said and there were some tears which she tried not to notice. Many of the unofficial families were gathered to see their people off. Alex was kissing Lisa; Alma and Jason were laughing while setting a .50 cal on one of the Humvees.

"You ready to go?" Miriam asked.

Miriam was dressed in body armor and ammo pouches. She didn't wear a helmet and her hair was tied back in a single long pony tail. Her multi-cam cargo pants were tucked into black combat boots she had gotten from an army surplus store near Lynchburg.

"I'm ready to go off and attack my former friends and allies. It's great."

"You're not having second thoughts, are you?"

"No, I'm in this all the way. It doesn't mean I have to like it."

"I don't like this either. This whole thing is pointless. There's enough space to spread out and not have to fight."

"We do what we have to do, Miriam."

"What we have to do is the right thing."

"And who decides what the right thing is? Not me."

Cassidy rode up to the assembled group in front of the Castle.

"Farmville is almost here. They're up by Walmart now," Cass yelled out for everyone to hear.

"Alright, people. Mount up and let's get rolling," Alex said.

Shakti climbed into the back of a deuce-and-a-half along with five other people amid crates of ammo and food. Miriam sat next to her with her Dragunov pointed down between her knees.

Miriam wasn't smiling and her eyes looked down but not at anything in particular.

"You okay, Miriam?"

"Do you think God or your gods are watching over us?"

"Just because mankind chose to destroy themselves doesn't mean the gods aren't heartbroken over this. I think I was meant to find you and we were meant to come here. That's good enough for me."

"But why? I thought it was to make a difference, but so far I haven't done much at all."

"That's not true. You saved that soldier when you probably should have shot him."

Miriam fell silent and the truck rumbled to life along with all the other trucks in their convoy. The Recovery vehicle was in the middle with a .50 cal armed Humvee at the front and another at the rear of their convoy.

The Farmville truck and armored vehicles came into the circle road around the parade ground and came in at the rear. Without ceremony, the now united convoy rolled out towards the highway.

Everyone fell silent. Soon the droning of the engine lured her to sleep. She'd wake up once in a while and look out to see rolling green hills and empty road. There was no way to tell where they were and it seemed like time and space no longer had meaning.

This could be what Nirvana was like, forever living the same moment but free to think. I hope that moment's a better one than this. At least give her someone else to talk to. Everyone else was asleep or close to it.

She fell asleep again and awoke to the same bright sunlight but different hills and trees. Everyone else was still asleep.

Shakti put her earbuds in and turned on some Punjabi music. Right now something familiar was needed. As she listened to the rapid beats of the cheerful music, she let her now awake mind wander off.

She thought back to her time with the PG and how she had ignored what the PG was doing because the ends justified the means. Yes, they had forced people to come to Ft. Knox, but civilization was at stake.

The rule was that deserters would be shot and she knew that when she left. She had stolen an M4, sidearm, ammo, food and water. That alone would have gotten her shot several times over.

And now she was going back there. Some of the people there she liked. They had been her friends and they didn't deserve to die. If there was a way to avoid fighting, she would take it.

But she knew that Senator McNeil, Shumate and Anderson weren't going to surrender. The new "Senate" was composed of three Type A, Alpha Males,

"I'm in charge" types that would never accept surrender. They'd rather see everything in flames before admitting they were wrong.

There would be no peaceful resolution.

Miriam sat up after an hour and rubbed her eyes.

"Where are we?" She asked.

"No idea." Shakti said.

Miriam crawled over the ammo crates to the rear of the truck and looked out. The hills were steeper and the trees were thicker, but she still couldn't tell where they were.

They were taking the long way to avoid the obvious routes to Ft. Knox and the recovery vehicle slowed them down.

She spent all day listening to music and setting her backpack solar panel near the rear of the truck where the sunlight could reach it.

At night, they stopped and camped along the side of the road. She stayed in the back of the truck and rolled her sleeping bag out.

"You think it'll actually come down to a fight?" Miriam asked in the dark.

"Yes."

"Think we'll win?"

"Yes."

"So, you're not worried?"

"I didn't say that."

"Any single Muslim men there?"

"None that I know of."

She heard Miriam sigh and rustle around in her sleeping bag.

"This sucks." Miriam said.

"I don't see any eligible Hindu men either. Most immigrants were in the cities where the virus hit hardest."

"I'm not going to be the last Muslim on the east coast."

"You're not, but the rest are probably up North where the cities used to be."

"This really sucks."

Before dawn, the convoy was on its way again. The sky was gray and dew covered everything. When she went to use the bathroom, she came back with her boots and pant legs soaked from the moisture. She had never been camping before and now she knew why. Nature was more trouble than it was worth.

She'd rather be someplace warm with a hot tub and a good movie.

Instead she found herself in the back of an army truck, driving towards a battle she didn't want to fight.

They arrived near Ft. Knox at five in the afternoon. The trucks came to a stop and behind them people were jumping out. She looked over to Miriam and nodded her head toward the rear of the truck.

She climbed out and Miriam handed her their weapons before climbing out herself.

Everyone gathered around their lieutenants and waited for orders. She was in the ambushing group. Farmville was in charge of the diversionary artillery position.

She met with Miriam and eight others. Lisa was in charge of her squad, with Cassidy and Alma each in charge of a five man team.

"Alright, we know our job. Let's get into position and stay out of sight." Lisa said.

They moved off into the woods to a position that allowed them to see both the front gate of Ft. Knox and the artillery firebase that was being set up.

She took a position next to Miriam, behind a log and got comfortable. It was going to be a while.

The Farmville people took their time setting the cannons into position. The self-propelled artillery created a line while the crews set up camo nets as slowly and obviously as they could.

The cannons were in the direct line of sight of the base because no one knew how to fire indirect fire and they didn't have the shells to spare to figure it all out.

"What if they have more helicopters?" Miriam asked.

"We have a stinger and .50 cals. We'll be fine." Shakti said.

"How many people do you think they have?"

"Less than us."

"Why are you so calm?"

"Because freaking out won't keep me alive."

The main Gate opened and she saw something large roll out. It just looked like a tan blur moving down the road.

"They saw us." Miriam said.

"And they're taking the bait. Get on your scope and tell me what that is."

Miriam removed her lens cap and peered through her Russian scope.

"It's a tank."

"An actual tank or an APC?"

"No, an actual tank. A big one."

Shakti waved Miriam to the side and took a look.

Sure enough, it was an Abrams main battle tank and it was coming right at the fire base. The artillery looked impressive but it wasn't designed to take out armor like that.

The muffled blasts of the artillery sounded through the woods and she saw explosions of smoke and sparks hit the tank without any effect at all.

The Bradley and recovery vehicle were hidden in the woods but now their ambush was ruined because the tank would never get close enough to spring the trap. It would just sit back and fire at will.

The crews of the Paladins turned to the side and went full speed, crashing into the woods and out of sight of the tank.

"Good thinking." Miriam said.

The tank then surged forward. It was going at a controlled pace watching for trouble.

There was nothing she could do but stay hidden. Her gun was useless against that metal beast and it probably had infrared to spot warm bodies.

"Stay down." Shakti hissed.

Miriam got down lower and held her rifle with both hands.

"This sucks, so bad." Miriam said with closed eyes.

She heard the tank fire and could hear the faint ripping sound of the round traveling through the air. A split second later, she heard an explosion across the road and had to fight the urge to take a peek.

Then the sound of an engine revving up to full made her look. The Bradley tore through the woods and came out into the road. The turret swung to face the oncoming tank.

The box on the side of the turret swung up and a blast of white smoke launched out. The missile streaked down the road and exploded on the Abrams. The Bradley then unloaded with its rapid fire cannon in a steady stream as it plunged back into the woods.

Shakti watched until the smoke cleared.

The Tank moved forward but it stopped.

"One of its tracks is off." Miriam said while looking through her scope.

"It's not going anywhere, but it's right in front of the gate."

"We can go to a different gate."

"But the point was to draw them out. If we attack them on their home turf, they'll murder us. They'll know where to ambush us, where to hide and where to attack us. No, if they don't come out, we're not going in."

"So, we just sit here?"

"For now. And try not to get shot by the tank."

In the distance, the tank opened fire with its machine gun and she heard a smaller explosion, maybe a grenade.

After that there was only silence. The tank waited in the road for anyone to show themselves.

"They're going to run out of food and water in there." Miriam said.

"It's a waiting game."

"They haven't sent anyone to help. That's a good sign, right?"

"Yeah, that's a good sign."

Sometime after sunset, Lisa crawled over to them with two MRE's.

"Here you go," Lisa said.

"Any word on what's going on?" Shakti asked.

"We're sneaking an AT-4 team to fire at its rear, but we don't know if that will work. If it doesn't, we're going to wait it out until the tank crew surrenders. It could be days."

"Can we wait that long?"

"We're set."

"Any contact with the PG leaders?" Miriam asked.

"Nothing. Alex is trying to get them on the radio."

"Still trying to stop the fighting, huh?" Shakti asked.

"I think it's noble of him." Miriam said.

"It's also useless. The PG won't negotiate," Shakti said.

She slept in her sleeping bag while Miriam kept watch. When it was her turn she looked out at the tank but couldn't see anything but a dark shape in the road. She knew some of their people had NVGs so if the tank was doing something funny, she'd find out.

In the morning, she was awakened by an explosion. She jumped up and looked. The rear of the tank was on fire but the turret was turning around. It opened fire with its machine gun but she couldn't see who or what it was shooting at.

The tank was crippled but not dead.

She sat back down and waited.

"What if they don't come out of the base? It's not like they're going to starve to death in there." Miriam said.

That was an excellent question. What was the plan?

Around noon, Alex came up to her and sat down, leaning against the log.

"We need some advice." Alex said.

"I'll do what I can."

"We're waiting for the tank to surrender. Once that happens Frank wants to go into Ft. Knox."

"That'll be disastrous." Shakti said.

"That's what I tried to tell him."

"The truth is that we can't stay here more than two weeks before we run out of food ourselves. We have to do something."

Miriam sat up.

"Any contact with PG leaders?"

"Nothing. I know they're listening, but I think they know we can't go in and they can't come out."

"But we're not going in, right?" Shakti asked.

"I don't know."

"What do you mean? It would be suicide."

"Almost everyone else wants to. We're going to bombard the place with our artillery until we're out of shells, then move in."

"Let me talk to them. Going in there will be too dangerous. Yeah, we'll probably win, but we'll lose too many people." Shakti said.

"Jason seems to think that if we take out the leadership, the PG will collapse."

"Maybe, but you'll never get to them. They're going to be deep underground away from the danger." Shakti said.

"Tell them not to hit the civilian barracks." Miriam said.

"Of course."

Alex hurried off and Shakti sat there wondering what they were supposed to do.

That night they held a meeting out of sight of the tank. A few were left behind to keep an eye on it to make sure no help came.

Alex laid the situation out for everyone. The tank wouldn't last much longer and when it was gone they would shell the base in preparation for an assault. Everyone cheered for the idea except a few.

Shakti didn't cheer.

The PG had to be stopped but this wasn't the way. They would lose too many people that were irreplaceable and she didn't want cousins marrying cousins.

She looked over to Miriam and saw that she wasn't smiling either.

23

ALEX PUT DOWN THE RADIO AND RUBBED HIS FACE. HE KNEW the PG were listening, they just weren't answering for some reason. They probably thought they wouldn't go into the fort.

Normally, they would be right but there was too much bad blood and his people wanted payback. The Farmville guys wanted their boy back and weren't going to leave without him.

Night was coming and nothing had happened since the AT-4 attack in the morning. The tank was still there and still alive. Their hope was that the PG would send a rescue team.

As night fell, they built a fire and ate their MRE's in a circle. Lisa sat next to him and Alma sat across from him with Jason. Not so long ago she would have been at his side. They had drifted apart and he still didn't understand why.

"The PG will come to an end, one way or another." Frank said.

"We'll move in and take them out. Maybe we can arm the civilians." Alma said.

"Too many civilians support the PG. We wouldn't know who was who." Alex said.

That night he lay in the back of the Humvee with Lisa. They were wrapped up in their sleeping bag.

"This is all going wrong." he said.

"It's not going according to plan, not the same as wrong."

"You think it's a good idea to go in? They probably have barricades and snipers all over the place."

"Probably, but we will win."

"That's not good enough."

"What would you do then?"

"We need eyes inside. We don't know what's going on in there."

"I'll go."

"Good, I was counting on you."

"Who else?" She asked.

"Miriam."

"Her? She's a good shot, but she's not cut out for that kind of work."

"I want Miriam and Shakti. Shakti knows the layout."

"Wouldn't Alma be better?"

"She's too eager to start shooting."

"Isn't that what we need?"

"Not for what I have in mind."

The next morning, the crew came out of the tank holding their hands above their heads. They were taken and zip-tied before the PG could do anything.

Frank slapped him on the back.

"See that? The gate is open. All we need to do is soften them up a bit."

"While you're blowing them up, have the Bradley go to the gate and have the commander get on a megaphone. Tell them to surrender."

"You think they will?"

"No, but we need to give them the chance."

"I'll tell them."

Frank gathered his men and after a short briefing they ran to their Paladins and rolled back into the street. Their guns raised and fired. In the distance, two spouts of dirt and smoke rose up in silence.

The Bradley rolled forward to the now defenseless gate. He could barely hear the commander on the megaphone demanding their surrender.

"Now, we sit back and wait," Frank said.

He unfolded a lawn chair and sat down with a cooler next to him.

"This isn't a game, Frank."

"No, it's not, but that doesn't mean I can't be comfortable."

Every half hour the Paladin's fired. Sometimes the shells fell on empty fields or parking lots. Other times they fell on buildings, they knew to be empty. But their accuracy was increasing and by the end of the day, they were shelling the populated area.

They had enough shells to last two days. After that, it would be a direct assault and he couldn't let it come to that.

He got back on the radio and flipped through every channel while sending out the same message. He asked them to talk and surrender.

No answer came.

As the Farmville people started a bonfire with singing and music, Alex took Lisa, Miriam and Shakti off to the side.

"You have a plan?" Shakti asked.

"I think so.

"Think? That's not reassuring." Lisa said.

"We are going to sneak in there and look around. I want to know what the civilians think and why no one's answering. What are their leaders doing?"

"And if we find the leaders?" Lisa asked.

"It depends on what we find. If they can be reasoned with, let's reason with them."

"That doesn't sound like a good idea. They're just as likely to shoot us on sight," Shakti said.

"That's why we need eyes in there."

"Are you going to tell Frank?"

"Yes. I'll tell him we're going on a recon with the PG expert."

"Let's do this." Shakti said.

Frank shook his head when he told him.

"That's a perfect way to get yourselves shot or captured. What if they use you as a hostage?"

"I'm going in. You can continue your bombardment if you want, we need to know what's going on in there before sending our guys in."

"Fine, do what you want. But in two days I'm ordering the assault whether you're captured or not."

"Deal."

"I still think you're being stupid."

"I've been accused of that before."

"I hope it won't be the last time."

He walked back to where Lisa, Miriam and Shakti waited.

"Alright, let's go." he said.

Shakti led the way. She knew where the best location was to sneak in under the fence. Miriam carried the wire cutters and Lisa kept watch with her NVGs.

They arrived at the edge of the woods and crawled on their bellies through tall grass that hadn't been mowed in two years. It was cold and his breath billowed up in front of him. The cold seeped through his clothes and spread through his body.

The moon was behind some clouds, something he was thankful for.

As soon as they reached the gate, Miriam began cutting a hole through the fence.

"See anything?" He asked.

"Nothing." Lisa said.

"They don't have any lights on." Miriam said.

"Because they don't want to paint big target signs on themselves." Shakti said.

There was one four story brick building in front of him. The abandoned cars in the parking lot looked expensive.

"Past this building will be another admin building. After that is the barracks where they keep the civilians," Shakti whispered.

"Should we expect help from the civilians?" He asked.

"Maybe. I know a few. Let me go in first."

He nodded his agreement and they ran at a low crouch to the side of the building. They made their way to the end and he peered around the corner. A one story building with tattered flags lay across the parking lot and beyond that was a cluster of larger, simpler buildings.

"Those are the barracks. There are going to be guards nearby." Shakti said.

"Lisa, you have the NVGs. Go first and find those guards."

Lisa nodded and led the way through the parking lot. They stayed low and went from car to car with Lisa watching out for any sign of activity.

He propped his M4 on the hood of a Mustang as the rest of his group moved. The windows of the admin building were black holes and the barracks beyond were a shadow land where anything could wait for them.

Maybe there was a whole platoon of soldiers or maybe armed civilians loyal to the PG.

Alma would say I'm being stupid. She'd probably be right.

They got to the flat admin building and Lisa looked in with her goggles.

"Clear," she whispered.

Lisa then went to the corner and looked out at the barracks. She watched for a few minutes while they waited in silence.

"Three guards. Sloppy. Not soldiers." Lisa said.

"Don't kill them," Shakti said. "They're civilians loyal to the PG. Kill them and the civilians won't like you at all."

"Lisa, can we get past them?"

"One at a time, yes. There's a door but it could be locked."

"It's not locked. They couldn't find the keys and they like to make surprise inspections."

"Okay, Shakti, you're up. We'll wait here."

Shakti waited for the guards to get out of sight. One of them looked no older than seventeen. They carried M4s without any attachments and didn't have uniforms.

She ran across the grassy field to the door and disappeared inside.

While he waited, Alex looked around. He saw the motor pool from Shakti's maps. There were only a few trucks and Humvees there. There were wooden guard towers surrounding the motor pool along with the destroyed armory and the barracks for the PG soldiers.

"Someone's coming." Lisa said.

One of the civilian guards was walking toward them. He had his M4 in one hand and a small flashlight in the other. His flashlight was off but he was moving at them in a slow and guarded pace.

"Stand back. I got this," Lisa said.

"Don't kill him." Miriam whispered.

When the guard turned the corner, Lisa grabbed his M4; butt stroked him in the groin and then kneed him in the face.

The man fell to the ground, knocked out cold.

"Is he alright?" Miriam asked.

"He'll be fine."

Alex took the man's ammo and threw it into his pack.

It was ten minutes before Shakti came out and ran back to their position.

"I found someone. She said that they armed the men they knew were loyal to guard the rest."

Shakti looked down and saw the unconscious guard.

"He's alive." Lisa said.

"Please keep it that way," Shakti said.

"For now, let's continue on. Maybe we'll come back and arm the ones that would support us."

"How can they be loyal to a government that treats them like servants?" Miriam asked.

"They'd rather be safe than free," Alex said.

He waved them forward. They went around the building away from the civilian barracks and toward the military section.

Shakti pointed out a building on the other side of the military barracks. It was a blocky three-storey building with small windows. She told them that that was where the senators most likely were. It was their command center and one of the sturdiest buildings around.

There were guard towers around the area and barricades made from old cars that blocked off road access to the motor pool and barracks. He saw armed men waiting behind the barricades. This was their inner keep and they were waiting.

"We can get around to the rear." Shakti said.

The PGs attention was focused toward the front where the threat was and the opposite side was lightly guarded. But it was guarded and he couldn't afford a mistake now.

Together they made their way in a wide circle past the burnt armory and the motor pool. Lisa watched the towers and told them when it was safe to move. They left the concealment of the trees and crept building to building until they reached a dark building next to the senator's HQ.

"What can we expect in there?" Alex asked.

"A body guard. Contractors. They never go on patrol or raids. They stay here and make sure no one gets out of line."

"How many?"

"Four."

Four well-armed, trained killers against his four. Unless they surprised them, they would lose the fight.

"Let me go in. I can take out the senators." Lisa said.

"No, I'm trying to avoid a blood bath here."

"We need to talk to them." Miriam said.

"That won't help. I know these men. They don't care about the people under them. They will let all of them die if it meant they lived." Shakti said.

"We have to try." Miriam said.

"It'll be useless." Shakti said.

"I don't know if they want to talk. I tried to get them on the radio." Alex said.

"Then let's sneak in there and find them." Lisa said. "If they don't want to talk, we kill them."

"And then the people loyal to them will come after us and I'll be looking over my shoulder for the rest of my life," Alex said.

"Then we kill them and the bodyguards." Lisa said.

"I'd like to avoid a firefight with four veteran contractors." Alex said.

"I can handle them." Lisa muttered.

"No, we're here to find a way to end this before the assault. Let's use our heads." Alex said.

He heard engines starting from the motor pool. He moved to where he could see and saw about fifteen people mounting up in Humvees armed with .50 cals.

"Looks like they're launching a sortie." Alex said.

"A what?" Miriam asked.

"They're going to attack in an effort to try to catch our people off guard. My guess is that they want to take out those cannons."

He watched the four Humvees take off. He counted three with .50's and one with what looked like a lighter machine gun. If not handled the right way, those four Humvees could do a lot of damage, but it was out of his hands now. Whatever happened, people would die.

24

ALMA LAY IN THE BACK OF THE PICKUP TRUCK NEXT TO JASON. Her backpack made a passable pillow.

"I'm going to punch him when he comes back." Alma said.

"He needed you to stay here and lead our forces."

"No, he runs off and has all the fun and leaves me behind like he always does."

"Alma, you're the head of the army. You wanted it. Now you have it."

"He still should have asked me."

She rolled over and laid her head on his chest.

"We will win this, right?"

"We will. We have to because if we let them alone, the next generation will have to contend with them. Better to destroy them as a power now and not leave it for our children."

"But what's the world going to be like then? How long will it take to get back to normal?"

"Not long. It will be a different normal though."

"How many kids are we going to have?"

He coughed and shifted his position.

"Haven't really thought about it."

"I always thought three at most, but now I want like eight."

"Eight?"

"Yes. More kids means a stronger family later. Our children will have more children until we're everywhere. Imagine a world where half the people are descended from us."

"I don't think we will be around to care."

"It would still be cool. Our own dynasty."

"Sounds like something Alex would say."

"I pay attention sometimes."

"Not to me."

"Always to you."

Then she heard shouting.

Alma sat up and looked toward the gate. Four dark shapes were tearing down the road toward them. Enormous muzzle flashes erupted from the approaching vehicles and the impact of large caliber rounds exploded all around her. Dirt flew up and she heard the sound of metal on metal.

A bullet blasted through the windshield of the pickup truck, spraying glass all over her. Sparks burst all around one of the Paladin's. From the momentary flashes of light created from the impacts, she could tell that the Paladin's armor was chewed up with holes.

She grabbed her rifle and fired at the dark shape.

"They're up armored." someone yelled out.

Crap.

Her gun wouldn't scratch the armor.

As she watched, the Humvees pulled into a line like a roadblock. The machine guns up top continued to lay down fire as she watched people get out of the Humvees and run into the woods.

Crap.

"Get NVGs. They're going into the woods." she yelled out.

She and Jason grabbed their goggles and put them on.

"Let's go hunting." Jason said.

They jumped out and ran to the woods for cover.

The surviving Paladin leveled its gun as people shouted to get behind it. The concussion and blast of the cannon firing was dangerous and no one wanted to be near that thing when it fired.

She covered her ears and waited.

The Paladin fired and struck the middle Humvee. The blast was like a toddler smacking his toy blocks. Two of the Humvees flew back and high into the air. One of them tumbled and the other was in too many pieces to count.

After gawking, she focused on the woods and looked for the escaped PG soldiers. Jason walked beside her at a low crouch. His AK shotgun was kept up at his shoulder, ready to fire. He moved smooth and quiet, not what she expected from such a large man.

The NVGs gave everything a ghostly green look. It was bright and clear as day though, so she would find the enemy.

Jason would stop every now and then to listen. She heard gunshots in the distance and some shouting, but it was faded like it came from another world.

The sharp crack of the Bradley's auto cannon sounded in rapid fire. She knew the other two Humvees were out of the game now.

Her world was right there in front of her. She had to focus on finding the enemy and not what was going on out there.

She got behind a tree and peeked out.

Nothing.

Jason tapped her on the shoulder and she turned to look where he was pointing. Through a dense section of forest, she saw five men making their way outward. It looked like they were trying to move away in order to come in around them and attack from the rear.

She turned around and saw that no one else was nearby. It was up to her and Jason.

They stayed low and went from tree to tree. The men didn't stop or look their way except for the occasional scan. She knew where they were but they didn't know where she was.

She moved to the next tree and peeked out.

Tree by tree, they made their way closer.

She stopped when Jason raised his giant shotgun. They probably couldn't get closer without being seen or heard. There were a lot of trees in the way but it would have to do.

She tapped him on the shoulder to tell him she was ready.

Then he opened fire. A second later she did as well.

Jason's shotgun spit out several blasts of buckshot tearing through the leaves and branches. It was like the forest exploded. She fired her more precise 5.56 at one man and saw him fall backwards.

Jason dropped at least two of them and the other two ducked down out of sight.

"They know we're here." Alma said.

"Stay here and keep their attention. I'll move around and get at them from the side." he said.

He was off before she could argue. She wasn't even sure why she wanted to argue but the idea of him running off on his own gnawed at her gut.

"Be careful, stupid." she whispered to him as he crept away.

She fired two rounds at the area where she knew they were, to remind them that she was out there and maybe get a lucky shot.

There was a big difference between cover and concealment. Cover was when a person was behind something that could stop a threat. Concealment just meant that the threat couldn't see the person. Many people made the mistake of thinking concealment was cover.

Trees, like cars, weren't the cover most people thought they were.

She fired two more times into the cluster of trees, hoping a bullet would hit one of them by chance.

She watched Jason creep closer and waited with her AR ready to go.

One of the men ran for it. The other man fired and she heard bullets plough through the branches around her. She ignored that and took aim the best she could with her NVGs on. She had to sight through the red dot sight that was turned off. Even at low power setting, it would have blinded her in the NVGs.

She fired and missed. Alma cursed and continued firing. A bullet clipped his leg and he fell forward.

Jason fired several blasts from his shotgun and then stopped. She looked over to make sure he was alright and saw him standing over the location the other man had been. His gun was pointing down at the man which meant the enemy was still alive.

"Hey, guy I just shot in the leg. You still alive?"

A gunshot rang out but didn't go anywhere near her.

"I'll take that as a yes. Surrender and we'll get you medical attention."

"Go to hell." the man shouted back.

"Look, we don't want to kill you." Jason said. "Do you want to die? Your friend made the smart choice and will live a long healthy life."

"Roger, you there?" The wounded man called out.

"I'm here, dude, it's not worth it."

The man stood up, leaning on a tree and held his hands up.

Alma went to him with her gun pointed at his head. She zip tied him and lead the bleeding men back to camp.

There were five other prisoners, three of them wounded. Frank stood over them with his giant revolver on his hip.

Her eyes went to the shredded Paladin. They had lost people tonight.

"How many dead?" Alma asked Cass as she walked up to her.

"Three. Two in the Paladin and another. Eric, one of our demolition guys."

"That had to be their swan song. I bet they don't have anything left." Frank said.

"I say we move in now and end this." Alma said.

"Hold on. Alex and the others are still in there." Cass said.

"She's right. We should wait for their report." Frank said.

"The gate's wide open. We should at least move forward and control their exit." Alma said.

Frank scratched his chin.

"Not a bad idea. Let's move in. Not to the central area where they are, but at least inside the fence. Maybe some direct fire by the Paladin will get them to rethink this 'fighting till the end' business."

Frank waved his hands and shouted for everyone to prepare to move out.

Alma leaned against Jason; his arm wrapped around her shoulders in a comforting embrace that she was growing very fond of.

"We're winning." she said.

Her eyes lingered on the smoking paladin.

"We are. It's insane that they haven't surrendered yet."

"Would you?"

"No, but I would be retreating about now. I'd take off on foot before I surrendered."

She thought about if this was happening to her. That night the PG attacked in force, she didn't know if she would survive. In her mind, she had imagined grabbing Jason and running off. He had been her first thought.

"Would you only think about yourself?"

He turned and looked down at her.

"I'd think about us."

They loaded the bodies in the back of a truck and put the prisoners in another truck. When everything was packed up and ready, they moved forward.

Their diminished convoy moved through the gate with the Bradley leading the way.

Alma rode shotgun in a Humvee while Jason drove. Cass and Chris were in the back.

"Keep that Broadsword ready." Alma said.

"It always is." Cass said.

The two people she wanted beside her in a fight were in that Humvee. Alex used to be number three.

"So, it's getting serious between you two." Cass said.

"Not the time, Cass."

"Are you sure you wouldn't want some kind of ceremony?"

"Cass, shut up."

She heard Cass chuckling in the back seat and wanted to reach back and strangle her.

They moved in through the open front gate and towards what the map said was the civilian barracks. Past that, she saw makeshift barricades and guard towers.

The convoy stopped in an open field behind a group of low buildings. The Paladin and Bradley moved to either side of one of the buildings so they could look out from behind cover. Their guns were trained on the barricades.

"We'll commence in the morning." Frank said as he walked through the camp.

"What's the plan?" Alma asked from Humvee's open window.

"We blow the barricades apart and move in nice and slow. Building by building, room by room."

"Sounds fun."

"I'll get on the megaphone and demand our boy back. If he's returned, we'll try to settle this peacefully. If not, then we'll kill everyone holding a gun."

There was a bright light and she turned to see a rocket streaking out of the third floor window of the military barracks.

The blinding rocket flew across the Motor pool and exploded on the Bradley in a burst of light and fire.

The Bradley opened up with its 25mm chain gun tearing holes into the third floor. If the shooter was still there, he was in several pieces.

Fire came from the front of the Bradley and the three men jumped out.

There went their armor support.

"Paladin, fire." Frank said over the radio.

A few seconds later, the Paladin's turret aimed for the barracks and fired. The bottom floor of the barracks exploded out in an eruption of smoke and dust. The shockwave sent a ripple across the dusty motor pool.

"Level that building." Frank said.

The Paladin fired again.

A gunshot rang out from a window of another building and people around her ducked for cover.

Cass jumped out of the Humvee and lay on the ground. She took aim with her large caliber AR and fired.

"Darn it." Cass said and fired again.

Others returned fired and people with NVGs kept watch.

"This isn't going to be a peaceful night." Alma said.

"They know that as soon as that sun comes up, we're coming for them."

"How many do you think they have left?"

"Can't be many. A handful at most.

"Nothing went right."

"It never does."

"You think this will be in a history book one day?"

"Alex is writing a history book, so yes, I do."

"He's writing a history book?"

"He's collecting notes, nothing finished yet."

"I didn't know."

"Because you never talk to him anymore."

"Because he doesn't care about me anymore. He's too busy."

"That's not true and you know it."

"No, I don't know it. You're my new family and that's all that matters."

25

MIRIAM HEARD THE GUNFIRE COMING FROM THE FRONT GATE and tried to get a look. All she could see were the distant muzzle flashes. People were dying and she couldn't stop it.

Men in uniform rushed out of the senators' HQ and to the barracks. One of them carried a missile launcher of some kind. Shakti probably knew what it was.

"Looks like they're preparing for their final defense," Alex said.

"We need to stop this," Miriam said.

"I don't see how, not without killing them," Lisa said.

"We need to get in to talk to the Senators," Miriam said.

"They don't want to talk to us," Alex said.

Alex had given up. Even if he didn't realize it yet, he had.

"I'm going in to talk to them," Miriam said.

"Just like that?" Shakti asked.

"Just like that."

Miriam took off her armored vest and unslung her SVD.

"You can't go in there," Alex said.

"Watch me."

"You're insane. They'll just kill you or use you as a hostage," Shakti said.

"I have to try."

She handed her SVD to Shakti and stood up.

"Miriam, don't be stupid," Lisa said.

Maybe it was stupid. Maybe she would be held as a hostage or worse. Back in Iraq, the person with the most armed thugs was the one that made the rules. She had seen how they perverted her religion to suit their own addiction for power.

Maybe these three Senators were just like that. Maybe they'd watch the world die around them before giving up power. But maybe there were others in there that would listen.

She handed Shakti her father's old Nagant revolver and stepped out into the motor pool with her hands up. The few soldiers running between buildings didn't notice her at first because all the lights were off. Then one of them saw her and snapped his M4 up.

"On the ground." he shouted and she obeyed.

He hadn't shot her on sight. That was a good start.

The man came up and put his knee on her back, crushing the wind out of her while he zip-tied her hands. He then yanked her on her feet and dragged her into the HQ building.

"Who the hell are you and what are you doing here?" The soldier asked.

It was the soldier she had spared. His eyes went wide when he saw her face.

"I need to speak to the Senators." she said.

"You?"

"Yes. I need to talk to them so we can stop this. Right now, my people are planning an assault that will kill lots of people. We have to stop it before it happens."

"You are here to negotiate?"

"Yes."

He thought for a few seconds.

"Alright, let's go."

He dragged her through the dark hallway until they came to a staircase that led down to a cement underground floor with all the lights on. There were a few civilian people milling about in what looked like a break room. Their eyes were wide and they were huddled together around a coffee machine.

They viewed her with white faces as she passed by.

They were just people. Normal people frightened about what was coming.

"What's your name?" She asked.

"Brian."

"I'm Miriam. We just want peace."

"That's what everyone says."

"Do your Senators?"

He didn't answer.

"Our leader has been trying to contact your leaders and discuss some kind of peace, but no one answered."

Brian still didn't respond.

He brought her to a conference room with an oval table, chairs and a painting of an aerial view of Ft. Knox on the wall.

Brian pushed her in; closed and locked the door behind him. She waited alone in the room. The minutes ticked by and the clock on the wall said it had been a half hour before Brian came back.

He wasn't alone. A man in a uniform with a star on his collar came in along with a man in a dark suit.

"This the prisoner?" The general asked. His nametag said "Baker."

"She came out unarmed and willing." Brian said.

"How did you get in?" General Baker said.

"I snuck in through a hole in the fence. I came alone and nobody knows I'm here."

"So, you don't have authority to negotiate." the man in the suit said.

"I came to talk sense into you. They're planning an assault and they will win." Miriam said.

The man in the suit snickered and shook his head.

"No, listen to me. There are over thirty men and women out there with heavy firepower. Just talk to them. All they want is the kidnapped boy back and a promise of peace."

"Peace? They're rebels. They killed soldiers of the United States government." the suit man said.

"They're defending their home. Either way it doesn't matter because they have more people and more guns. They will kill you if you don't talk to them." Miriam said.

"And why do you want us to give up if your forces are so strong?" Baker asked.

"Because I don't want to see anyone else die."

"Isn't that sweet. But the fact is, they're attacking our home and we're going to defend it to the last man," Baker said.

"They don't want your home. Return the child and promise to leave them alone," Miriam said.

A soldier ran up to the open door, almost out of breath.

"Sir, the attack failed. They still have one Paladin and the Bradley left."

They had destroyed a Paladin. That meant people had died.

"Sir, their assault is only a matter of time. I only have six men left." Brian whispered.

She hadn't been meant to hear it but she did and did her best to pretend she hadn't.

"You hold them off and make them pay for every inch." Baker said, not even attempting to be quiet. "If they're stupid enough to come in here, they'll be slaughtered."

"It won't be enough," Brian said. "Senator McNeil, lend us your bodyguards."

"Absolutely not. We need them in case they get this far."

"They will but with their help we can hold them off long enough for them to consider negotiations. Give the boy back."

"He's a hostage." McNeil said.

"He's ten years old."

"Sergeant Staker, you're out of line. You don't get to give orders to a senator." Baker said.

"Please, listen," Miriam said. "No one else has to die. Give back the boy and promise not to attack again and everyone can go back to normal."

"They have resources we need to restart the United States. Don't you traitors have any sense of patriotism?" McNeil asked.

"I'm trying to save lives here." Miriam said.

"There are more important things than lives right now."

McNeil left and waved the messenger back out.

"What should I do with her?" Brian asked.

"She'll be a second hostage. When the rebels get close, we'll parade her and the boy out and threaten to kill one. If they continue forward, we shoot her."

"But sir…"

"Do as you're ordered."

Then the general left and she was alone in the room with Brian.

"You're going to shoot me?" Miriam asked.

"It won't come to that."

"But you would shoot me?"

"I don't know."

"They will come here and they will kill anyone that fights back." Miriam said.

He looked at her but didn't answer.

"You know I'm right," Miriam said. "Fighting now will only mean more lives lost and the world has lost too many already."

"We'll arm the civilians then."

"And then they will die. We can't afford to lose anyone else."

"Wouldn't you die for your country?"

"I would, but right now you're dying for three old men in suits, not your country. Your country is those people out there. We have to protect them."

"I've already got my orders."

"Convince them that what they're doing is wrong. Tell the other soldiers that this can all be over if they just lay down their weapons. We don't want to occupy you or control you. We just want to be left alone."

"I have work to do."

With that, Brian left her in the locked conference room.

****

Rebekah waited for the sun to rise and held her Tavor in both hands. Her dead eye still ached after all this time and she tried not to let it distract her.

Dew covered the ground and the smell of cooking fires filled the camp. She saw the same, tired expressions on everyone's faces. Some people laughed in spite of the deaths but most stared at their fires or in the direction of the enemy.

There had been no more gunshots or attacks from the PG. They were all in hiding now. Their barricades had been destroyed and the barracks were now a smoking ruin. There were a few other buildings around but most of their attention was on the Senator's HQ. The thick building with narrow windows waited for them.

It was going to be a final stand and she hoped it went as well as Custer's.

She remembered Jen's lesson on Custer. He had been an idiot and these PG guys were idiots too. They thought they could just roll in and bully everyone they wanted and when those people fought back they crumbled.

Alma was talking to Cass, Frank and Jason about the plan of attack. Alex and the others still weren't back and she tried not to worry. Alex and Lisa could take care of themselves.

She walked up to Alma's group.

"When do we attack?" Rebekah asked.

"In just a little while. Let it get light enough," Frank said.

They all held cups of coffee, a luxury that they awarded themselves for being at war. Also, no one slept that night and big decisions weren't good to make on a clouded head.

The sky was turning a lighter gray as the sun rose and the end of the battle approached. Home was waiting for her. Only a little more work and she could go back.

It was time to end tyranny before it began. Yes, people would die, but it was better that they die than generations live under an incompetent dictatorship. They claimed to be the United States, but they were just three rich senators that knew the virus was coming. They wanted to keep their power. Founding

Fathers they were not.

She checked her magazines and got into position with her squad. Most of them had M4's but one had a FAL and an old coot had a scoped lever action.

The Paladin was the first to move forward. Its cannon was ready to blow up anything that moved.

It only had three shells left, but that would be enough.

Her squad moved in behind the Paladin, using it as cover. A Humvee with a .50 cal moved forward on her right and another squad to her left used the buildings for cover. They kicked doors down and searched them room by room.

She waited outside while the largest men kicked the doors down. Alex had told her to stay out of harms way. So she stood by and took notes of everything that happened. This had to be recorded accurately for history.

They found nothing. Whatever was left was in the HQ.

Frank was on the Paladin shouting through his bullhorn for the PG to surrender and give the boy back. Nobody answered.

As they moved forward, four men came out. With them they dragged a boy and a woman.

The woman she recognized. Miriam. A man in a uniform held a gun to Miriam's head. Without thinking, she raised her gun and leveled the sight at the man holding a gun to her friend's head.

If she was in charge, there would be no peace treaty, she would kill their leaders and take the people back to the Promised Land.

****

Miriam watched her people move down the parking lot toward her and the HQ. The Paladin's giant 155mm cannon pointed right at her. She saw that all of their soldiers had their guns trained on the four PG men behind her.

"Don't be afraid, John. This will all turn out okay." Miriam said.

The boy didn't say anything. Like her, his hands were tied and his eyes wide and mouth closed.

What kind of monsters threatened to shoot a little boy?

In the distance, she saw Alex and the others meet up with the approaching army. The Paladin stopped and he saw Frank lean over to talk to Alex. They were probably arguing about what to do.

Frank would fight at all costs. What was one life compared to victory?

General Baker held her arm and his M9 to her head. Brian was behind her somewhere. She had spared his life and for a moment thought that he would do the right thing. But now here he was, taking orders like a robot.

She had tried. She said a silent prayer to Allah that he would forgive her for failing. Whatever mission he had for her, it would have to be done by someone else.

It was all in Allah's hands though. Whatever her fate was, it was according to His will. She had done her best.

She began whispering the prayer in Arabic and the old familiar language soothed her mind.

"Sir, let me hold the girl. You'll be less of a target." Brian said.

She wanted to break off her prayer to say something rude to Brian, but she forced herself to continue with her prayer. There were few things better to be doing than praying when death found her.

It wasn't her place to judge him. Only Merciful Allah could do that.

"Will you do what needs to be done?" Baker asked.

"Yes, sir. My head's in the game."

He let her go and stepped out of the way while Brian took her arm.

"This is Frank Tetrelli, Mayor of Farmville," he said through a bullhorn. "We demand that you release your hostages and lay down your arms. We need to talk, face to face."

"Leave now or your woman dies." General Baker yelled.

"Kill her and I guarantee that you won't leave here alive. Let her go and I promise you won't be harmed."

Alex then crawled up on the Paladin and grabbed the megaphone.

"Let them go and give us a promise to leave us alone for good and we'll talk. We can work together to rebuild civilization. This is tearing it apart."

"No negotiations until you leave. I will shoot." Baker said.

Miriam felt something tug at her bonds and felt them fall loose. Something cold and metal pressed into her hands.

"You have to shoot the general. I'll take care of the others," he whispered in her ear.

She nodded and felt the pistol in her hands. She was unfamiliar with whatever kind it was and hoped it was ready to fire.

Shooting someone up close was different than a distant target through a scope.

I have to do it. There's no other choice. I've killed before and this could end the war. I have to do it.

"Now!" Brian said.

She shoved the black pistol into the general's chest and pulled the trigger. The gun bucked in her hand. In what felt like the same instant, there was a flash of smoke and the general stumbled backwards. Warm hot liquid splashed her face. He still had a gun in his hand and he looked up at her. She fired again and again until he fell down to the cement of the parking lot.

Behind her, she heard Brian shouting for the other men to freeze and drop their weapons. She didn't look. Her focus was on the dying general in front of her. She couldn't turn away no matter how awful the sight. She did this and she had to watch as her punishment.

Alex and other people ran up and zip-tied the men. Alex put a hand on her shoulder and looked her in the eye. He said something but she didn't hear.

"Huh?"

"Are you alright?"

"Yeah, sure. I'm fine."

He took her off to the side and sat her down with a canteen of water and a package of MRE Skittles.

She sat there as she watched her people move into the HQ. They were after the senators and their bodyguards. She listened to what people were saying around her and heard that the civilians were safe, but she couldn't connect any meaning to it.

Shakti walked up and sat down next to her.

"How you feeling?" Shakti asked.

"Fine."

"You will be."

"We won, right?"

"We did."

Shakti wrapped an arm around her and watched the swarming activity around them.

"I did the right thing, right?" Miriam asked.

"Yes you did. He wasn't going to surrender. We want a peaceful world and he wouldn't allow it as long as he lived. You're a hero, Miriam."

She didn't feel like a hero at all.

26

ALEX GATHERED THE CIVILIANS INTO A DINING HALL THAT could fit almost a thousand people. His people and Farmville were on one side and the civilians of Ft. Knox were on the other. Some of them thanked them and others cursed them.

Frank stood in between the groups explaining why the war had been necessary and how they didn't want any more bloodshed.

The PG prisoners were locked away for now and he had no idea what to do with them. One of the Senators had shot himself and the other two were tied up.

Lisa patted him on the knee and gave him a rare smile.

"We did alright." she whispered.

"I suppose."

He looked over at Alma who was whispering something into Jason's ear that made him suppress a smile. Rebekah was talking to one of the armed PG civilians and Shakti and Miriam sat next to each other in silence.

Yeah, we did good.

After a full day of persuading and promising, a treaty was signed. The PG would remain a separate government and there would be peace between them. They left the problem of what to do with the senators up to the new PG government.

After spending the last night there, their convoy rolled back to Virginia. They siphoned the remaining gas out of the recovery vehicle and Paladin and left them there.

He took out his notebook and wrote it all down.

The battle of Ft. Knox was the last battle in which armored vehicles from the old world were used. The next battle will probably be with horses and hand made ammo.

He showed Lisa his note and she nodded her approval. She was his unofficial editor.

Adam was driving while Rebekah had shotgun.

"You think they'll keep their word?" Adam asked.

"I believe so. They have too much rebuilding to do to worry about us. They have to form a new government and find a better place to live."

"Three separate countries, huh?" Rebekah said.

"It looks like that," Alex said.

"Miriam's right. We need a new constitution. Oh, I know, we need a new flag."

He hadn't thought about that.

"What do we call ourselves?" Adam asked.

"Democratic American Republic?" Lisa said.

"Sounds like a Communist dictatorship," Adam said. "No offense."

"None taken."

"The Free American Republic?" Rebekah said.

"Sounds like a political movement," Alex said.

"Just go with Promised Land," Rebekah said.

"I like it," Adam said.

****

They got home and the celebration was mixed with the mourning. Two more funerals. The next one needed to be from old age.

Over the next few weeks, Alex held several meetings with the people asking what they wanted from their government. The general consensus was that they wanted the American Constitution with some added assurances that their rights would be protected. They tried to find a way to prevent the apocalypse again, but by the time the world got to the point it could destroy itself again they would have forgotten the lessons.

There would be a Congress and judges and for some reason they voted to keep him on as President.

He refused to let Lisa call him that.

Three weeks later, a delegation from the Appalachian Cherokee came by. It was the man, his two kids, three women and an old man with white hair.

"Glad to see you again," Alex said as they walked in through the front gate of the Castle.

They shook hands and Gary smiled.

"Good to see you. I understand that there will be peace now."

"That's correct. No more fighting, no more tanks."

"Our chief would like a word with you."

He stood aside and the old man stepped forward.

"You are the chief?" The old man asked.

"I am."

"I am Edward Hanging Down. We have decided to stay. These mountains have been our home for too long. As we planned we found that we did not want to leave. So, since we're staying, we need to trade with you. We have things you don't have and you have things we don't have."

"Sounds like an excellent idea."

"But there must be a few conditions."

"Very well."

"You will never enter our territory uninvited. We will shoot you on sight. Our ancestors were nearly wiped out and I will not allow the same to happen to us. We know these mountains and if you, your children or grandchildren ever try to take our lands, we will come in and kill you in your sleep. Understood?"

"Crystal clear, sir."

"Good. With that out of the way, let's talk."

He led them to a room they had set up as a meeting room with a big table and lots of chairs. There they talked about what resources they had. It turned out that they had a lot of meat in freezers and used wind turbines for power.

Wind turbines made more sense. Eventually the solar panels would break or go bad and there would be no replacements. But wind turbines would work.

"The biggest thing though, is people," Alex said.

The old man chuckled.

"I know that. Our young people have been begging to come meet yours. Cabin fever, I guess. No more Facebook."

"How about a big party in the spring? May first. Your young and our young meet together."

"We'll be there."

****

Rebekah stood off to the side, taking notes on the meeting. Alex would want them for the history book he was writing.

"What's your name?" The Cherokee boy asked.

He looked about seventeen. He had long black hair in two braids and a big toothy smile.

"Rebekah."

"Skyler."

He held out his hand and she shook it.

"I guess we're staying around."

"Good. We could use the company."

"Tired of all the same old faces, right?"

"Yeah. Big time."

"I guess I can't give you my phone number or anything."

Wait, is this guy flirting with me?

"I guess not," she said. "But you know where I live."

"We'll be back to visit."

"I hope so."

The meeting adjourned and the group went out to the courtyard.

"I'll see you again, Rebekah, until then."

"Looking forward to it."

He smiled and waved as he followed his people out of the Castle.

"What was that about?" Jen asked.

"Nothing. Just talking."

"Are you sure that's all?"

"Yeah."

She watched Skyler leave out the gate and out of view.

A party in the spring. She couldn't wait.

"Did you take good notes or were you distracted by the flirting?" Alex asked as he walked up to the two of them.

"Oh, I...I took a lot of notes."

Alex laughed.

"It's okay, Rebekah, you deserve a break. Things are going to be different now. Relax and take it easy for a while."

"Alright."

A guy flirted with me. A good looking guy. Okay, he's not Jewish, but I kind of don't have a choice here. We'll see what happens in the spring.

****

Alma watched their new flag rise on the pole in front of the Castle. The old United States flag flew beside it.

Alex stood in front of everyone alongside Lisa, Cass, Jen and herself. Her people waited to applaud and burst out in song. The band with their marching band drum, guitar, accordion and trumpet itched to play.

"On this day, we formally announce the creation of the Promised Land, a new country that continues the great traditions of the United States of America but with the hopes of learning from history and avoiding the same mistakes.

"This is a time to begin anew and from this time forward we will create the world we always wish we had. Set the course of history straight at the beginning. This is our chance to do it right."

The crowd erupted in applause and the band began playing a new song they had written for this occasion.

She looked up at the flag that waved in the humid breeze of the April morning. The blue flag with white dove facing a red eagle had been one of the kids' designs, but it worked and was voted on.

It looked good. Her idea of a black background and a white gun didn't get many votes.

She looked down at her belly. Nothing was noticeable but she knew something was different. It had been two months without her period and she knew enough to know that wasn't normal.

Jen had helped her find a working pregnancy test and so far she was the only one that knew.

There were no fancy hospitals or MRI machines anymore. Anything could go wrong. In history, the mortality rate for childbirth was insane. If the baby had problems, they wouldn't have any way to help him.

She looked up at Jason who stood in the audience and wondered how he would take the news.

When the official ceremony ended, she walked over to Jason and threw her arms around his neck.

"I found a house I think you'll like," he said. "Lots of farmland, a place for a good rifle range, and even a small pond."

"After the party, let's go take a look."

It's what everyone was doing. With a few exceptions, people were spreading out and getting their own farms with their family groups. Instead of one town, it was becoming a spread out cluster of farms. The horses and livestock had been distributed evenly among the different households and the Town Square of Promised Land was no more.

But the new country of Promised Land grew.

The Castle had most of the shops and was the center of attention. The Murray River wound through the Promised Land's undefined territory so over the summer people started calling it "Murray Town."

"Alma, hold on," Alex said.

He jogged up and put on a smile she knew was forced.

"Maybe we'll get some peace and quiet now," he said.

"You're staling. I hate it when you do that. Just spit it out, *hermano*."

He sighed.

"Alma, I'm sorry."

"Huh?"

"I'm sorry for everything. You have every right to be mad at me. I didn't show my appreciation enough. You're my sister and always will be. If you need anything, just ask."

That wasn't what I had expected. Not sure what I expected, but it wasn't that.

She didn't know what to say.

"Oh…well…"

"Thank you for everything, Alma. You're stubborn and reckless and sometimes rude, but you're the best sister I could ask for."

"You have your moments too."

"Not as many as you though."

"Of course not," she laughed.

"I'll see you around. Got some photos to take."

He gave her a quick hug, the first hug in several months and then hurried off.

"You two finally made up, huh?" Jason said.

"I guess so."

Then her mind snapped back to the news she had for him.

"Walk with me."

She led him away from the crowd and toward the Washington and Lee Campus. The entire time she thought about what she could say. It wasn't as if she had done this before.

"Jason, where do you see yourself in the next two years?"

"Here. With you."

She was about to contain her smile before he noticed how emotional she got, but this time she let the smile grow. It was a large, toothy smile, but it was real and she wanted him to know.

"You mean that?" She asked.

He stopped and faced her.

"Alma?"

"Yeah?"

"There's something that I…" he cleared his threat and cracked his knuckles. If she didn't know any better, she'd say that he looked nervous.

"Something wrong?"

"Wrong? No. Not at all. That's what worried me. But I'm not worried anymore."

He reached into his pocket and pulled out a gold ring with a diamond that caught every ray of sunlight. He got down on one knee and the realization of what was happening swept over her. She couldn't breath or even think.

Is this really happening? No way. No way. I didn't think he would. I wanted him too, but this is too much. Too wonderful.

"Alma, will you marry me?"

She threw her arms around his neck and kissed him all over the face.

"Yes, yes, yes."

****

"**A**re you going up to Murray Town and the Castle?" Her neighbor asked one day as she passed by on a horse.

Alma leaned on the rails of her porch and sipped the chocolate milk she had been craving all morning. She had never craved chocolate milk before.

"Not feeling well. Jason might," Alma said as she held her giant stomach.

Being pregnant sucked. She couldn't run or demonstrate the obstacle course for training. All she wanted to do was lounge around all day and eat.

Fortunately there were several teenagers that would be more than happy to babysit the Promised Land's first born once this awful pregnancy business was over.

I like that I'm having a baby, I just don't like the actual pregnancy part. Why couldn't it be like a delivery from Amazon?

If it was a boy, his name would be David, after Jason's father. If it was a girl, her name would be Maria, after her mother.

Jason was off at the meeting about the country's new Constitution. That was all anyone talked about these days. It seemed that everyone had their own idea of what the country should be like.

She would have gone but today she had just been too sick to go. Instead she sat on the porch overlooking the fields that surrounded her house. Rebekah would be there any minute. She stopped by every day to see if there was anything she needed.

But she was fine. She had everything she could want. For once in her life, she was at peace.

****

Miriam rolled up her prayer rug and stowed it in the closet. Shakti and Rehka were coming in from the fields and it was her day to prepare lunch.

They had spam sandwiches from one of the few remaining cans left. Their shelves were looking barren but any month the crops would come in and they'd have plenty to last them till next year.

"I'll be at the Constitution meeting tomorrow." Miriam said.

"We'll take care of the cows." Rehka said.

"Are they close to a final draft?" Shakti asked.

"Maybe in another week."

Rehka leaned over and looked over Miriam's shoulder.

"What?" Miriam asked.

She turned around and saw that someone was riding a horse down the old driveway toward the house.

"Who the heck is out at noon in this heat?" Shakti asked.

Miriam grabbed her old SVD that stood beside the door and walked out on to the porch.

When the rider got closer, she saw that it was Brian. He wasn't wearing a PG uniform anymore. He wore jeans, a black T-shirt, baseball cap and sunglasses.

"Who's that?" Rehka asked.

"Someone I met in Kentucky," Miriam said.

"Inside, Rehka. Finish your lunch." Shakti said and escorted the girl back inside.

Brian climbed down off the horse and walked to the porch's steps.

"What are you doing here?" Miriam asked.

Brian smiled and took off his sunglasses.

"I came to see you."

"That's…that's a long way to go."

"I'm with a trading convoy. I volunteered to come see you though."

"Me? Why?"

"You saved my life."

"Well, you saved mine in return."

"Exactly. We've got a lot in common."

She wanted very much to talk to him.

"Come inside. We're having lunch."

She took her guest inside where she wouldn't have to be alone with him. There they talked all evening even after Shakti and Rehka went to bed. She spared the lamp oil for light as they sat out on the porch watching the fireflies give them a light show.

He came up with every convoy after that. The summer after that, they had a wedding at the house. The place was decorated in streamers of flowers that Shakti and Rehka had made. Alex, Lisa, Alma, Cassidy and the entire population of Promised Land was there. Lisa held her new baby girl while

Alma held the hand of her toddler, keeping him from running off and getting into trouble.

She sat with her new husband as the town roasted a deer. Adam had slaughtered the animal following the rules for Halal. Then he worked his magic and created a feast. Shakti sat beside one of the men from Farmville and she knew another wedding would be soon. There were so many babies now. No one could take a step without fear of stepping on one. Cassidy had twin girls, red heads.

God was indeed merciful and He watched over her and her people. She didn't know what else their future had ready for them, but she knew they would make it through somehow. This was a new world and if it continued like this, it would be a better one.

About the Author

Zachary Hill has written stories as long as he can remember. In high school he filled up notebooks full of stories. In army basic training, after lights out, he wrote using his flashlight and notebook. During his two deployments to Iraq he wrote stories in his down time.

Zachary Hill graduated from Southern Virginia University with degrees in History and Art. He taught English in Italy and fell in love with Rome and Venice. He has done illustration for Larry Correia's *Grimnoir Chronicles*. He loves pizza and Mountain Dew.

You can find him at his blogs at *Broken World* and *Minimum Wage Historian*.

Here's a list of other great
White Feather Press Titles !

Sins of Prometheus by Zachary Hill

The Lost Promise by Zachary Hill

Uprising USA by George Hill

Uprising UK by George Hill

Uprising Italia by Zachary Hill

Blood and Tequila by Colin Webster

Blood on the Mississippi by Colin Webster

Available on amazon
and anywhere books are sold.